"Joyce _____ used
with fa_____ real
flavor o_____ rm-
ing my_____ and
smooth _____, *To Brew or Not to Brew* is sure to appeal
to mystery readers and beer aficionados alike."

—Jennie Bentley, *New York Times* bestselling author of
the Do-It-Yourself Mysteries

"A heartwarming blend of suds and suspense, featuring a
determined heroine and her big Irish family. Tremel knows
and loves her Pittsburgh setting, making the mystery all the
more real and enjoyable."

—Cleo Coyle, *New York Times* bestselling author of
the Coffeehouse Mysteries

TO
Brew
OR NOT TO
Brew

JOYCE TREMEL

BERKLEY PRIME CRIME, NEW YORK

An imprint of Penguin Random House LLC
375 Hudson Street, New York, New York 10014

TO BREW OR NOT TO BREW

A Berkley Prime Crime Book / published by arrangement with the author

ISBN: 978-0-425-27769-0

PUBLISHING HISTORY
Berkley Prime Crime mass-market edition / December 2015

PRINTED IN THE UNITED STATES OF AMERICA

10 9 8 7 6 5 4 3 2

Cover illustration by Bruce Emmett.
Cover design by Jason Gill.
Interior text design by Kristin del Rosario.

To my wonderful husband, Jerry.
I couldn't have done this without you. I love you forever!

ACKNOWLEDGMENTS

This book would never have been written without the help and input from so many people. I am forever grateful!

First, I want to thank my wonderful agent, Myrsini Stephanides, at the Carol Mann Literary Agency. I'm forever grateful she doesn't seem to mind my sometimes dumb questions. I'd also like to thank her predecessor, Eliza Dreier, who took me on in the first place. Thanks also to my editor, Kristine Swartz, and former editor Andie Avila for taking a chance that someone might like some beer with their cozy.

Speaking of beer, there are two local brewers whose help has been invaluable: Scott Smith at East End Brewing and Shawn Setzenfand at Hofbrauhaus Pittsburgh. Back when I was writing the proposal for this book, Scott showed me all the good places to kill someone in a brewery. He is also quick to answer when I have brewing questions. His beer is really tasty, too. Shawn is the head brewer at the Hofbrauhaus and he gave my husband and me a tour of the brewing operation there and answered a lot of questions. Their monthly keg tapping ceremony is a must if you're ever in the area. It would take me years to learn all there is to know about brewing beer. Any mistakes I've made in the book are entirely my fault. Don't blame the brewers!

Great big hugs to my pals in the Pittsburgh chapter of Sisters in Crime and my former critique group, The Mysterywrights. I would list you all by name, but I'm sure I'd inadvertently miss someone. Just know that I truly appreciate your support and I don't know where I'd be without you. Yinz guys are the best.

Last, but definitely not least, thank you to my husband, Jerry, and our sons, Andrew (and his beautiful wife Anna) and Josh. I love you guys! Prost!

NOTE TO THE READER

Anyone familiar with Pittsburgh will recognize some of the neighborhoods in this book. While Lawrenceville and Butler Street are real locations, the block where Max's brew-pub is located is purely a figment of my imagination. You won't find the Allegheny Brew House, Cupcakes N'at, Jump Jive & Java, or any of the other businesses along the real Butler Street. I tried to pick everything that is wonderful about Lawrenceville and squeeze it all into Max's neighborhood. I hope I succeeded.

The Steel City Brewery mentioned in the book is also fictional. The name does bear a resemblance to the Iron City Brewing Company, but that's where the similarity mostly ends. I borrowed a tiny bit of their history, but they never smuggled and sold bootleg beer during Prohibition. But they did make ice cream. The rest I made up.

Thanks for reading!

CHAPTER ONE

If looks could kill, the plumbing inspector giving me the bad news would have been in big trouble. "What do you mean there's a crack in the water line?" I said. "That's just not possible."

"Right here." He pointed. "You're going to have to replace this whole piece."

Sure enough, there was a one-inch gash in the line running to the brand-new stainless steel brew kettle, which we'd just installed a few days ago. I was hoping to brew a batch of pale ale tomorrow, but that was now out of the question.

The inspector brought me back down to earth. "You'll have to schedule another inspection after you get this taken care of."

This should have been the final plumbing inspection. The brew kettle we'd been using had been a hand-me-down from a local brewery that had upgraded their equipment. I hadn't planned on a new brewing tank for another year, but this one had come up at a price I couldn't pass up. Everything else, from the kitchen to the restrooms to the tanks we'd installed previously, had all passed weeks ago. I couldn't afford a delay right now. The opening of my brewpub—the Allegheny Brew House—was only a month away.

"When I call to schedule it, how long will I have to wait until you come out?"

He shrugged. "I'll try to get out the same day, but it really depends on how busy I am."

That eased my mind a little bit—provided I could get the plumber in tomorrow to fix it.

The inspector passed a clipboard to me. "I need your signature that you acknowledge that you didn't pass."

I signed where he indicated.

He studied my John Hancock. "You don't look like a Max."

I'd heard that so many times, I'd lost count. I couldn't help it that I was born the only girl in my family. I had five older brothers and my parents assumed they'd have another boy when I surprised them twenty-nine years ago. My brothers all had normal first names—Sean, Patrick, Joseph, James, and Michael. I had no idea why they decided Maximilian would be a good name for a baby. It wasn't even Irish. Anyway, I ended up Maxine, but I preferred plain old Max.

"I'd get that fixed first thing tomorrow if I were you, Miss O'Hara."

As I watched him leave, I fought the urge to beat my head against the steel tank. All I could see were more dollar signs before my eyes. Although my plumber happened to be my brother Michael, he still needed to be paid. I got the family discount, but it was still money I hadn't planned on. Now I was second-guessing my decision to buy this tank.

"Another problem?"

I started at the sound of my assistant's voice behind me. Truth be told, Kurt Schmidt was more than an assistant. I didn't know where I'd have been without him. The son of one of my instructors in Munich, he knew just about all there was to know about brewing beer. He was also an accomplished chef who made the best apple strudel I'd ever tasted. He was easy on the eyes, too—tall, blond, and blue-eyed. There was no romance between us. He was more like my sixth brother, and he was completely devoted to his fiancée back in Germany. "I'd say so," I answered. "There's a crack in the water line." I showed it to him.

"That's very strange. It wasn't there yesterday," he said. "It should not have split like that. It is not a high-pressure line." He removed his wire-rimmed glasses and examined it closely. "Someone cut this."

"Impossible. No one's been near these tanks except the two of us. It was probably just defective."

"Do you really think Mike would have used a defective pipe?"

"Maybe he didn't see it." At this point, I was just relieved it wasn't a line that was turned on all the time. It might have flooded the whole pub.

"You don't think that any more than I do."

"There's no other explanation. Like I said, we're the only ones who have been near it."

Kurt put his glasses back on. "I suppose you still don't believe the loose electric breaker, the broken mirror, the scratched bar top, and the half dozen other little things aren't connected. I'm telling you, someone is trying to keep us from opening."

This wasn't the first time I'd heard this line of reasoning. Sure there'd been some minor annoyances, but they'd been bound to happen. Even during construction, things hadn't always gone according to plan. It went with the territory. There were always surprises. "You're right," I said. "I don't believe it." I turned and went down the metal stairs of the elevated platform that served to reach the higher sections of the tanks. I'd considered installing all the equipment out of sight, but decided half the fun of going to a brewpub was seeing how what you were drinking was made. I wanted a wall of glass, but because of the cost, I'd opted for a large window instead. Eventually, I planned to give brewery tours, but that was a long way off.

I went through the swinging wooden door of the brewery area, crossed the pine-plank floor, and sat down at the oak bar. I couldn't let myself believe we were being sabotaged. If I did, I'd be giving in to all those who said I'd never succeed in this endeavor. The first time I set eyes on the former Steel City Brewery, I knew it was what I'd been waiting for. When I returned to Pittsburgh from Germany after earning my brewmaster certification, I spent months searching for the perfect spot to open my brewpub. It had taken even longer to get financing, even though I had a nice inheritance from my grandmother for a down payment. No one wanted to take a chance on a five-foot-two female brewmaster. I finally found a lender that specialized in financing women entrepreneurs, and the rest, as they say, is history. At least I hoped so.

Seconds later, Kurt took the stool beside me. "It is not a coincidence."

"You don't know that," I said.

"Explain it, then."

"I can't any more than you can. Don't you think if someone was sabotaging us, they'd come up with something a little more elaborate? It's been annoying, but it's all fixable. And how are they getting in? None of the doors have been tampered with."

"That doesn't mean anything. Maybe whoever it is has a second career picking locks. At least the alarm company is finishing up soon. Then, when the alarm is set off, you'll see that I'm right." Kurt stood. "It's almost five o'clock. Why don't you go home? I'll lock up tonight. I want to work on that *kirschtorte* recipe."

"But it's delicious already." My mouth watered just thinking about it.

Kurt shook his head. "Not quite. It tastes like every other chocolate cherry cake. It's missing something. I want it to be perfect."

If it turned out half as good as the apple strudel, he could do whatever he wanted with it. The kitchen was his domain. I'd stick with the beer.

I took Kurt's advice for a change and left a short time later—after I called Mike, who promised to be there bright and early in the morning. Once outside, I turned to admire the building, like I did at least once daily. Sometimes I had to pinch myself to realize that all this really was mine. It was hard to believe that, not long ago, this had been an empty, forlorn shell. The former Steel City Brewery had been bought out by a large conglomerate, and the first thing the big boys did was shut down the Pittsburgh operation. All the equipment was auctioned off, and the buildings had sat empty for several years before the brewing plant itself had burned to the ground.

The single-story redbrick building, which was now the Allegheny Brew House, had been used as offices for the company. It was at the end of the row of buildings housing various shops and other businesses. It had taken quite a while to tear out everything down to the brick walls. I hoped my patrons would love the exposed brick inside as much as I did. A nice find had been pine-plank floors underneath the industrial linoleum. It had been much cheaper to have them restored than to install new boards.

Both the brewery and my loft apartment were in the Lawrenceville section of Pittsburgh. Since Children's Hospital had moved from near the University of Pittsburgh in Oakland to the Bloomfield-Lawrenceville border, the area was booming. It was no longer considered a "bad" neighborhood. Real estate values had skyrocketed, partly because of the medical professionals wanting to move close to work. Developers who bought up all the distressed properties and rehabbed them were likely making a killing on the resale. New shops and cafés opened constantly. It seemed like every time I walked up Butler Street to head home, I spotted something that hadn't been there the week before. On my block alone, there was a cupcake bakery, a flower shop, several boutiques, a deli, and a coffee shop.

I was tempted to stop for a treat when I passed the Cupcakes N'at bakery next door to the pub, but talked myself out of it. Out of towners always questioned the name of the bakery. The cupcake part they got, but inevitably someone wanted to know what *n'at* meant. I actually looked it up once and found it was short for *and all that*. Many of the expressions known as "Pittsburghese" originated with either the Scots-Irish or the Pennsylvania Dutch.

The owner, baker extraordinaire Candy Sczypinski, had become a good friend and apparently thought she was helping when she brought her creations over for us to sample, but my waistline couldn't handle much more. Between the cupcakes and other goodies, and sampling the menu items Kurt was coming up with, I was going to have to start walking more than just to the brewery and back. I considered joining the new gym a few blocks away, but I didn't know when I'd actually have the time to go.

Instead of a cupcake, I grabbed a turkey sandwich from the deli across the street. The deli was owned by Ken Butterfield, who manned the counter most days, but since it was after five, he was gone for the day. As I climbed the two flights of stairs to my apartment with my low-calorie sandwich in hand, I felt downright virtuous. That feeling was replaced with guilt when I unlocked the door. I'd moved here three months ago, but the place was still littered with boxes that I hadn't had time to unpack. I kept telling myself I'd get to them tomorrow, but after putting in twelve-hour days at the pub, I was too exhausted to do much of anything else.

But at least I had furniture. Sort of. Grandma O'Hara's traditional wingback sofa and chairs didn't exactly go with the modern style of the apartment. The dark mahogany end tables didn't match the bleached-oak laminate flooring. Gram's antique dining room set didn't even fit—it was stored in my parents' basement. It would have looked ghastly with the white cabinets and stainless steel in the kitchen anyway. She always said *Beggars can't be choosers*, and while I certainly wasn't a beggar, I was glad to have the hand-me-downs whether they matched or not. Besides, it was comforting to have a little part of her with me. I'd been in Germany when she passed two years ago, and I still regretted that I hadn't made it home for her funeral, although Gram herself would have been upset with me if I had. A waste of good money, she would have said. She'd never squandered so much as a dime. It was thanks to her that I'd had a nice down payment for the brewery.

When I finished eating my sandwich, I sat at the kitchen island and wondered what to do with myself. I wasn't used to this. I reached for the pen and pad beside the phone and made a list of things I had to do over the next week. The plumber was already taken care of. I had to schedule some waitstaff interviews. The alarm company needed to finish and activate the alarm. Kurt had already started training the kitchen staff, so I should probably touch base with how that was going. There were other miscellaneous deliveries that I needed to be present for. I hoped I wasn't forgetting anything.

The phone rang just then, and I picked it up.

"Wonder of wonders, my baby sister is at home." It was my oldest brother, Sean. Father Sean to his parishioners. Some people thought he had gone into the priesthood because he was the oldest Irish Catholic son, but it was truly a calling for him. He'd broken more than a few hearts when he decided on the seminary. We'd both inherited Mom's black hair and blue eyes, and they gave him a debonair movie-star look, especially when he wore the collar. If Hollywood ever remade *The Bells of St. Mary's*, he'd be a shoo-in to play Father O'Malley. Twelve years my senior, he was my favorite brother, although I'd never tell the others that. A little sister had been a novelty to him, and he became my protector from the day Mom and Dad brought me home from the hospital.

"You can always call my cell phone if I'm not at home, you know."

"I missed you at Mass yesterday," he said.

He obviously couldn't see me, but I felt my face flush anyway. I would have liked to tell him I went to another parish, but I couldn't very well lie to a priest, even if he was my brother. "Sorry about that. I got tied up at the brewery."

"You're working too hard. We missed you at dinner, too."

Sunday dinner was a long-standing family tradition. Most of the time I loved it. Since three of my five brothers were scattered across the country, Mom liked to keep the rest of us close. I often thought it was because Dad was a police officer. Even though he was a homicide detective now and not on the front lines as much as when he'd been in uniform, she still worried. I'd already talked to Mom that morning about missing dinner and she understood. At least, she'd told me she did.

"With the opening so close, I had a lot to do," I said.

"Anything I can do to help? Believe it or not, I haven't forgotten how to wield a hammer or a screwdriver."

"Don't let your parishioners know you can do that. You don't want the contributions to drop because they think you don't need to pay a handyman."

Sean laughed.

"Thanks for the offer," I said, "but we'll be fine if we stay on schedule. I'll be sure to make it to dinner next week."

"And Mass, too?"

"Hopefully."

"Maxie . . ."

Sean was the only one who dared call me that. When I was five, I busted the next-door neighbor kid in the chops for doing it. "Fine. I'll be there," I said.

"Good. I'll see you on Sunday."

I puttered around for a while and actually cleaned out a few boxes of kitchen items. It was nice to see the cabinets fill up. There was a small collection of German beer steins in one of the boxes, and I washed and arranged them on one of the built-in bookshelves in the living room. It was a nice touch, even though the rest of the shelves were almost empty. I vowed to make a better effort to get things unpacked. It was never going to look like home until I did.

By ten o'clock, I was tired and decided to call it a night. The phone rang as I finished brushing my teeth. I almost didn't answer it, and when I did, I was surprised to hear Kurt's voice.

"Is everything okay?" I asked.

"I was right."

"About what? Your *kirschtorte*?"

"No. The sabotage."

Not this again. "There is no—"

"Yes, there is. I know what's going on, and I know exactly who is doing it."

I would have argued more, but something in his voice stopped me. "What happened?"

"I have proof. I heard a noise and found . . . You need to come down here. It'd be better if I showed it to you. Then we can turn it over to the police and get to the bottom of this whole thing."

I still wasn't convinced anything was going on, but Kurt wouldn't have called this late if he didn't think it was urgent. So much for an early night. "I'll be right there."

"**K**urt?" I called as I dropped my purse on the bar. The lights were all on, but he wasn't in the main room of the pub. Upset as he was, I thought he would have met me at the door. Maybe he was in the kitchen. I crossed the plank floor to the other side of the room and pushed open the swinging door. The scent of chocolate and cherries made my mouth water. His latest torte creation sat half-decorated on the stainless steel counter. A bowl of thickened tart cherries was beside it, along with a plastic piping bag that looked full of whipped cream. It was odd he'd walk away without putting it back into the refrigerator. I put the cherries and whipped cream in the fridge, then went looking for Kurt.

He wasn't in my office. I opened the door that led to the basement, but the lights were out. I stopped outside the men's restroom and knocked on the door. Twice. I didn't want to just barge in. Kurt was a good friend, but not that good. When he didn't answer, I peeked in. It was empty. I stood in the hallway and tapped my foot. I went back down the hallway to the pub. I could see through the window that the brewery was dark. Where could he be? Surely he wouldn't have taken off and left the place unlocked—especially after asking me to come down here. Could he have stepped out for a quick snack? I went back to the bar and sat down to wait.

Fifteen minutes later, Kurt hadn't returned. The longer I waited, the madder I got. Why had he bothered calling me if he was going to leave? Apparently, whatever he had to tell me wasn't all that important after all. I snatched my cell phone from my purse and tapped his number on the speed dial with a lot more force than I needed. He'd better have a good explanation. Seconds later, the sound of his phone ringing made me jump. The sound was muffled, so I couldn't figure out where it was coming from. I got up, and as I crossed the room the sound got louder. The ringing seemed to be coming from the brewing area. It didn't make sense that Kurt would leave his phone in the darkened brewery. I pushed the swinging door halfway open and paused. The ringing stopped, and Kurt's voice mail picked up. There was another sound, however—the mash tun was operating. A prickly sensation went down my spine. Why was that tank running? We had cleaned out the spent mash earlier when I'd brewed a batch of hefeweizen. There was no reason for it to be turned on, especially at this time of night.

"Kurt?" I fumbled for the light switch. My fingers found it and the overhead lights blazed on. I blinked a couple times at the sudden brightness and spotted Kurt on the platform bent over the large opening at the top of the mash tun. Something wasn't right about that. I was about to call his name again when it registered. His feet weren't touching the floor. Heart in my throat, I raced up the metal stairs, the clangs echoing through the room with each step. I reached for the switch beside the tank. My hands shook horribly. I missed the switch. I tried again and turned it off.

It wouldn't have mattered if I'd missed it again. There was a good reason why Kurt hadn't been waiting for me or responded when I called him.

He was dead.

CHAPTER TWO

Kurt hung halfway into the tank opening. The neck piece of his kitchen apron was twisted tightly around his throat, and the rest of it was caught in the rake in the bottom of the tank. I gagged as I spun around and stumbled down the steps, my whole body shaking. I couldn't catch my breath. Somehow I managed to make it into the pub and pull a chair down from one of the tables. I collapsed onto it. The room spun before my eyes. I bent down until my head was between my knees. When the feeling passed and I could breathe again, I called 911.

I choked back a sob as I waited by the door for the police. If I cried now, I was afraid I'd never stop. Tears wouldn't do me any good. They wouldn't bring Kurt back. I stared out the window and concentrated on the Butler Street traffic. Even at this late hour, the street and sidewalks were busy. People going about their business, not knowing a good man was dead. I hadn't known, either. Why hadn't I looked harder for him when I arrived? All the time I'd spent waiting and complaining to myself that Kurt wasn't here, he'd been stuck in—oh God—what if Kurt was still alive when I got here? What if he had been caught in the rake and couldn't call out for help? His death could be my fault. I could have saved him if only I'd thought to check the brewery. The tears I'd been holding back burst like a dam. I was still sobbing when the police arrived.

"Here, drink this."

I took the cup of tea offered to me. "Thanks, Dad." I was sitting at one of the square wooden tables in the pub waiting for the investigators to finish. My father was the detective in charge. Dad could have retired when he'd turned fifty-five, but I didn't think he ever would. He loved his job and he was good at it. I'd lost count of how many commendations he'd received over the years. Sean O'Hara Sr. looked like an older version of my brother, Michael. They both had red hair—although Dad's was white now—and green eyes. I took a sip and made a face. "What did you put in here?"

He pulled out a chair and sat down beside me. "I thought you could use a little something."

A "little something" was most likely a splash of Jameson. I didn't need to ask where he'd gotten it. When I bought the place, he'd given me a bottle as a gift. It had sat unopened on a shelf in the office ever since. I often wondered if he gave it to me because he was disappointed that I'd turned to brewing—German-style no less—instead of distilling. When I went to Ireland after grad school with my masters in chemistry, my plan was to learn all there was to know about Irish whiskey. After a side trip to Germany, I discovered great beer and a new career. I took a large swallow of tea.

"Feeling any better?" Dad asked.

Ever since the tears stopped flowing, I'd been unable to stop shivering. I was finally warming up, thanks to the doctored tea. "Yes, I am."

"Good enough to answer a few questions?"

I nodded. "Especially if it helps you catch whoever did this to him."

"Did what to him?"

"Killed him," I said. I'd done a lot of thinking while Dad and the others were back in the brewery and I'd been relegated to the pub. I thought about all the little things that had happened over the last few weeks and how Kurt had been convinced we were being sabotaged. I hadn't believed him. If I had, and if I'd reported the incidents earlier, Kurt would be alive. It was no coincidence that he figured out who it was, and an hour later he was dead.

Dad took my hand. "Honey, no one killed Kurt. This was a tragic accident. Nothing else."

I pushed my mug aside with my other hand. "It was no accident." I told him about the vandalism and today's cracked water line. "Kurt called me tonight and said he knew who was behind everything going on—what he called sabotage." My voice caught, but I continued anyway. "I didn't believe him. I didn't believe someone would actually come in here and do those things to try and keep us from opening. I should have believed him."

"Even if someone was trying to keep you from opening, that doesn't mean there was any foul play in Kurt's death."

"But—"

Dad put up a hand. "Wait a minute. You know why homicide gets called out when something like this happens."

"Of course I do." It was to make sure the victim hadn't been murdered.

"Then trust me to do my job."

"I do, Dad, but I'm sure it wasn't an accident. Kurt said he had proof. That's why he called me to come down here. He had something to show me."

"Something in that tank? What did you call it?"

"The mash tun. That's where we mix the grain with water. Don't you see? The tun was clean. There was absolutely no reason for it to be turned on."

He was quiet like he was thinking about that. "What did Kurt want to show you?"

"That's just it. I have no idea. He wouldn't tell me over the phone—he said it would be better to show me." I felt the tears coming again, and I pressed the heels of my hands against my eyes. "It's all my fault. If only I'd believed Kurt sooner, this wouldn't have happened."

"Honey, it's not your fault. Don't ever think that." He put an arm around me. "I'll tell you what. I'll keep this open and won't call it an accident just yet. But if the autopsy report doesn't show anything suspicious, I'll have to go by the medical examiner's findings."

It was four in the morning by the time I got back home. I knew I should try to get some sleep, but there was no way it was going to happen. I made a pot of coffee instead.

Poor Kurt. What was I going to tell his father and his

fiancée? Mr. Schmidt hadn't been crazy about the idea of him coming over here. He'd wanted Kurt to follow in his footsteps and take over the family brewery, not come to America and work with me. His fiancée hadn't minded, though. She'd been excited about the prospect. I told Dad I should be the one to call and tell them about Kurt, so he retrieved their phone numbers for me from Kurt's cell. I smoothed the scrap of paper out on the table in front of me and stared at it, dreading making the calls. It was late morning in their time zone, so I'd probably reach at least one of them. I took a gulp of coffee and picked up the phone.

An hour later I had no tears left. Both of them had answered their respective calls, and they'd gone exactly how I expected they would. Mr. Schmidt was angry and used every German cuss word I knew and some I didn't. I kept silent and let him yell, partly because he was right. If Kurt hadn't moved here to help me, he'd still be alive. He'd cooled off a bit by the time I hung up. I was grateful he hadn't broken down. I couldn't have taken that. Not with him.

The call to Maura had been much worse. She was devastated. She'd just made airline reservations to visit Kurt and be here for our launch. All I could think about was how unfair it was—it was unimaginable that all the plans they'd made to be together for their whole lives could be snuffed out in an instant.

And that fact made me angry. The more I thought about it, the madder I got. By the time I'd showered and dressed, I was determined to find out who was responsible for the incidents at the brewery. Even more so, I wanted to find Kurt's killer. Despite what my father said, I knew his death wasn't an accident. Kurt had been Mr. Cautious—sometimes to the point of driving me crazy. He'd double- and triple-check everything. He'd never in a million years do anything careless around the equipment.

By the time I returned to the brew house, I felt energized with a renewed purpose. Unfortunately, that energy only lasted until I saw the aftermath of the investigation in the brewery area. Dad had released the scene to me when we left to go home, but I didn't have the heart to go back there then. Now I wished I had. I would have locked the investigators in and insisted they clean up after themselves. My formerly immaculate sealed concrete floor was covered with dusty footprints, and there were smudges all over the stainless steel tanks. Not just on the mash tun, mind you. Every tank was dirty. Kurt would have had a conniption. *Oh, Kurt, I miss you already.*

Before I started bawling again, I pulled out the hose and a bucket. I was halfway through my cleaning when Mike showed up to fix the water line to the new tank. I'd forgotten he was even coming until I spotted him heading my way. I dried my hands on my jeans, and when he reached me he folded me into a hug. His white T-shirt was soft and the scent of Ivory soap reminded me of racing him to the bathroom sink to wash up before dinner. Although he was married with two toddler girls, he still looked like that kid. Maybe it was the freckles and tousled red hair. Even the laugh lines from his near-perpetual grin didn't seem to age him. He was thirty-two going on fifteen. I gave him a squeeze and stepped back.

"How you holding up, baby sister?" he said. "Dad filled me in."

"I'll be okay."

"Mom said she'll stop by later."

"I meant to call her this morning, but after I called Kurt's fiancée and his dad, I was all talked out."

Mike nodded. "I can imagine. You sure you're okay? You know, no one would care if you actually took some time off. You can delay the opening."

There was no way I was going to do that. Kurt and I had worked too hard to stay on schedule. If he had been in my place, he'd keep going. I wouldn't dishonor my friend by wimping out just because I didn't feel up to working.

Mike must have seen my expression. "Yeah, I guess you don't want to do that." He glanced around. "So, where's the cracked water line?"

I showed it to him without mentioning Kurt's suspicion. It wasn't that I doubted him at this point, but I wanted verification from a professional, even if that said professional was my brother.

"What the heck did you do? How did you manage to cut it like this?"

"We didn't."

"Someone sure did."

I wanted to tell him about Kurt's—and now my—suspicions, but I held back. He'd not only go into big-brother mode, he'd get all my brothers to do the same. Even worse, he'd tell Mom. They'd find out sooner or later, but at the moment later sounded pretty good. "It doesn't matter how it cracked. I just need you to fix it."

"Why do I get the feeling you're not telling me something?" When I didn't answer, he shrugged. "You're the boss."

I patted him on the shoulder. "And don't you forget it."

* * *

"**Y**oo-hoo! Max?"

I smelled Candy Sczypinski—or rather her treat of the day—before I saw her. I was in the office seated at the old oak teacher's desk I'd picked up cheap at a local place that sold recycled building materials and household items. While Mike repaired the water line, I'd started making calls to reschedule the plumbing inspection and the new hires that Kurt had been training. Before Mike left, I told him I was concerned about training the kitchen staff, as that had been Kurt's domain, and I didn't know how I'd ever find another assistant. He said he had a great idea and not to worry. Knowing some of the ideas he'd come up with in the past, I was reasonably sure I had cause to worry.

"Max?" Candy called again.

"In here." I stood and stretched. It felt good when my back cracked.

Candy whooshed into the office carrying a clear glass plate holding two chocolate chip muffins. These were definitely not ordinary muffins. They were twice the size of most and topped with pecan slivers and drizzled with a dark chocolate glaze. She put the plate down on my desk and crushed me into a bear hug.

"Oh, Max," she said. "I just heard. I am so sorry! That poor boy. And what you must be going through."

I seriously doubted Candy "just heard" about Kurt. She almost always heard about things the minute they happened. I wouldn't be surprised if she sometimes knew in advance. Her information-gathering skills were second to none. She should have been working for the NSA. I disentangled myself and backed up far enough that she wouldn't hug me again. Ordinarily, I didn't mind hugs but Candy's were a little too enthusiastic to suit me. She was a good bit taller than me, so my head ended up smashed against her ample bosom. The rest of her was fairly ample, too.

Before we met, I'd pictured a statuesque blond bombshell when I first heard her name. She was as far from that as one could be. She was tall, but that's where the similarities ended. Picture Mrs. Santa Claus in black and gold. She was a rabid Steelers fan and wasn't afraid to show it, no matter how outlandish the outfit. Today she wore lemon yellow pants and a black T-shirt with a large photo of Troy Polamalu on the front. Her black orthopedic shoes were tied with yellow Steelers laces. Even her fingernails had team decals.

"I'm all right," I said.

"It must have been so traumatic." Candy lowered herself into one of the chairs I'd picked up at a yard sale, and I reclaimed the seat at my desk.

"It was." I knew she was waiting for the particulars. As much as I liked her, I didn't want the events of the previous night to be fodder for gossip. Candy knew everyone and everything that happened in the neighborhood. She wasn't malicious about it; she just liked to talk.

"I just can't believe it," Candy said. "Kurt was such a nice young man. Did you know we exchanged recipes?"

I shook my head and broke off a chunk of muffin. One piece wouldn't be too many calories.

"I gave him my aunt's recipe for German chocolate cake. Maybe I'll make some in his honor." She picked up the other muffin and split it in half.

"That would be nice." I picked off another piece of muffin.

Candy went on about a few more recipes they'd shared. While she talked, my mind wandered and I only half listened. I couldn't help thinking about Kurt's last words to me. He'd known who was behind the sabotage. I only came back to earth when Candy stood up.

"I need to get back to the bakery," she said. "And you look like you need some rest."

"I'm sorry I'm not very good company right now," I said. As I walked with her through the pub to the front door, I had a thought. I hadn't wanted to tell her the whole story because she might gossip, but Candy was the eyes and ears of the neighborhood. Maybe she knew who might not want the brewery to open. "Did Kurt ever mention anything about some of the strange things that happened here lately?"

"Like what? Ghosts? I'd love to have a ghost."

I told her what had been going on and what Kurt suspected, including what he told me when he called.

"It wasn't an accident, then," she said.

"I don't think it was."

Candy was silent, studying me. It was long enough to make me wonder what she was thinking and if I'd made a huge mistake by confiding in her.

"It really doesn't surprise me," she said finally. "Not one bit."

CHAPTER THREE

𝓘t was my turn to stare. "What do you mean you aren't surprised?"

Candy put a hand on my arm. "That didn't come out quite right. Of course Kurt's death is a shock. I surely didn't expect anything like that. It's just that not everyone in the neighborhood wanted this brewery to open again."

I walked over to a table, pulled out two chairs, and motioned for Candy to sit. "I don't understand. Why wouldn't they? Look how this part of town went downhill when Steel City closed. This building was nothing but an eyesore. Another business, especially a potentially successful one, will be a boon to this neighborhood."

"I know, dear. Not everyone thinks that way."

"You keep saying that. I want to know who."

"Off the top of my head, one would be Dominic Costello."

I didn't recognize the name. "Who is he?"

"Dom owns the Galaxy down the street."

The Galaxy was a small neighborhood bar two blocks away. It was a shot-and-a-beer kind of place that had been there since I was a kid. It certainly didn't attract the same type of customer I hoped the brewpub would.

Candy continued. "Dom is afraid you'll steal all his customers. I heard he's telling everyone he sees to boycott this place. He's even considering adding something besides peanuts and pickled eggs to his food selections."

"That's ridiculous. I seriously doubt anyone who frequents the Galaxy would be interested in coming here." I leaned back in my seat. "I'm going to have to talk to him."

"He's likely to toss you out on your keister."

"I'll take my chances. Anyone else?"

She tapped two of her Steelers-decorated fingertips on her lips. "Hmm. Let me think." She tossed a couple more names my way, but they were all neighbors I was on good terms with, like Daisy Hart, who owned the flower shop, and Adam Greeley, who owned three boutiques across the street.

We talked for a few more minutes, but in the end, I didn't have much in the way of suspects. The most promising one—really the only one—was Dominic Costello. I planned to have a chat with him as soon as I could. But first, I had work to do.

I hadn't been back to my chores for long when my mom came by. I'd propped open the door to the brewing area, and I spotted her as soon as she entered the pub. Mom was an older version of myself—as long as I aged as well as she has. One of the only things that gave away her age was her salt-and-pepper hair. She refused to color it—she said it gave her character. I waved and she rushed over. As soon as she pulled me into a hug, my eyes opened like a faucet again. So did hers.

"Oh, Max," she said when we finished. "I am so sorry."

We sat across from each other at the same table Candy and I had vacated earlier, with a box of tissues between us. I snatched up another tissue and passed the box to Mom. She took one and patted it under her eyes.

"I still can't quite believe it," I said.

"Kurt was such a nice boy. Just the thought of what your dad told me . . ." She shuddered and reached for my hand. "Such a horrible accident."

So Dad hadn't mentioned my suspicions to her. Either he'd completely dismissed them or he just didn't want her to worry. Mom was definitely a worrier, even if she tried not to show it. We sat quietly for a few minutes, then Mom suddenly smiled. "Remember when you first met Kurt and called me because you were mad he kept correcting your German?"

I nodded. "I thought he was making fun of me. It turned out he was only trying to help. He was appalled that I thought badly of him." I told her a few more stories about Kurt, and by the time she stood to leave, I felt a thousand times better.

By six in the evening, I couldn't do another thing. The stainless steel tanks were gleaming and you could probably eat off the concrete floor, which was the way it should be. Cleanliness is everything in a brewery. In a way, I was glad I was so exhausted. Maybe I'd be able to sleep without having visions of what had happened last night swirling around my brain. I needed to be back here bright and early. The alarm company was coming at eight to install a state-of-the-art system. I had called them earlier to see if they could move the installation up a few days. If whoever had killed Kurt returned after tonight, he'd be in for a surprise.

I locked up for the night, and as I started down the street, someone called my name. The male voice sounded familiar but I couldn't quite place it. He called me again, and then said, "Wait up." With those words, I put the face together with the voice.

Jake Lambert had been my brother Mike's best friend. We'd played together as kids, and by the time I reached puberty, I had been sure I was madly in love with him. I had also been sure he didn't return the feeling. As I was leaving for college eleven years ago, he'd told me to "wait up." I'd hoped he would kiss me good-bye. Instead, he ruffled my hair and told me to behave myself. The only time I'd seen him since then was at Mike's wedding six years ago. Jake had been his best man.

He reached me as I turned around. I half expected him to ruffle my hair again, but this time he hugged me. He stepped back, grinning. "You look great," he said.

He needed to get his eyes examined. That wasn't the word I'd have used to describe myself after cleaning all day. "You, too." And I meant it. He'd gotten better looking—if that was even possible. He wore khaki cargo shorts and a navy polo shirt. His chocolate brown hair still had the same waves I remembered, and although there were a few lines around his brown eyes now, he didn't look much older. A little bulkier, but that no doubt was from playing hockey with the New York Rangers. It made me wonder what he was doing in Pittsburgh right now. The last I heard he was living in Brooklyn and engaged to a future supermodel. I'd been too busy to follow hockey or any other sport lately, but maybe the Rangers were in town for a playoff game.

"I'm glad I caught you," Jake said. "Mike said you're usually here late."

"I'm actually leaving early tonight. It's been a long day."

"He told me what happened," he said. "I'm sorry for your loss."

"Thanks."

"Have you had dinner yet? I'd like to talk to you about something."

"No, I haven't." Now that he mentioned dinner, I realized I was starving. I never got around to eating lunch, and as tasty as Candy's muffin had been, it hadn't satisfied for long. Besides, I couldn't imagine what he wanted to talk to me about, and I was dying to find out. I suggested a small restaurant a few blocks away. They had a good beer list and great burgers. We exchanged idle chitchat while we walked. After we were seated, he asked me what was good on the beer list. I recommended a couple from a local craft brewery.

"Isn't that the competition?" Jake asked.

"Sure it is. But it's a friendly competition. I know most of the brewers around here. We all think we have the best beer, but we're not above recommending another's. We even give one another pointers on improving our products."

Jake grinned, showing the dimple on his left cheek that I remembered so well. "Kind of like hockey."

"I thought the different teams hated each other."

"Nah. We saved the fights for during the games. Once in a while it carried over, but most of us were pretty good friends."

I couldn't help but notice he used past tense. What was that all about? "Speaking of hockey, haven't the playoffs started? Are the Rangers in town?"

"No, they're not."

The server brought our drinks then and we both ordered burgers. Jake tried the beer and it met with his approval. When he didn't elaborate on why he was in town during the playoffs, I came right out and asked.

He took a long pull on his beer before he answered. "I moved back here a few weeks ago. My parents moved to Florida last year, and their house has been empty. They didn't want to sell it until they were sure they were staying. I'm living there—at least until I find another place."

I must have missed something. "So you're playing with the Penguins now?"

"I'm not playing hockey anymore."

As my Gram would have said, you could have knocked me over with a feather. Jake not playing hockey was like the Pope not being Catholic. Jake had been skating since he could walk, and he lived and breathed being on the ice. For someone who'd put up with hockey practice at three in the morning all through high school because that was the only ice time he could get, it didn't make sense that he'd quit the game. "You retired already? I thought you had a few more years to go."

"Yeah, well, things happened." He took another drink and pushed his glass aside. "Tell me about your brewpub."

Nice way to change the subject. I guess it was none of my business. I really wanted to know what had happened, though. Maybe Mike would tell me. Unless he'd been sworn to uphold some supersecret best-friend code. "What would you like to know about the pub?"

"Everything," Jake said. "What kind of beer, what kind of food. Your plans for the place."

I took him at his word and told him everything. I stopped myself before I got too far into the brewing process. He wasn't a chemistry geek like I was.

"Sounds like it's going to be great," Jake said when I'd finished. "You learned to brew in Germany, didn't you?"

I answered with the German form of *yes*.

He laughed. "Why there?" he asked. "Couldn't you have learned brewing here somewhere?"

"Yeah, I could have. There are some brewing schools in this country, or I could have just gotten a job and learned the ropes at a microbrewery. Kind of like an internship. But I loved Germany, and the country is synonymous with good beer, so I figured why not learn it from the experts?"

Jake lifted his glass. "To the experts." We clinked our glasses together, and then he said, "What do your Irish parents think of you brewing German beer?"

"I think Dad was a little disappointed at first that I wasn't going to come home with the secret recipe for Jameson whiskey. He got over it quickly when I promised to learn how to brew an Irish stout. My assistant, Kurt, was afraid to tell his dad back in Germany we were brewing an Irish beer." I teared up thinking about Kurt. Jake put his hand over mine and I felt like I was back in high school.

"Were you two close?" Jake asked.

"Not romantically—he had a fiancée back home. He was like having another brother."

"Are you seeing anyone?"

"Not at the moment," I said. "I haven't had much luck in that department. As soon as a guy finds out my dad's a cop and my brother's a priest, it pretty much scares them away." I didn't mention that I hadn't yet met anyone I wanted to be in a long-term relationship with. I couldn't blame it all on my family. "How about you?" I said. I knew about the fiancée but wanted to hear it from him.

Before he could answer, our meals arrived and we moved on to reminiscing about our childhoods. By the time we finished eating, I had forgotten about it. When the server cleared our plates and brought the check, Jake passed him his credit card over my objections. After the server left, Jake said, "Mike told me you're going to need a new chef."

"Yes, I am. Do you know someone?"

Jake cleared his throat. "That's what I wanted to talk to you about."

"I need someone who can start right away. Like tomorrow. Kurt was completely in charge of the kitchen from the food all the way to hiring the kitchen staff. And because he practically grew up in a brewery, he knew that end, too. If the person you know has brewing experience, that would really be helpful."

Across the table, Jake was grinning at me again.

"Sorry, I'm rambling, aren't I?" I said.

"You always did."

I threw my napkin at him. "Thanks a lot."

The server brought Jake's card and the receipt back. As

he signed the slip, I said, "So, are you going to tell me who this person is? I'd like to schedule an interview as soon as possible."

He leaned forward. "You don't need to bother with an interview. You already know the person."

"Great! Who is it?"

"It's me."

CHAPTER FOUR

"You?" This had to be a joke. I wondered if Mike had put him up to it. Put one over on his baby sister. "You're a hockey player."

"*Was* a hockey player. I'm also a certified chef."

"You. A chef." Hockey and cooking just didn't go together. At least not in my mind.

Jake nodded. "Yep. I had to do something during the off-season. I always liked to cook. And I figured I'd need to do something when I retired. I thought I'd open a little café or something, but the brewpub sounds like just the thing for me right now."

He was serious. This could be the answer to my problem. With the opening coming up so quickly, I needed to act fast to hire someone. But could I work with Jake? Sure, I'd known him forever and we seemed to get along. More important, could he cook pub fare? I didn't want someone who wanted to make fancy dishes or put more decorations on a plate than there was food. And I liked him. Seeing him again brought back so many memories of pining for him all through my teen years. I'd need to get over that if I was going to work with him every day—especially since those feelings were definitely one-sided.

Jake stood, reached for my hand, and helped me up. "You don't have to decide right now," he said as we headed for the exit. "Just think about it and let me know."

He held the door for me and we stepped outside. Despite my misgivings, I didn't have much of a choice at this point. I needed a chef now. Jake was available. I'd worry later about what to do if it didn't work out. I could at least give him a tryout and see what he could do. "I don't need to think about it," I said. "Come in tomorrow at ten and we'll see if you really know your way around a kitchen. If you do, you're hired."

Jake's smile stretched from ear to ear. "I'll be there." He leaned over and kissed me on the cheek. "You won't regret this, Max."

As I watched him walk away, I reached up and felt the spot on my cheek where his lips had touched. I headed home thinking maybe working with Jake wasn't such a bad idea after all.

I slept like a log. I'd dropped into bed as soon as I'd gotten home and fallen asleep in minutes. If the alarm hadn't awakened me, I think I could have slept until noon. Two cups of coffee and a hot shower got me moving, though, and

I was ready to take on the day. As I walked up Butler Street, I made a mental list of all that I needed to accomplish. By the time I reached Cupcakes N'at, I decided fortification was in order.

I got in line behind two other customers. The first was a woman in a business suit. The other was an older bald man wearing jeans and a white T-shirt. Candy waved to me from behind the glass counter. She was decked out in her usual Steelers duds, complete with a black and gold apron.

The man in front of me sighed loudly when Candy asked the woman she was waiting on about her kids. "For cripes sake. Hurry it up, would ya?" he said. "I don't got all day."

"Keep your pants on, Dom," Candy said. "You'll get your jelly donut."

"Yeah, but in what century?"

Candy rolled her eyes. "Don't mind him, ladies. Dom's always this cranky."

Dom? I wondered if this was the bar owner Candy had told me about. There was one way to find out. I tapped him on the shoulder. "Excuse me, but are you Dominic Costello?"

He turned around. "That depends. Who's asking?"

"Don't let him fool you, Max," Candy said. "He's the one and only."

"Max." His gray eyes narrowed. "You're the one that's trying to put me out of business."

"Nothing of the kind." I smiled and extended my hand. "Maxine O'Hara."

Dom ignored it and instead shook a finger in my face. "Don't think you're going to get away with it."

I forced myself not to step back and stood my ground. "Mr. Costello, I'm not going to put you out of business."

"Darn right you're not. I've owned the Galaxy since 1962 and have worked long and hard to keep it going. Even when this part of town went to hell in a handbasket, I stuck with it."

Candy finished waiting on the other customer, who made a wide path around us, no doubt expecting a fight to break out. Without asking what Dominic wanted, Candy put two jelly donuts in a bag and held it out to him.

"You know I only get one," he said. "I'm not paying for two."

"It's on the house," Candy said. "Maybe it'll sweeten you up a bit."

He snatched the bag out of her hand and turned back to me. "You better leave me alone. I'm not about to have some youngster serving girlie beers steal all my clientele."

"I don't think—"

"You'll be sorry you ever messed with Dominic Costello." He stomped to the door and shoved it open so hard the frame shook.

The encounter rattled me. I jammed my hands into the front pockets of my jeans to stop them trembling.

Candy came around the counter and put her arm around me. "Don't you let him get to you. I know we talked about Dom yesterday, but the more I think about it, the more I think it's someone else causing your problems."

I couldn't believe it. "How could you say that? You saw what just happened."

"You don't know him like I do. He's a grumpy Gus. That's it. He wouldn't be happy if he didn't have something to complain about. On rare occasions, he can even be pleasant."

"I don't buy that at all."

She patted my arm and went back behind the counter. "Just keep an open mind."

I told her I would, but as I walked next door to the brewery after buying a couple of bagels, I couldn't help thinking about what Dominic had said to me. He would make me sorry I'd messed with him. Was killing Kurt part of this plan?

The plumbing inspector arrived at eight while I was eating my bagel. I offered him the second one I'd bought but he declined. It took him less than five minutes to check the repair Mike made the day before, and it passed inspection. Not that I doubted my brother's work, but it was a relief anyway.

The alarm company came just after that and went to work. While they fished wires and installed motion detectors, I checked the batch of hefeweizen I'd brewed the other day. It smelled a bit like banana bread when I entered the brewing area. I tried to keep my mind on the task at hand, but I couldn't help thinking about Kurt every time I caught a glimpse of the mash tun. I needed to use it within the next day or so, and I didn't know how I could. I couldn't bear the thought of even turning it on. But I had to. Kurt would have told me I was being ridiculous. He would have cleaned out the tank and moved on. He wasn't one for sentiment. The most sentimental thing he'd ever done was ask Maura to marry him. Even she'd been surprised at that.

I was checking the gauge on the fermentation tank when I heard Jake calling my name. "In here," I hollered.

He pushed through the swinging door. "Good morning." He was dressed in black chinos and a crisp white shirt. It wasn't the traditional chef's tunic, but he looked ready to work. He sniffed the air. "Bananas in your brew?"

"Nope." I waited for the inevitable question.

"It sure smells like it. And maybe cloves. Why is that?"

And there it was. "Do you want the long explanation or the short one?"

"How about the short one for starters."

"The beer I brewed the other day is a hefeweizen, which has a distinct banana taste and aroma—sometimes clove, too—even though the only ingredients are water, yeast, hops, and a wheat malt in place of a good portion of the usual barley." I explained that esters released from the type of yeast used caused the banana scent as the beer fermented. While I talked, he strolled around the room checking out the various pieces of equipment.

"So you don't add flavorings of any kind to the beer?" Jake asked when I was finished.

"Heavens, no." I laughed. "I would have been expelled for even thinking something like that. There are some craft brewers who do it, but I'm not one of them. I like things pure and simple." I shrugged. "But that's me."

"I've found that with food, too. The simpler things are, the better. Use fresh, good quality ingredients."

He asked a few more questions about brewing and I gave him a mini lesson on the process and showed him the different tanks in reverse order. When we got to the mash tun, I stopped. I couldn't seem to find the right words.

Jake put a hand on my shoulder. "I'm sorry, Max."

I gave him a slight smile. "Kurt would have been the first

one to tell me to get a grip." Which I needed to do. And fast. "So, are you ready to see the rest of the place and then do some cooking? I expect to be awed, you know."

His eyes sparkled. "Oh, I guarantee you will be." He held the swinging door into the pub open for me. "Lead on, milady." He bowed as I walked through.

I never realized he was such a ham. I liked it. As we entered the pub area, I waved to one of the alarm installers, who was up on a ladder in the hallway where my office was located. The entry from the street was in the center of the room with two large windows on either side. The windows had wood blinds that matched the plank floors. I pointed out the table arrangement in the pub. "There are twelve of the square tables that seat four, and two round ones that seat six to eight, plus eight stools at the bar." Since the floor and the bar were darker wood, I'd chosen a clear finish for the oak tables to lighten things up a bit. I considered having a variety of mismatched chairs, but in the end just picked plain straight-backed ones that matched the tables.

We went behind the oak bar, and I showed him the taps for the various beers. "I'm planning on having four beers year-round—a lager, a stout, a weizen, and an IPA. I'll add two others, depending on the season."

"So you'll have six total year-round."

I nodded.

"Sounds like a good plan," Jake said. "I like the idea of the seasonals."

"I do, too. They won't be the same all the time, so people will have to keep coming back. At least I hope they will."

"I don't think you'll have to worry about that."

Before we reached the kitchen, he picked up two grocery

bags from one of the tables. "I stopped to get a few things. I wasn't sure what you had on hand."

"It's a good thing you did. Kurt only bought enough for whatever recipe he was trying out. I should have thought of that. I'll reimburse you for whatever you spent."

"You've had other things on your mind. And there's no need to reimburse me. It wasn't that much."

"This is nice," Jake said when we entered the kitchen. "The stainless steel and the tile floor will make for easy cleanup."

I let him check out the equipment on his own. If he stayed on, this would be his domain, just as it had been Kurt's. He opened the refrigerator and lifted out a bowl of cherries.

"Kurt was working on a *kirschtorte*. I don't know if they're still good. We'd better throw them out. The whipped cream, too." I reached for the bowl and Jake shooed me away.

"I can take care of it," he said.

I decided to let him.

He closed the refrigerator door, and said, "Anything in particular you want me to make?"

"I'll leave it up to you." I wanted to see what he'd come up with, hoping it would fit in with my idea of what we'd be serving—especially since the menus were already at the printer. I left him to his own devices and went back to the brewery.

A short time later, delicious aromas emanated from the kitchen as I sat at my desk going over some bills that had come in the day before. My stomach growled loudly just as one of the alarm installers poked his head into my office.

He grinned. "Whatever's cooking smells mighty good."
I agreed.

He told me they were almost finished and wanted to
give me a lesson on how everything worked. I followed
him out to the pub, and he showed me the keypad near the
front door, how to arm and disarm the system, and how to
change and add codes. He also showed me where the motion detectors were located. He had one aimed at the front
door, another at the back door, and one more in the hallway
near the office. He handed me a thick packet of information
and said that if I forgot anything, it was all in the owner's
manual.

As soon as they left, I headed for the kitchen. It was almost noon. Surely, Jake was finished with whatever dish
he'd decided to make. I burst through the door and stopped
cold. There were a half dozen plates lined up on the warmer.
Jake was placing a stainless cover on the last one. I stood
there with my mouth hanging open.

Jake grinned, most likely at the incredibly dumb look on
my face. "You're about a minute too early."

"I didn't expect all this." I waved my arm over the table.
"One would have been enough."

"Hey, you were the one who said you wanted to be awed.
I took you at your word."

No wonder it had smelled so good in the brew house. I
removed the covers one by one. The first dish held a juicy
hamburger with the works on a pretzel bun with a side
of some of the best-looking fries I'd ever seen. The next
plate had a club sandwich made with marble rye and more
fries. Three different sausages and a large mound of German
potato salad rested on the third plate. The others contained

a grilled chicken sandwich, a steak hoagie, and the ever-popular Pittsburgh staple—the fried fish sandwich.

"How did you manage all this in a little more than an hour?"

He stood back, looking very proud of himself. "I made some of this at home. After I left you last night, I asked myself, *What would Max have on her menu?* I came up with a list of meals—which was much longer than this, by the way—went to the grocery store, then went home and started cooking."

"In other words, you cheated."

"I'd call it being prepared. Just like when I was a Boy Scout."

"You were never a Boy Scout."

"Okay. Just like hockey, then. There was a big opening up ice and I went for it. He shoots! He scores!"

I had to laugh. "You're really something, Jake Lambert."

He winked. "That's what all the ladies tell me."

The heat level in the room went up a notch, and not because of the cooking. That was not good if we were going to be working together. I couldn't let an old crush interfere with our working relationship. After all, I wasn't a teenager anymore. Far from it.

I didn't have time to ponder that any further, because I heard Candy calling my name. I poked my head into the pub. "In here."

Candy pushed through the door. "Are you cooking? I smell something heavenly." She stopped when she spotted Jake. "I didn't know you weren't alone, Max. I'll come back later." She turned to go and I stopped her.

"You're actually just in time. You can help me sample these dishes."

She hesitated. "Are you sure? I don't want to intrude."

"I'm sure. There's no way I can eat all this." I took her by the arm and led her to the table where Jake was standing and watching our exchange. "Candy, meet my new chef, Jake Lambert."

He reached out his hand. Candy took it, then dropped it like it was a hot potato. "Oh, my gawd!" she squealed. "You're—you're—"

Jake bowed. "The new chef."

"No!" Candy said. "You're that hockey player! For the Rangers!" She fanned her face and turned to me. "Max, do you know who this is?"

"Of course I do. Jake and I grew up together."

"I can't believe it." She fanned herself again. "This is almost as good as meeting Troy."

"Troy?" Jake seemed completely puzzled.

"I'll explain it later," I said, knowing Candy meant her beloved Steeler.

Candy grabbed Jake's hand and pressed it to her face. "Mr. Lambert, I am so pleased to meet you."

Jake's face was as red as the tomato on the hamburger. "Jake, please. My dad is Mr. Lambert." He managed to disentangle his hand and took a step backward.

I probably should have warned him about Candy but, truthfully, I didn't realize she'd be so gaga over a hockey player, especially one who didn't play for the Penguins, let alone the dreaded Rangers. I was under the impression she was all Steelers, all the time. Come to think of it, though, I

vaguely remembered her wearing a Pirates cap at one point.
She must be an equal opportunity sports fanatic. Before she
went after Jake again, I steered her over to the door. "Why
don't you have a seat in the pub and we can try some of this
food?"

She took one last adoring glance at Jake and disappeared
into the pub.

Jake started laughing. "Who—or better yet—what the
heck was that?"

"Shh! She'll hear you," I said, but I couldn't help laughing, too. I explained my next-door neighbor as best I could
while I helped him re-cover the plates and put them on a
tray, which Jake carried into the pub. I followed him through
the door, fingers crossed that it all tasted as good as it
looked.

CHAPTER FIVE

The food was as good as I'd hoped. After we'd put a pretty good dent in the six dishes Jake had made, Candy reluctantly went back to the bakery, but only after Jake promised her an autographed hockey puck. We cleaned up while I filled him in on exactly what his duties would be. Before he left, I gave him all of Kurt's paperwork, which included information regarding the kitchen staff he'd been interviewing and training. I told him if he had any questions, we could talk about it tomorrow.

Five minutes after he left, my phone rang. It was my brother, Mike. "Jake just told me the good news," he said.

"That was fast."

"He wanted to thank me for giving him the heads-up about the job," Mike said. "He couldn't say enough nice things about you."

I felt myself blushing. "Well, that's good, since we'll be seeing each other every day."

"Uh-huh."

I'd never told him, but I had a sneaking suspicion he knew I'd always had a thing for Jake.

"How's the repair I made?" he asked.

Happy he changed the subject, I filled him in. He told me if I needed anything else to give him a call.

After I hung up, I checked the tanks. Everything was in order, and for once I didn't have anything pressing that needed attending to. Figuring this might be a good time to talk to some of the neighbors, I made sure the kitchen door to the alley was locked, then grabbed my purse and headed for the main entrance. Before I reached it, the door opened and Adam Greeley stepped inside. I set my purse on the bar. This would be one neighbor I wouldn't have to visit. It was definitely better on my pocketbook—I wouldn't be tempted to buy anything.

Adam owned three boutiques on the other side of the street. Handbag Heaven sold designer handbags—everything from Vera Bradley to Coach. Fleet of Foot sold—no surprise—designer shoes. His third store, This and That, carried a little of everything.

"I heard about the accident and wanted to offer my condolences," he said.

"Thank you. I appreciate it." I pulled out a bar stool and motioned for him to sit.

He shook his head. "I can't stay. I don't like to be away for too long. Can't trust anyone nowadays. My employees will steal me blind."

Every time I talked to Adam, he seemed to get more

cynical. He was friendly to his customers, less so to his clerks. He'd always been cordial to me and to his other neighbors. I watched him as his gaze roamed the room. It was hard to guess his age, but I'd put him at mid-fifties. He was pencil slim, and he wore his steel gray hair pulled back in a ponytail. He was dressed in black pants, a red shirt, and a black tie, loosened at the neck. Very befitting a boutique owner.

"I see you finally got an alarm system," Adam said. "Very wise move—especially the motion detectors. I don't see any cameras, though. I keep mine running whenever I'm not there."

Considering his previous comment about his employees, it didn't surprise me.

The front door opened just then and my dad came in. "Am I interrupting?" he said.

"Not at all." I made the usual introductions and the men shook hands.

"I'd best be going," Adam said. "If you need anything, remember I'm right across the street."

Dad and I sat down at the bar. "I stopped to make sure you were doing all right," he said, "and to tell you Mr. Schmidt has arranged to have Kurt returned to Germany."

I assumed that was what Kurt's father would do. I wouldn't get to attend his funeral, but maybe I could do some kind of memorial here. I liked that idea. "Have you heard anything from the medical examiner yet?"

He didn't answer right away, and I knew he was trying to decide how much to tell me.

"Dad, I'm not a child."

"I know that. But you're still my little girl." He patted

my hand. "We got the preliminary findings from the medical examiner."

"And?"

"The ME said Kurt had some slight trauma to his head."

"I was right." I put my hands in my lap so my dad wouldn't see them shaking. "He was murdered."

"That's not likely."

"But you just said—"

Dad held up his hand. "Let me finish. The ME said the wound on his head could have occurred any number of ways, that, in his opinion, it was likely Kurt hit his head when he fell into the tank."

I shook my head. No way. Not super-careful Kurt. "That's not possible."

"We didn't find anything that someone could have hit Kurt with, and there was nothing to indicate that anyone else was even there."

"That doesn't mean no one was." Dad was silent, and I didn't like the expression on his face. There was something else. "What aren't you telling me?"

"Kurt hitting his head wasn't the cause of death," he said finally. "The ME thought it was hard enough to daze him, though."

My stomach lurched. He didn't have to spell it out for me.

"I'm sorry, Max."

I tried to wrap my mind around what Dad had just told me. It didn't fit the events of that night. Kurt was in the kitchen making his torte. Why would he leave perishable cherries and whipped cream out on the counter, go into the brewery, and climb the steps to look into the mash tun? The answer was that he wouldn't. I didn't care what the medical examiner thought. His conclusion was wrong. Kurt had been murdered. I couldn't sit any longer. I slid off the stool and paced back and forth. "What about Kurt's phone call to me?" I said. "It's too much of a coincidence that he said he found something and knew who was out to get us, and an hour later he's dead."

"Do you know what that something was?" Dad asked.

"No. Kurt wanted to show it to me."

"Do you know for sure someone was sabotaging the pub?"

"Not exactly, no. But Kurt did. He was sure of it, and I believe him."

My dad sighed. "I know you don't like it, but unless I discover otherwise—or find some new evidence—it will be ruled an accident." He got up and hugged me. "I'm sorry, sweetie. It's not what you wanted to hear. But if there's any new evidence, or something else comes up, we'll take another look. And definitely let me know if you have any more problems with vandalism."

After he left, I collapsed into a chair. I was stunned. Not to mention angry. There was no way Kurt had fallen into the mash tun. Even if he hadn't been hit over the head, someone had pushed him into that tank. I just had to prove it.

The flower shop, Beautiful Blooms, was next door to Cupcakes N'at, so I decided to start there. I liked flowers, of course, but didn't buy them all that often. Usually, I'd drop a bouquet into a vase and promptly forget all about it until all that was left were sticks and wilted petals. The shop was owned by Daisy Hart, who was outgoing and friendly and always had a smile on her face. I was sure she wasn't the one resorting to sabotage and murder, but she might have known something. I needed to order plants and flowers before the opening anyway, and this was as good a time as any to do it.

Daisy looked up when the bell on the door rang as I entered. "Max!" She dropped the lily she'd been trimming and rushed over to me. I wasn't too surprised when she pulled me into a hug. "I am so sorry about Kurt. Candy told me all about it. Such a horrible thing to happen to someone. I just can't believe it."

"Thanks. I can't, either."

Daisy looked like her name implied. She had shoulder-length blond hair that she wore in pigtails today. Together with her denim overalls, she could have been twelve years old instead of thirty. She took my hand and pulled me over to the glass counter, where she practically sat me down on a vintage piano stool.

The shop was decorated in a hodgepodge of vintage and hand-me-down items that somehow looked as if they belonged. There was even an old 1930s refrigerator that Daisy had taken the door off and now used to display small knick-knacks and tiny bud vases. She pulled out another stool and sat down.

"I wanted to come over to see you," she said, "but I didn't want to get in the way, and I didn't want to bother you."

"You wouldn't have been in the way. I spent yesterday cleaning and today hiring a new chef."

"Really? You hired a new chef?"

"You seem surprised."

"It's just that, well, I didn't expect it. Especially not so soon."

"I didn't have any choice with the opening so close. Besides, my brother recommended the guy, and I've known him all my life. It just seemed to be the right thing to do."

Daisy got up and went behind the glass counter. "So you'll be opening after all?" She picked up the lily she'd been holding when I came in. "I thought—I mean, I heard—" Her phone rang just then and she answered it.

While she took care of business, I walked around the shop looking at the plants and flowers and wondering why Daisy seemed to think I wouldn't be opening the brew house. Was that what everyone was thinking? It wouldn't have surprised me. In the months I'd been working on the brew house, I'd come across more than one person who thought Kurt was really in charge. A female brewmaster was as alien as, well, an alien. I wasn't going to let that bother me now.

Daisy finished her call. "Sorry about that."

"No need to apologize. Business should come first." I smiled. "Although I do plan on being a paying customer. I'm going to need to order some plants, and maybe some special arrangements, for the opening."

"Wonderful!"

I told her what I had in mind, and she showed me what she thought would work. I was more than pleased there would be no ferns. Not that I had anything against them, but I didn't want the pub to be anything like the yuppie hangouts of the eighties and nineties. I had painstakingly gone for a traditional pub look with a bit of industrial thrown in for good measure. I wanted it to feel like the Allegheny Brew House had always been there. With the plank floors, the oak tables, the brass foot rail on the bar, and the exposed brick and ductwork, I liked to think I'd accomplished it.

When we finished, Daisy said, "Is there anything else I can do for you?"

"Actually, there is." If I was going to find out anything to solve Kurt's murder, now was the time. "Have you seen anything strange going on near the brewery lately?"

"Strange? I'm not sure what you mean by that."

"I mean anyone hanging around who shouldn't be. Someone going in when no one is there. That sort of thing."

Daisy chewed her lip. "I haven't noticed anything. Other than the workmen you've had going in and out. But that's when either you or Kurt were there. Why?"

I couldn't very well come out and say Kurt had been murdered, especially when the police were calling it an accident. "We've had a few instances of vandalism. I was just wondering."

"Probably kids. Every time I put bouquets outside, some little brat will go by and grab one. I finally wised up and stopped putting them out." She reached under the counter and pulled out a dented aluminum baseball bat. She grinned. "The last time one of them tried to lift something from in here, I brought this baby out. They haven't been back since. You should at least get yourself one of these."

I laughed. "It's not quite as dramatic, but I did have an alarm system put in today."

"Now, why didn't I think of that? Of course, watching them run when I lifted the bat was a lot more fun."

* * *

After I left Daisy, I went home and retrieved my old Co-rolla from the parking lot. The poor thing probably felt neglected, since I hadn't driven it much lately. The upside to living and working in the same neighborhood was that I could walk most days. Unfortunately, I still needed a vehicle for everything else. The city has public transportation, but it didn't always go where I wanted to go. A car was much more convenient, especially when I needed groceries, which was where I was headed now.

Two hours later, I had restocked my fridge and cupboards and fixed a salad for dinner. I had eaten way too much of Jake's offerings at lunch, so I needed to make up for the excess in calories. Every extra pound showed on my small frame.

I'd had time to do a lot of thinking since leaving the flower shop. Daisy's surprise that I was still planning to open the brew house continued to bother me. I tried to recall her exact words. If I remembered right, she said she *heard* something. From whom? Candy liked to gossip, but it wouldn't have been from her. She knew my plans. Adam Greeley was a possibility, but he was more likely to complain about his employees. Dominic Costello was a better choice, but unless Daisy stopped at the Galaxy for a shot and a beer, he was probably out. I hadn't had a chance to talk to the other store owners yet to have opinions about them. Now that I'd given it some thought, I wasn't sure it mattered. It wasn't going to get me any closer to finding out who had murdered Kurt.

As the daughter of a homicide detective, you'd think I'd

know how to go about it, but the truth was, I had no idea. Dad had never brought his work home with him and never talked about cases with my brothers or me. Only one of us followed him into law enforcement. Patrick, my second oldest brother, was a police officer in Richmond, Virginia. He and Dad talked shop when we all got together, but only until Mom and Pat's wife put a stop to it. I considered calling him, but I was pretty sure he'd squeal to Dad and I didn't want that. I guess I could start by asking some questions, like I had this afternoon. I hadn't learned much from Daisy, but maybe I'd have better luck with the others tomorrow.

With that much decided, there was one more thing I wanted to do before the day was over. I grabbed my purse and headed out again.

My brother, Sean, was the pastor of Most Holy Name of Jesus parish in the Troy Hill section of Pittsburgh. The church was one of the older in the city, built in the late 1860s. The parish included St. Anthony's Chapel, which had the largest collection of relics outside the Vatican. The neighborhood sat on a bluff overlooking the Allegheny River, so I crossed the Fortieth Street Bridge and took Route 28 to Rialto Street. Rialto was known as Pig Hill or Pig Alley by the old-timers, because it had been the route used to drive pigs to local slaughterhouses. Neither the pigs nor the slaughterhouses were around anymore, thank goodness. Rialto was also one of the steepest roads in the city, but it was a convenient shortcut to the top of the hill. It shaved at least ten minutes from the drive.

Troy Hill didn't look all that different from some of the

residential sections of Lawrenceville. There were a few businesses along the short main drag, but the area was mostly
small single-family homes. Like many older, working-class
sections of the city, the houses were built close together.
Holy Name sat right smack in the middle of it all.

There were about a dozen cars in the asphalt parking lot,
and I wondered if maybe I should have called Sean first. I
knew there was a weekly novena in St. Anthony's Chapel,
but I thought that was on Tuesday nights, and this was
Wednesday. If it was tonight instead, I'd probably give Sean
the shock of his life. I hadn't been to a novena since I was
in high school. I went to the chapel first but found the door
locked, so my brother was safe for now. When I reached the
door of the main church, I heard singing. Inside, I discovered
the choir practicing, and I went searching for Sean. I definitely should have called first—he could be anywhere.

He wasn't in the church, but before I could slip out, one
of the choir members spotted me and asked if she could help
me. She told me Sean was probably in the rectory, so that's
where I headed. I probably should have gone there first. I
was just about to ring the bell when the front door opened.

"Max!" Sean said. "Is everything all right?"

"Everything's fine. I just wanted to see my big brother."

The expression of alarm on his face disappeared. "I was
worried for a second. I don't think I've ever seen you here
on a weeknight. As a matter of fact, I'm sure of it." He put
his arm around me. "I only have a few minutes. I'm heading
down to Allegheny General. One of my parishioners is
scheduled for heart surgery tomorrow and he asked for the
Anointing of the Sick."

"I only need a minute." I walked with him to his car and

told him about Kurt's dad having him returned to Germany for burial. "Kurt wasn't Catholic, but I'd like to have some kind of memorial service for him. I thought maybe you could help."

Sean nodded. "Definitely. Let me check my schedule and I'll get back to you either tonight or tomorrow sometime."

"Thanks."

He kissed me on the cheek and squeezed my shoulder. "And I *will* see you here on Sunday."

I watched him drive away and returned to my Corolla. I'd just started the engine when my cell phone rang. I didn't recognize the number. I answered anyway, ready to yell at whatever telemarketer was calling me even though I was on the Do Not Call Registry. I was wrong about who the caller was. It was the alarm company. My motion detectors had been set off.

CHAPTER SIX

Thankfully, traffic was light and I made it to the brew house in record time. A Pittsburgh Police Zone 2 squad car was double-parked on the street near the front entrance. I screeched into the lot beside the building and raced to meet the officer at the door.

"You the keyholder?" He looked me up and down like there was no way this place was mine.

I straightened in an attempt to make myself taller than my five-foot-two. "Yes. I'm the owner."

"I checked the doors already," he said. "They're all locked. No sign of forced entry. I'll check inside if you'd like."

"I would. Thanks." I unlocked the door and he went inside. I followed and punched in the alarm code.

"Wait there," he said.

I did, taking deep breaths to slow down my heartbeat, which could have kept time with a Spanish flamenco. I couldn't help replaying Monday night in my mind. It seemed like hours before Officer What's His Name returned, but I knew it was only minutes.

"You're all clear, miss."

"Are you sure?" I said. "The alarm company said the motion detectors were activated. Wouldn't that mean some-one was in here? How did they get in? How did they get out?" I was rambling, but I couldn't stop.

"Probably just a glitch of some kind. It happens all the time."

"I only had the alarm installed today, so I wouldn't know."

He suggested I follow up with the alarm company in the morning, then asked for my information for his report. When I told him my name, he looked at me again. "That name sounds familiar." He snapped his fingers. "Wasn't there an incident here the other night? I think I saw something on the call log."

I was not only jumpy, I was a little cranky by this point. I pulled myself up to my full height again, which was almost a foot shorter than he was. "My assistant was killed. I'm the one who found his body. So it was a lot more than an inci-dent, as you put it."

The officer had the good grace to blush and apologize to me. He even offered to do an extra drive-by before his shift was over. After he left, I locked the door behind him, then went to take a look around myself. Maybe I'd see something he missed.

Thirty minutes later, I hadn't found anything out of order.

Either the officer was right and there was a problem with the alarm, or my intruder was a magician. I went into the kitchen to get a drink of water. I turned the faucet on for the water to get cold while I retrieved a glass, and when I turned back to the sink, water was pouring out from the trap and onto the floor. I quickly shut off the water and grabbed a mop and some paper towels. After I dried the floor and under the sink, I inspected the trap. It was a good thing Sean wasn't within earshot, because I spat out every swear word I knew.

A nut on the trap had been loosened and there was a gap between the pipes. There was no problem with my motion detectors. They worked just fine. Someone really had broken in. But how in the world had he gotten in? And out? I was a little spooked about the whole thing, but I managed to put the trap back together and tighten the nut. I ran some water and there was no leak for now, so I washed my hands, reset the alarm, locked up, and headed home.

The more I thought about the break-in, the madder I got. Unable to sit still, I paced the floor in my living room. I really believed that, after Kurt's death, the vandalism would stop. Apparently, it wasn't enough that he'd killed Kurt. I didn't understand this person's motivation. If he was trying to keep me from opening, there were other—and probably better—ways to go about it. There were permits and inspections out the wazoo. Surely, a complaint or two— even a false complaint—to the right person would go further than messing with the plumbing.

And it totally baffled me how the person had gotten into the pub with no telltale signs. He hadn't set off any door or window alarms, only the motion detector. So how had he done it? I suddenly had an idea. I picked up the phone and called my dad's cell.

"Hey, sweetie," he said. "How are you?"

"I'm okay. I have a question. Do you happen to have Kurt's keys for the brewpub?"

"I can double-check, but I didn't see them in his personal effects. Why?"

I told him what happened. "I thought maybe someone stole his keys. That would explain how they got in."

"I don't like this at all. You need to change your locks, just in case. I'll call a locksmith I know and have him get in touch with you," he said. "I'm also going to see if a unit can do some extra drive-bys. And you shouldn't be there alone at night."

"Do you believe me now that Kurt's death wasn't an accident?"

He paused before answering. "I won't go that far, but I do agree something is going on."

He hadn't exactly said he'd keep Kurt's case open, but this was better than nothing. We talked a few more minutes, and I promised him I'd be careful. Five minutes later, the locksmith called and we agreed to meet first thing in the morning. Hopefully, between new locks and the alarm system, there would be no more vandalism. It didn't, however, get me any closer to figuring out who had killed Kurt.

The locksmith came as promised, and by nine a.m. I had brand-new locks and two sets of keys. I considered giving Candy a third set, since she was right next door, but changed my mind. Until Kurt's murderer was behind bars, Jake and I would be the sole key holders. Only Kurt and I had access before, and even that didn't turn out well. There was no sense complicating things any further by giving out extras.

Jake arrived as the locksmith was leaving. Today he was dressed in faded jeans and a black T-shirt. His hair still looked damp from the shower. My stomach did a little flip. "Something going on I should know about?" he said.

"Sort of." He worked here now, so it was time to tell him what was going on.

As he listened, his expression grew dark. When I finished, he said, "And you didn't think to tell me any of this before."

"Well, I—"

He swore. "Let me get this straight. Someone's been breaking in, he may have killed your previous chef, and he broke in again last night."

I felt my face flushing. "That pretty much sums it up."

Jake ran a hand through his hair. "Great. Just great."

"I understand perfectly if you want to quit. Maybe I should have told you—"

"Maybe? Maybe you should have told me?"

"I'm sorry," I said. "In retrospect, I should have said something, but I honestly didn't think the vandalism would continue. I didn't want to scare you off. And my dad thinks Kurt's death was an accident."

"But you don't."

"I'm sure it wasn't. There are too many things that don't fit for his death to be an accident." When Jake didn't say anything, I went over to the bar and picked up my purse.

"I'll pay you for yesterday of course, and today, for coming in."

Jake sighed. "Put that thing away."

"No, really. I want to pay you."

He walked over, took my purse from me and placed it back on the bar. "I didn't say I was going to quit."

He was close enough that I could smell the soap he'd used. I couldn't place the brand, but I liked it. I also liked the fact that he didn't feel the need to douse himself in cologne or one of those horrid body sprays. "You're not?" It came out like a squeak. So much for sounding like a boss. I was Max the teenager again.

"I'm not." He pulled out two bar stools and we sat. "It just would have been nice to know everything that's been going on. I had no idea. Mike never mentioned anything, either."

"Mike doesn't know, except for maybe the water line he had to fix. He saw that it had been cut, but I didn't explain anything about it. My dad knows, but that's it. And I'd kind of like to keep it that way. I don't want my mom to worry, and you know how my brothers get."

"They just want to take care of their baby sister."

"Yeah, well, baby sister is perfectly capable of taking care of herself."

"I'll try to remember that."

"You'd better."

Jake grinned. "Yes, boss lady." A serious look returned to his face. "But you have to promise me one thing."

"What's that?"

"If Kurt really was murdered, you could be in danger,

too. Any time you're planning to be here late, tell me. I don't want anything to happen to you."

The way he was looking at me made my stomach flip again. "I will."

"Good." He hopped off the stool and reached over and ruffled my hair. "Besides, I have no idea how to make beer. This place would flop without you running it."

So much for any hope of a future romance between us. I was back to being his best friend's little sister. In his eyes, I guess I always would be.

Jake was on the ball. By ten o'clock, he had talked to the kitchen staff Kurt had hired and scheduled two more interviews for that afternoon. He asked me to sit in on the interviews—he wanted me to have final approval. Although technically they'd be my employees, not his, he was the one who had to work with them day in and day out and I told him that. In the end, I agreed to sit in. It was a change from Kurt's way of working. He had preferred to do everything himself. Not a bad change, but it was one more thing for me to get used to.

Kurt had been very organized and Jake told me the files I'd given him the day before contained everything he needed. There were several recipes for each item on our menu, as well as names and numbers of all the restaurant suppliers. While Jake chose a few recipes to try out and made some calls to the various vendors, I decided it would be the perfect time to visit a few of my neighbors. I'd just gotten off the phone with Sean and we'd set up Kurt's memorial service for Monday evening, so it would give me an opportunity to extend an invitation. And to question them about anything suspicious they may have noticed near the brewery.

Jump, Jive & Java, the coffee hotspot on the opposite side of the street and next door to one of Adam Greeley's boutiques, seemed like a logical place to start. It had nothing to do with the fact that I had a sudden craving for their mocha java topped with whipped cream and chocolate jimmies. Or maybe it did. The fragrance of freshly ground coffee beans and the sound of Benny Goodman playing the clarinet welcomed me as I stepped inside. The place wasn't quite as busy as it was on most mornings, but there was still a good crowd—a mix of senior citizens, college students, young mothers with children, and a writer or two.

Barista and owner, Kristie Brinkley, looked up from her spot behind the counter. She always introduced herself as "Kristie with a K," although I'm sure no one would mistake her for the former supermodel. Not that she wasn't gorgeous—she was. She was African American and bore a striking resemblance to Halle Berry—if Ms. Berry wore dreadlocks, that is. Burgundy ones at that.

"Well, if it isn't my favorite brewmaster," Kristie said with a grin as I reached the counter.

"And exactly how many other brewmasters do you know?"

She pretended to think about it. "Zero. You're the one and only."

I laughed. "I thought so."

She reached over and squeezed my hand. "How are you? You doing okay?"

"I'm all right."

"I knew you would be. It's just such a shock." She reached for a cup. "Do you want the usual?"

"Yep."

While she fixed my mocha, I told her about the memorial service and she said she should be able to make it. No one else was in line after me, so she poured herself a cup of plain old coffee and joined me at the table next to a poster of *Casablanca*.

"Do you want to talk about it?" Kristie had a master's degree in psychology, and although she'd chosen not to pursue her doctorate and hang out her shingle, she often threw in a bit of counseling along with a cup of java. "It's healthy to get your feelings out."

"My feelings are out, believe me," I said.

"That's good. Can I help you with anything?"

I spooned the last of the whipped cream from the top of my mocha, licked the spoon, and set it down on the table. "Maybe." I told her about the vandalism, including the incident last night, and asked if she'd noticed anything out of the ordinary.

Kristie thought for a moment. "I can't say that I have, but I'm not usually here at night unless there's some neighborhood thing going on."

The fact that no one was open all night was throwing a wrench into my strategy of asking my neighbors if they'd seen anything. They couldn't very well see anything if they weren't there. I thought I might have to rethink my strategy.

"I can ask around. Some of my early morning customers are out and about all night. Maybe one of them saw something."

"That would be great," I said.

The door opened just then and Kristie got up. "We can talk about it tonight—if you're still coming."

I'd almost forgotten. Thursday was our monthly book club meeting at the Lawrenceville branch of the Carnegie Library of Pittsburgh. The group included Candy, who always supplied the goodies; Kristie's mother, Pearl; Amanda Morgan, the children's librarian; and Elmer Fairbanks, the only male in the group. I wasn't quite sure how Elmer had gotten involved other than that he was ninety-two years old and practically lived at the library. He'd attached himself somehow.

On the way to the counter, Kristie turned back and grinned. "If worse comes to worst, we can always stake out your place. I'm always up for an adventure."

I finished my mocha thinking about her suggestion. It wasn't a bad idea at all. As a matter of fact, it might be just the thing. The more I considered it, the more I liked it. I left the coffee shop with a plan in my head and a smile on my face.

The rest of the day passed quietly. The kitchen staff interviews went well. Jake seemed to know the right questions to ask and in the end decided to hire one of the two candidates. The other one had no cooking experience at all—I was reasonably sure he was just hoping for free beer. He smelled like he'd already had more than his share.

After that, I checked the beer I had fermenting but put off starting a new batch of anything. I couldn't delay it much longer, but I still couldn't bring myself to use the mash tun. I told myself I'd brew tomorrow. Back in my office, I sorted through some waitstaff applications and made a few phone calls to schedule interviews. We'd hired a few people already, but we needed to hire more. I couldn't put it off any longer.

I'd just finished up when Jake poked his head into my office. "How about we both call it a night and I take you out to dinner to celebrate my first full day as a chef?"

The idea was tempting, even if it did sound too much like a date and Jake didn't mean it that way. If I didn't have book club, I'd probably have taken him up on it. "Can I take a rain check? I already have plans tonight."

"Hot date?"

"No such luck, unless your idea of hot is an evening at the library with four other women and a ninety-year-old man."

"Well, now. That would depend on the women."

I laughed. "I guess it would."

Jake perched on the edge of my battered desk. "What about tomorrow night? I'd really like to celebrate."

In all the conversations we'd had, he hadn't once mentioned his fiancée in New York. I leaned back in my chair. "You mean you don't have a hot date on a Friday night? I thought you were engaged."

The smile left his face. "Not anymore."

Nothing like putting your foot in your mouth, Max. "I'm sorry to hear that."

"So was I."

"Do you want to talk about it?" Yikes. Now I sounded like Kristie.

"Not really. Let's just say it didn't work out, like a lot of other things."

Like hockey?

Jake stood. "You didn't answer my question. How about tomorrow night?"

I didn't have any reason to turn him down, so I said okay. After he left, I tried to push my second thoughts away. Just because Jake had no romantic interest in me was no reason not to go out with him. We were friends and coworkers. People who worked together went out all the time. We were just two friends having dinner.

By the time I got home, I had almost convinced myself. Almost.

CHAPTER SEVEN

"The football players today are a bunch of babies," Elmer Fairbanks said. "Back in my day, they didn't have all the fancy pads and hard helmets like they do now. Bunch of sissies, if you ask me."

"Well, we didn't ask you," Candy said. "And Terry Bradshaw isn't exactly one of today's players."

It had been Candy's turn to choose the book for discussion this month, so her choice had been a biography of Terry Bradshaw, who had been a Steelers quarterback in the seventies. I hoped Candy didn't ask me any questions, because I hadn't read the book. I scanned the dust jacket five minutes before the meeting. The discussion had barely begun when Elmer made his comment. Every month he had some complaint about the book, except when it was his turn, of course. I'd only been with the group for a few months, but I'd heard his picks varied between Zane Grey or Louis L'Amour and anything about World War II. I had a feeling he was a cowboy at heart. When he wasn't wearing his 101st Airborne ball cap, he wore a Stetson.

I liked the variety of genres. I'd been an avid reader as a child, but I'd had so much academic reading to do throughout college and grad school, I'd set pleasure reading aside. It was fun to get back to it. Ordinarily, I would have read this month's book, even though it wasn't a topic I was interested in. I had just gotten busy and forgotten about it until Kristie reminded me about the meeting. I was slowly learning the participants' tastes in reading. Since I joined the group, Kristie picked the latest women's fiction. Her mother, Pearl, liked historical fiction. Amanda, the children's librarian, had chosen a young adult novel. It would be my turn next month—my first time—and I had no idea what to have everyone read. I did know, however, that whatever the book was, Elmer would be sure to complain.

"I learned a lot, Candy," Pearl said. "I didn't know anything about Mr. Bradshaw before I read the book."

The other comments were more of the same. Needless to say, I didn't add much to the discussion. When it seemed like we were winding down, I excused myself to use the restroom, and when I got back, Candy and Kristie were standing in the corner, deep in conversation. Everyone else was digging into the cupcakes Candy had brought. I grabbed one for myself and sat down beside Amanda.

"These are delicious," Amanda said. "And so cute with those little footballs. I should get some of these for next week's story time. The children would love them."

Elmer made a face. "In my day we weren't allowed to eat in the library. These kids today—"

"We know, Elmer," Candy said, returning to the table with Kristie. She shoved another cupcake at him. "Stick this in your yap. The rest of us have something important to talk about."

"We sure do." Kristie tapped me on the arm. "You've been holding out on us, Max."

I had no idea what she meant.

"Why didn't you tell us Kurt was murdered?" Kristie said.

So that's what they'd been talking about. I'd figured Candy would spill the beans eventually. Actually, I was surprised she'd kept it to herself this long. The problem was, I didn't want everyone in Lawrenceville to know—at least not yet. Not until I had some proof to show my dad. I put my cupcake down on my napkin. "The medical examiner said Kurt's death was likely accidental."

"I take it you don't believe that," Pearl said.

Candy spoke up. "Of course she doesn't. Tell them what you told me, Max."

"I don't think—"

"Oh, no you don't," Kristie said. "You're not getting out of it now. You told me your place was getting vandalized. You didn't say anything about murder. Spill it, girl."

"It's true someone has been vandalizing the brewery. I didn't believe Kurt at first, but now . . ." I swallowed the lump forming in my throat. I should have been used to telling the story by now, but I wasn't. "There were a few minor things that were more annoying than anything."

"Like what?" Kristie asked.

"One morning, the mirror behind the bar was cracked when I arrived. Another time, some of the lights wouldn't turn on and Kurt found a problem with one of the breakers. Just the other day, a water line had been cut. Things like that."

"They don't sound minor to me," Pearl said. "Couldn't that breaker have started a fire?"

"That would depend," Elmer said. "But, yeah, it could."

I continued my story. "On Monday night, Kurt stayed late to work on a cake recipe that he didn't think was perfect yet. He called me and said he knew who had been causing the problems. He'd found something but wouldn't tell me what it was. He thought it was better to show me." My voice shook and I paused.

Candy patted my arm. "You're doing fine."

"When I got there, I didn't see Kurt anywhere. I thought he'd left for some reason. I should have known something was wrong when I found cherries and whipped cream sitting out on the counter. Kurt would have put them in the refrigerator if he'd gone anywhere. I finally called his cell phone and heard it ringing in the brewery. I followed the sound and found him."

The room was quiet when I finished. Elmer was the first to speak up. "Yep. Sounds like murder to me. If you need a bodyguard, young lady, I'm available."

It was the nicest thing I'd ever heard him say. "Thank you, Elmer. I appreciate the offer. I'll keep it in mind."

"What about suspects?" Elmer asked. "Do you have anyone in mind?"

"There's a bar owner who thinks I'll run him out of business." I was surprised that Candy only made a face at this and didn't jump to his defense. "Other than that, I'm at a loss. Everyone else in the neighborhood seems to like the idea of the pub. It'll bring more traffic to their stores."

Kristie agreed. "The busier the street is, the more business I get."

"Same here," Candy said. "It could be someone who doesn't want the extra traffic, or someone who plain just doesn't want a pub in there."

Pearl drummed her fingers on the table. "The killer doesn't necessarily have to be someone from the neighborhood. Your father is a police officer, isn't he?"

"Yes, he is."

"Perhaps someone has a grudge against him and is taking it out on you," Pearl said.

"I don't buy it," Elmer said. "If someone had a grudge against her pop, he'd come after Max. He wouldn't waste his time messing with the pub."

We went through a few more options but didn't come up with a thing.

One of the librarians opened the door and motioned for Amanda. She excused herself and said she'd be right back.

"I'm sorry we weren't more help," Pearl said. "Is there anything else we can do?"

I was out of ideas. "Just keep your eyes and ears open, I guess."

"I still think we should stake out your place," Kristie said.

"Ooh," Candy said. "That's a great idea. We'd be just like Charlie's Angels."

"The Three Stooges would be more like it," Elmer said.

I had to agree with him. The last thing I wanted was help to stake out my own pub. If I came right out and told them no, they'd try to talk me into it, so I just said, "Let me think about it."

"What's to think about?" Kristie asked.

"I have to check my schedule," I lied. We went back and forth a couple of times, with both Kristie and Candy insisting I never did anything but work.

Kristie attempted to get in the last word. "I say we meet at eleven tomorrow night. We can sit in the coffee shop and watch the front of the building."

"What about the back?" Candy asked. "Someone needs to watch the alley."

"You may as well count me in," Elmer said. "I'll keep an eye on the back door."

This was ridiculous. I jumped up. "No. Absolutely not. I appreciate the offer, and I appreciate you wanting to help, but I can't allow it. You're forgetting that Kurt was murdered in cold blood. I am not going to put any of you in danger just so you can play detective."

Amanda took that moment to come back to the room. "I'm sorry about that. Someone had a question about a new children's book." No one said anything, and she looked at me. "Did I miss something?"

"Nothing important," I said.

"Max is being a spoilsport, that's all," Kristie said to Amanda. She turned to me. "I still think it's a good idea."

Maybe it was, but every word I'd said was true. I couldn't risk anyone else getting hurt. Or worse. If anyone was going to stake out the pub, it would be me. Alone.

* * *

I went right home from the library. I planned to take a two-hour nap, then head to the brewery. Other than last night when the alarm had gone off, I had no idea what time the break-ins had occurred. Whoever it was seemed to know my schedule—or at least when the brewery was empty. Except for the night Kurt was killed, that is. Had the killer expected it to be empty? Or had he gone after Kurt because Kurt had figured out his identity?

I changed into old jeans and a T-shirt, stretched out on my bed, and closed my eyes, but my mind wouldn't stop racing. I tried some deep breathing but I was still wired and couldn't fall asleep. Thirty minutes later, I gave up. I guessed I'd start my stakeout early.

Butler Street was busy no matter the time of day or night. It was one of the main arteries through Lawrenceville and eventually merged with Penn Avenue, which ran into downtown Pittsburgh. Between the cars driving by and those that were parked, my car wouldn't be the only one on the street. Not that my old Corolla was all that recognizable. I just didn't want Kurt's killer to see it. If he knew it was my car, he might change his mind. I didn't want to park in the lot beside the pub because it would be too obvious, even though that would be the best vantage point to see both the front and back of the building. Parking on the street would limit me to watching the front of the pub only. If I couldn't find anything on the street, my default plan was to park in the lot across the street beside the deli. I drove around the block once before choosing a spot three storefronts up on the opposite side of the street. It was late, so the deli, as well as Adam's boutiques next to it, was closed.

I could see the front door and windows easily from my vantage point. If the killer had stolen Kurt's keys and tried using them on the front door, he'd have a surprise coming. I realized then I should have brought a camera with me. I could always use the one on my phone, but there was no zoom feature on it. I made a mental note to bring the camera next time. If there was a next time.

Shortly after eleven, a police car drove by and slowed as it passed the pub. I slid down in my seat, even though I was on the opposite side of the street and the officer was looking in the other direction. The last thing I needed was for my dad to discover what I was doing. By midnight traffic had dwindled a bit, and I was having trouble keeping my eyes open. Not to mention the fact that I'd forgotten to bring a jacket and I was shivering because the temperature had dropped into the fifties. I didn't want to call it a night just yet, so I decided to spend the next hour inside the pub. I'd have to keep the alarm off, but I could always use the panic-alarm button if I had to. Or I could lock myself in my office and call 911.

Inside, I locked the door behind me and took a quick walk-through. Finding everything in order, I went to my office. I flipped through the bills that were due and put them in the order I wanted to pay them. I jotted down some notes for what I needed to do over the weekend and soon found myself nodding off. I leaned back in my chair and closed my eyes. I'd just rest them for a few minutes.

When I opened my eyes again, it took a few seconds to

remember where I was. I glanced at the clock on the wall—two o'clock. I'd been asleep for an hour. Sheesh. Time to go home. I gathered up my purse and keys, then went to make sure the back door was locked. I rattled the knob, and as I turned away I thought I heard a scratching sound outside the door. I shook the knob again and the sound repeated. I did so once more, but this time the sound was accompanied by a faint mew.

"What the heck?" I said out loud. There was a dusk-to-dawn light outside the door, but I flicked on another light anyway, then unlocked the door and eased it open a few inches. A cat—really just a kitten—sat outside. It let out the most pitiful mew I'd ever heard, and my heart melted. We'd had various dogs growing up and I'd always wanted a cat, but my mother had insisted a dog was more than enough. With the large household she had to take care of, she was probably right.

The kitten meowed again. It was holding one front paw up and the leg didn't look quite right to me. I reached down and scooped him up. "Well, hello, little fella." I turned him over on his back and held him like a baby. "Make that hello, little girl. You're a girl kitty, aren't you?"

The mostly gray tabby yipped in response. The fur on her belly and up her neck was white, although a little dirty. Her paws looked like she was wearing white boots or socks. I gently touched the leg that didn't look quite right—the one she'd been holding up. She squirmed and let out a whimper. I couldn't see exactly what was wrong, but something definitely was. She wasn't wearing a collar, but that didn't necessarily mean she didn't belong to someone. Even if she did, I wasn't about to leave her to fend for herself. She couldn't be more than three months old. I'd take her home with me and figure the rest out tomorrow.

On the way home, I stopped at the Giant Eagle grocery, which was open twenty-four hours. I locked the kitten in the car while I went inside and purchased some kitten food, two bowls, and a small box of litter. I had plenty of boxes at home that would substitute as a litter box until I found out whether she belonged to someone. When I returned to the car, she was curled up on the passenger seat, sound asleep.

CHAPTER EIGHT

Two tiny green eyes stared at me when I woke up the next morning. The kitten sat on my chest and made a noise that sounded more like a chirp than a meow. Maybe she was letting me know she was hungry. I'd fed her when we got home last night, and after she'd wolfed down a good bit of food, I sat her in the improvised litter box I'd made from a cardboard box lined with a plastic bag. It took her only seconds to figure it out.

I picked her up, put her on the floor, and she limped behind me to the kitchen. She still wasn't putting any weight on her front paw. Poor little thing. I thought I should take her to see a vet as soon as possible. She ate all the food I put in her dish. When I went to shower, she followed me into the bathroom and sat on the lilac throw rug until I finished. She followed me to the bedroom and somehow managed to claw her way up the side of the bed. My blue-and-white-striped comforter was in a heap at the foot of the bed. I thought she'd make herself comfortable on there, but she plopped down on the jeans I'd laid out instead. I moved her so I could dress, then she decided my shirt would be a good place to sit. I couldn't help laughing—she was so comical. Any thoughts I'd had of leaving her here when I went to the pub vanished. There was no way I could leave her alone.

When we got to the brewery, I made a bed for the kitten in the corner of my office out of an old blanket I brought from home. I'd need to make sure the office door stayed closed. I didn't want to be accused of any kind of health violation with an animal running loose in a restaurant—even if we weren't open yet. I put her food and water dishes out and placed her litter box in the other corner of the room. As soon as I was sure she was asleep, I closed the door and went over to Cupcakes N'at to get something to eat. I really needed to stop making a habit out of eating Candy's treats on a daily basis. Either that or start running again. I wasn't sure what would be worse. I liked most forms of exercise, but running wasn't one of them. I guessed I could always get a bike. We were a pretty bike-friendly city.

The bakery wasn't busy like it was the last time I'd been here. As a matter of fact, I was the only customer at the moment, which was perfectly fine with me. Candy came out of the kitchen when she heard the bell on the door. "Just the person I wanted to see," she said.

That could be good or bad, depending on why she wanted to see me. "Really?"

"I may have come up with another suspect. I definitely don't think it's someone trying to get revenge on your dad.

I can't believe I'm saying this, but I agree with Elmer on that one."

"I do, too. Who did you come up with?"

"What about Ken Butterfield from the deli? He could be afraid everyone will go to the pub to eat instead of his place."

"I don't know. . . ."

"It makes as much sense as Dom thinking you're going to steal all his customers."

She had a point, but Ken had never threatened me. He had always been cordial and excited about the brewery. I told her that. "Anyone else?"

"What about someone Kurt had crossed?"

"That's possible, I guess," I said, "but I have no way of knowing who that could be."

"I'm out of ideas, then. But I'll come up with something." She crossed her arms over her ample chest. "And I'm a little miffed that you don't like our stakeout idea. Why, the three of us—"

I didn't let her finish. "I never said I didn't like it. I said it was too dangerous. Big difference."

"We'd be sitting in our cars or in the coffee shop. I don't see how that could possibly be unsafe. If anyone showed up, we'd call 911. We wouldn't be dumb enough to confront him. Or her. Or whoever."

I wasn't so sure about that. It was easy to imagine Candy jumping out of her car and tackling the guy. I tried another tactic. "It would be a waste of time. I have an alarm, and the police are doing extra drive-bys. Time would be better spent talking to possible suspects, which I plan to do."

"And when do you think you'll have time to do that?"

"Today. I hope."

"Hoping doesn't make it happen." Her voice softened. "We just want to help. Kurt was a good man. I didn't know him anywhere near as long as you, but I liked him a lot. Let us help you with something, even if it's just brainstorming ideas or trying to come up with some more suspects."

I blinked away the tears that suddenly formed in my eyes. I'd met a few generous people in my life, but Candy really took the cake. No pun intended. Kristie, too. "Thanks," I said. "I could use a few new ideas."

Candy beamed. "How about tonight, then? We could all meet at my house."

I started to agree, then remembered dinner. "I can't tonight. I already have plans."

"You do?"

"Don't sound so surprised."

"I'm sorry. I didn't mean to, but I can't remember the last time you did anything but work on a Friday night. You—and Kurt, too—were always there late. Well, maybe not always, but most nights. Not that I keep track of your comings and goings or anything." She smiled. "Who am I kidding? Of course, I do. Someone's got to watch out for our little Max."

Like I didn't already have my brothers doing that. "Jake wants to buy me dinner to celebrate his hiring."

Candy clapped her hands together. "That's wonderful! You have a date! And with a famous hockey player, too."

I should have known she'd get the wrong idea. I had to set her straight or, before I knew it, everyone in Lawrenceville— or more like everyone in Pittsburgh—would think Jake and I were an item. "It's not a date. Jake is just being nice."

"You don't seriously believe that, do you?"

"Of course I do." She gave me a look, so I told her more about our background and how we'd grown up together. "He still thinks of me as Mike's baby sister and always will. I'm okay with that."

"I'm not buying it," Candy said. "There's something there. You mark my words." The door chimed then, as another customer came in. She leaned over the counter, and whispered to me, "You had better invite me to the wedding."

I laughed and shook my head. "Never gonna happen." With that, I bought a half dozen sweet rolls and left.

Outside the pub, I almost bumped into Adam Greeley. Or I should say he almost bumped into me. He was walking fast with his head down, not paying attention to where he was going. I dodged him by jumping to the left and in the process dropped my bakery box. At the last minute, he realized what happened and halted before he tramped on it. "Sorry," he said. "I guess my mind was on something else."

Obviously. "Nothing bad, I hope."

"Nothing I can't handle."

I bent over to pick up the box, but Adam beat me to it. "Here you go," he said.

When I took the box from him, I noticed his right hand was bandaged. The gauze wrapped around his entire palm up to the wrist. "What happened?" I asked.

"This?" He held up his hand. "A mere scratch."

The way it was all wrapped up, it looked like more than that to me. I would have just slapped a Band-Aid on a scratch, but then I wasn't the fussbudget Adam seemed to be. From what I could tell, he went overboard on most things. I unlocked the door and Adam followed me inside.

"I'm glad I ran into you," he said, then smiled. "I guess I should say almost ran into you. I've been wanting to talk to you about something."

I deactivated the alarm. "Really?"

"Maybe we could set something up for next week. After the memorial service, of course."

Word traveled fast. I hadn't even told him about the service yet. Candy had probably taken care of that for me. Before I could ask what he wanted to talk about, he glanced at his watch and said he had to run. I'd find out eventually. I put the bakery box on the bar. I had one more stop to make before I went back to work, and I didn't want to leave the kitten alone for too long.

I jaywalked across the street to Jump, Jive & Java and made it to the other side unscathed. Pittsburgh drivers were used to pedestrians crossing anywhere they pleased. Sometimes the drivers even stopped and waved you across. If the city ever started ticketing for jaywalking, like some other cities, they'd have a regular revenue stream. And probably a major revolt.

Kristie was at her usual spot behind the counter. I made my way through the tables thinking how much easier it would be if Candy and Kristie would only combine their businesses. Jump, Jive & Java did have prepackaged items, but I'd have to be nuts to choose one of those over one of Candy's creations. I waited in line while the customer in front of me paid for his coffee.

"Hey, Max," Kristie said. "The usual?"

"I think I'll live dangerously today and have some plain old coffee. With an extra shot. I could use the caffeine."

She grinned. "Book club too much for you last night?"

I couldn't very well tell her what I'd really been up to, especially since it had been her idea. "Not exactly. Just didn't get a lot of sleep."

"Ooh. Tell me it was because of that new chef of yours. Candy told me all about him."

Surprise, surprise. "Nope."

"Dang." She passed my coffee across the counter. "Have you changed your mind yet about my plan?"

I told her the same thing I told Candy.

"Did anyone ever tell you you're no fun?" Kristie said.

"All the time."

Kristie picked up a rag and wiped an imaginary spot on the counter. "I saw you talking to Adam Greeley before."

"Yeah. It was weird. He was in a bit of a hurry, but he said he had something he wanted to talk to me about. That maybe we could get together next week after the memorial service. I can't imagine what it would be. It's not like we have anything in common."

"Maybe he has the hots for you."

I rolled my eyes. "He's old enough to be my father."

"That doesn't stop some people."

"True. But even if he were younger, he's not my type."

"So, what is your type, Max?" Kristie wiggled her eyebrows. "Maybe your new chef?"

I felt my face turning red.

"Oh ho! I'm right!"

"No. Not exactly, anyway. Jake and I go way back. I had a teenage crush on him. That's all."

"Seems to me the crush is still on," she said. "Especially since I hear you two have a date tonight."

Candy. Again. Did everyone on Butler Street know about

this now? The answer to my own question was most likely yes. I sighed. "It's not a date." I wondered how many times I was going to have to repeat that sentence.

"I want a full report on this non-date in the morning." She gave me an evil grin as another customer came in. "Or maybe I should wait until the afternoon." Her suggestive tone underscored the innuendo.

I couldn't help laughing. "Keep dreaming," I said.

It was the middle of the morning rush hour and traffic was heavy, which actually made it easier to cross. I didn't have to dodge anyone trying to go fifty in a twenty-five-mile-per-hour zone. Once inside the pub, I retrieved the bakery box from the bar and headed straight to my office to check on the kitten. When I reached it, the door was open several inches.

"Oh no," I said aloud. I pushed it open the rest of the way and made a beeline for the kitten's bed. It was empty. I put my coffee cup down and dropped the box on the desk and frantically searched every inch of the room with no luck.

Somehow the kitten had escaped.

CHAPTER NINE

"Kitty? Where are you, kitty?" Like she was going to answer me. She couldn't have gotten far. Between her bum leg and the doors separating the restaurant area from the brewery and the kitchen, she had to be in the pub. But where? And how had she managed to open the door? I could have sworn I'd closed it tightly. I stood in the middle of the pub, turned in a circle, and eyed the areas under the tables. "Here, kitty. Come out, come out, wherever you are." I checked behind the bar and in every nook and cranny I could think of. She was nowhere to be found. "Where are you?" I said aloud.

The door to the kitchen opened and Jake came into the room—with the kitten in his arms. Relief washed over me. That and the thought that he looked really cute holding a kitten.

"I found this cute little guy in your office," he said.

"Girl."

"Huh?"

"It's a she. A girl." I reached over and took the kitten from him.

Jake grinned sheepishly. "I really do know the difference. I just didn't get that close of a look." He moved next to me and scratched the kitten on the head.

His hand bumped mine, and it was suddenly very warm in the room. Oh boy. That wasn't good. He was close enough that I could smell his soap again. Or maybe it was his shampoo. His hair was still damp and a stray lock hung over his forehead. It took everything in me not to reach up and brush it away. Definitely not good.

I backed away, saying to the kitten, "I was so worried about you. I thought you got lost."

"Sorry about that," Jake said. "I went looking for you and instead found this little guy—I mean girl. Friendly little thing. She came right over to me and started rubbing on my leg. I should have left her there, but . . ." He shrugged. "I guess I'm just an old softie. She looked so pitiful with her hurt leg, I picked her up and took her with me."

"I know what you mean."

"Where did she come from?" Jake asked.

I told him the story, leaving out the part about staking out my own pub. I also didn't tell him how late it had been when I found her. It would lead to a lecture, and that was the last thing I wanted from Jake. And if he said anything to Mike, I'd get one from him, too. Then one from Mom. And probably Dad. "I need to take her to a vet today.

And see if she has an owner. Someone could be looking for her."

"Do you think she's a stray?"

"I don't know. I kind of hope she is. I'm not sure I could give her back if she belongs to someone. I might have to ask for visitation rights."

"You two look like you belong together." He smiled. "Makes me feel a little jealous."

I stared at his back as he turned and headed to the kitchen, wondering which one of us he was jealous of. Surely not the cat.

There was a veterinarian located several blocks north of the brew house. I called and explained the situation and made an appointment for early that afternoon. In the meantime, while the kitten napped again, I decided to start another batch of beer, which meant I had to face the mash tun. I'd put it off long enough.

I thought about brewing a dunkel, a dark lager, but decided on an India Pale Ale instead. IPAs weren't my favorite. The abundant hops gave them a bitter taste, which I didn't especially care for, but if I wanted to sell my product, I needed to brew what customers wanted. The fact that an ale took only a couple of weeks to ferment, as opposed to eight or more for a dunkel, helped sway me, too. Besides, I had several barrels of dunkel already.

In the storage area, I stacked a few bags of barley malt on a dolly, wheeled them into the brewing area, and lugged the fifty-five-pound bags one by one up the steel stairs to the

platform by the mash tun. I repeated the process until I had
what I needed, and by the time I finished, I was sweating.
Whoever said beer makes you gain weight had obviously
never worked in a brewery.

I checked the clock and did a quick calculation in my
head. The grain needed an hour in the mash tun, then time
for sparging, and about ninety minutes to boil. While it was
boiling, I'd take the kitten to the vet, then come back and
finish the process by getting the wort to the fermentation
tank. If Kurt had been here, he would have been able to do
the last part if I wasn't back in time.

Kurt.

A lump formed in my throat as I gazed down into the
tun. I wasn't ready for this. But I had to be. I had a business
to get off the ground, and Kurt would have been the first
one to tell me to suck it up and get back to work. I swallowed
hard, took a deep breath, and did just that.

The kitten made a noise that sounded like "murp" as I
carried her into the veterinarian's office. I checked in
with the receptionist, who made a big fuss over the kitten.
When she asked me her name, I didn't quite know what to
say. "She doesn't have one" didn't seem right, so I settled for
"I haven't decided yet," which was partly true. I would have
to pick one if she didn't belong to anyone and I ended up
keeping her, but I was afraid it would make it harder to part
with her if I gave her a name. So I waited.

We'd only been seated a few minutes when the door
opened and we were called to go in. Or rather "Kitten
O'Hara" was called. I guess I was just along for the ride.

And to pay the bill, which I hoped wouldn't be astronomical. The vet tech weighed the kitten and got us settled in an exam room, then left. Less than a minute passed before the door opened again.

"Hi, I'm Doctor Perry." The doc was about my age. He was average height—not tall and not short. He had a nice smile.

"Max," I said, reaching out my hand for him to shake.

"And who's your little friend?" He gently took the kitten from my arms and placed her on the exam table. She purred as the doc gave her a one-finger neck rub.

I explained how I'd found her the previous night and that I wasn't sure if she was a stray or if she belonged to someone, but I thought her leg needed some attention. He examined her while I talked, and when he got to her leg, she whimpered.

"Hmm," he said.

"What does that mean?"

He reached over and pressed a button on the wall. "I'd like to x-ray that leg. If it's all right with you, that is."

Ka-ching. "Of course." What else could I say?

After the x-ray had been taken and developed, Doctor Perry put it up on the light box. "Look right here," he said, pointing at the film. "You can see her leg is fractured in two places."

"Oh, the poor thing! I had no idea it was that bad. She didn't even complain all that much. She just didn't use that leg. Shouldn't a fracture hurt more than that?"

"Cats are very stoic creatures. They don't show pain like we mere mortals do." He gave me a patient smile. "You told me she was most likely a stray."

I nodded.

"I tend to agree with that. She hasn't been microchipped, which most people do nowadays. Although, since she's so young, it's possible that her human family—if she has one—just hasn't gotten around to it yet. My question is: What are your intentions? Do you mean to keep the kitten if no one claims her?"

I didn't hesitate. "Yes. I want to keep her."

We discussed treatment, which involved a cast for a couple of weeks and then a soft splint until the leg was completely healed. The office manager came in with a consent form and a paper detailing the costs, which almost gave me a heart attack. I signed both papers. Thank goodness they had a payment plan. I didn't think a broken leg of my own would cost as much. I sincerely hoped that, if it turned out she did have a family, they would reimburse me.

Doctor Perry planned to sedate her to set the bone and put the cast on. He also wanted to give her some intravenous antibiotics in case an infection had started in her leg, so she'd be staying overnight. He promised to call and keep me posted on her progress. There were tears in my eyes as I patted her on the head and said good-bye. How in the world had I gotten so attached so quickly?

"Murp." The kitten batted my hand with her head.

I scratched the area above her nose. "You behave yourself, Hops."

Doctor Perry smiled. "Hops? I guess you decided on a name after all."

I guessed I had.

* * *

𝔍ake came into the brewery as I was about to add the finishing hops to the IPA. "Hey," he said. "I thought I heard you come in. How's the kitten? Where is she, by the way? I didn't see her in your office."

I filled him in on the visit with Doctor Perry. "I'll be able to pick her up tomorrow," I finished.

Jake pointed to the tank. "What are you brewing?"

I told him it was an IPA and explained what I was doing. "These are the finishing hops. They're what give the taste that lingers after you drink the beer."

"I didn't realize there were different kinds of hops."

"More than you can imagine."

"Looks like I have a lot to learn," he said. "What's next with this batch?"

"I have to separate the wort—the liquid—from the solids, then drain it. It goes to the fermentation tank, where it's cooled, and then I test the specific gravity . . ."

"That sounds suspiciously like chemistry."

I grinned. "That's exactly what it is."

"I guess I never thought much about it. Why do you need to know the specific gravity?"

"I actually measure it twice," I explained. "The first time is to get a base reading. That's called the original gravity. I do it again at the end of fermentation, and that reading helps determine what the alcohol content is."

"Interesting. Then what?" he asked.

"The yeast is added and we wait for it to ferment." I could have gotten into more of the chemistry of how sugar is converted to ethyl alcohol, but I didn't want to overwhelm him, so I kept it simple. "The type of beer determines what temperature we keep the fermentation tank and how long to leave it in there. This beer is a pale ale, so it'll ferment for about two weeks." I showed him the temperature gauge on the tank. "I'll keep the temp at about sixty-eight degrees." I pointed to the other tank, where the hefeweizen was fermenting. "That one's also at sixty-eight."

"What about a lager?" Jake asked.

"Forty-eight degrees for six weeks."

"Stout?"

I gave him a look. "What is this? A test?"

He laughed. "I'm only making sure you know your stuff."

"Uh-huh."

"Seriously, I'd like to know more. I don't have the background you do, but I'd like to learn brewing anyway."

A man after my own heart. I'd almost said it aloud. I felt my cheeks reddening, so I turned away and checked the pressure gauge on the fermentation tank. "That would be a big help."

I talked through the next steps in the process as I did them. He asked good, intelligent questions, and before I knew it we were done. Except for one thing.

"So, what's next, boss lady?"

I grinned and pointed to the hose. "Cleanup."

I called it quits for the day around four. Doctor Perry had called at three to let me know Hops was doing fine and I could pick her up at ten the next morning. Jake had already left and was picking me up at six-thirty for dinner. That gave me plenty of time to shower and change. I had no idea where we were going—only that I should dress casual, which was how I usually dressed anyway, so it wouldn't be a problem.

The closer it got to six-thirty, the more nervous I became. I tried to tell myself I was being ridiculous. This wasn't a date. Like I'd told Candy, we were merely two friends and coworkers going out to eat. It was no different than the other night when I'd first run into Jake. I kept repeating this to myself. By the time I'd tried on and discarded my third outfit, I gave up.

I plopped down on my bed in my underwear, clothes strewn around me. This was crazy. What in the world was I doing? So what if I had a crush on Jake? I had always had one. The fact that I was older now didn't matter. I could like him all I wanted. I could imagine . . . well, anything I wanted. I could even write *Mrs. Jake Lambert* on notebook paper like I had when I was fourteen if I wanted. Just because it wasn't mutual didn't mean I couldn't feel this way. Jake didn't have to know. The thought was rather liberating. I smiled to myself as I tugged on the charcoal gray chinos and the raspberry cotton sweater set that had been my first choice. I finished getting ready as my doorbell rang.

I was glad I'd worn the chinos instead of jeans. The place Jake had chosen was casual but definitely upscale casual. The restaurant was named Chrome, and it was located in the Strip District in downtown Pittsburgh. The Strip, as we natives called it, stretched for almost twenty blocks. It was easy to reach from Lawrenceville, as the same streets ran through both. Originally, this section of the city was home to factories and the Fort Pitt Foundry, which made cannons for the Civil War. Because of its location next to the Allegheny River and the railroads, it soon became the hub of commerce with numerous wholesalers and produce yards. It was still a vibrant shopping area full of stores that sold ethnic food, meats, cheeses, fresh fish, and produce. There were street vendors selling just about anything you could think of, from Steeler jerseys to jewelry to incense. It was also the home of Primanti Bros. restaurant, famous for serving French fries and coleslaw *on* the sandwich.

Chrome was nothing like Primanti's however. It was sleek and modern, and kind of industrial-looking. The space now occupied by Chrome had been a rowdy nightclub that was shuttered after numerous bar fights, including an incident where three people were stabbed. The final straw was a shooting that resulted in a fatality. The place had been up for sale the following week. The lack of bar fights was one of many reasons I preferred a brewpub over a bar or nightclub. Very few brewpub customers were there to get drunk. They came to enjoy the craft beer and get a tasty bite to eat. Once in a while someone had one too many, but it was rare. And I'd make sure the staff knew how to handle them.

Jake had made reservations, and the hostess seated us in a booth halfway between the entrance and the kitchen in the back. I automatically picked up the drink list and checked to see what beers they had. I was disappointed they were all brand-name domestics. Not a craft beer to be found. Not that I would have been able to order one. I barely had time to read the list when a waiter brought over a bottle of champagne.

I looked at Jake

"I hope you don't mind," he said. "I thought a celebration was in order. You know, you taking a chance on me."

I knew he meant me hiring him, even though I wanted to imagine the other thing. "I don't mind."

The waiter poured and stood beside the table.

Jake raised his flute. "Here's to a long and happy relationship."

We clinked glasses and took sips, then Jake nodded to the waiter. The server set the bottle on the table and leaned over. "Congratulations. I hope you're very happy and have a long life together."

I almost dropped my glass. I felt the heat in my face and was sure it was fire engine red. Jake thanked the waiter and didn't bother setting him straight.

"Jake! Why didn't you correct him?"

His eyes twinkled. "Why should I?"

"He thinks . . ." I couldn't even say it. *He thinks we're a couple. Engaged to be married.*

Jake's grin was wicked. "So? Is that such a revolting idea?"

My face flamed again. "No! Not at all." *On the contrary.*

Jake picked up his menu. "Then it doesn't matter what he thinks. I got over caring about what people think when I went to play for the Rangers. I was called a traitor—and much worse."

I had been a huge sports fan as a kid and through college—I mean, who wouldn't be with five brothers? I even had a Lynn Swann jersey that had been my dad's. But living overseas for five years, I'd lost touch with American sports. Until I'd met Candy, that is. Believe me, she filled me in. I knew all the teams that were hated rivals to the Steelers, Pirates, and Penguins. The New York Rangers were up there near the top. I hadn't realized, however, how that would affect a hometown boy playing for them.

"It was that bad?" I said.

He made a face. "Only if you consider threats to break my legs and arms, and shove the stick—"

"I get the picture. What about now? Do you still get threats, since you're not playing anymore?"

He shook his head and smiled. "Nope. Now I'm like the prodigal son. Hometown kid comes back to his roots."

"Do you miss playing hockey?"

"Yes."

"Why did you retire so early, then? Wouldn't you have had a few more years to play?"

"Things don't always work out the way we want them to." He opened his menu. "So what looks good to you?"

That topic apparently was off-limits. It wasn't the first time he'd changed the subject when I asked about his retirement. I didn't understand why he wouldn't talk about it. It wasn't like I was a complete stranger, or a reporter wanting a big scoop or hoping for a scandal. I guess I'd just have to be patient. Or ask Mike, like I'd thought of doing before. Knowing my brother, though, he wouldn't tell me anything if Jake told him to keep it a secret.

I stole peeks at Jake while I perused the menu. His baby blue oxford shirt was a nice contrast to his brown hair and eyes. He had wide shoulders and muscular arms. Not playing hockey sure hadn't hurt his physique any. I forced my gaze back to the menu before he caught me staring.

All in all, it was an enjoyable but unremarkable dinner. We talked about plans for the pub, and Jake told me about a few new recipes he wanted to try. As we were leaving,

Jake's cell phone rang. I smiled at the ring tone—it was the song they played at the start of the Penguins' games.

Jake wasn't smiling, though. He frowned when he glanced at the display. I was standing right beside him and caught the caller's name: Victoria. My stomach dropped at least to my knees, and I felt like someone had dumped a bucket of ice water over my head. The supermodel. I'd forgotten about her. Totally and completely. He hit the ignore button and pocketed the phone.

"Don't you have to get that?" I asked.

"It's not important."

"But isn't that your—"

"Ex-fiancée," he said before I even had the word out. "Yes. And I'm not interested in anything she has to say."

CHAPTER TEN

Jake put up a hand. "Before you ask, I don't want to talk about it. She's history. End of story."

As much as I wanted to hear the whole tale and not just the end, I kept my mouth shut. From the set of Jake's jaw, he was still angry about the breakup. I couldn't help wondering if Ms. Supermodel had dumped him or if she'd done something to cause Jake to break up with her. I told myself to mind my own business. He would tell me eventually. I hoped.

He was distracted on the ride back to my place and conversation was practically nonexistent. I gave up trying to get him to talk the third time he said, "Huh?" to one of my questions. I gave him credit for at least walking me to my door instead of just dropping me off. A good night kiss, or even a friendly peck on the cheek, was out of the question.

I couldn't fall asleep, although I should have been exhausted. I had too much on my mind, between thinking about Kurt's death, getting the brewpub up and running, the kitten and her broken leg, and now Jake's situation. I finally dozed off around four and woke up at eight. I dragged myself out of bed and headed to the kitchen to make coffee. Extra strong. I had a lot to do today.

After I showered and dressed, I went to pick up Hops at the vet. I was shown to an exam room, and minutes later Doctor Perry brought the kitten in and put her down on the exam table. She scrambled over to me, holding her hot pink soft cast out in front of her like she was saying, "Look what I got!"

"She did great," Doctor Perry said. "She's quite a charmer. I had three staff members arguing about which one of them would get to take care of her." He gave me instructions, told me to bring her back in two weeks, and to call if there were any problems.

"You look very fancy in your little pink cast," I said to Hops when we got back to the car.

"Murp." She circled a few times, then settled down in the passenger seat.

I debated whether to take her home or to the brewery with me, and I finally decided on the brewery. I'd put her in my office again. She'd be just as comfortable there, and I could keep an eye on her.

When I reached the brew house, I parked in an empty spot on the street instead of the lot around the side of the building. Between the businesses, shops, and apartments in the area, there was rarely a place to park on the street. Saturday was usually the worst day to find a spot, as most people were off work and took that day to hit all the stores. In other words, I got lucky. As I locked up the car, I spotted Daisy Hart coming out of Handbag Heaven. Her hands were empty. One of these days I'd have to find out how she managed to leave that store without buying anything. I avoided going in there because it was too tempting. I'd never come out of the store without doing damage to my credit card.

Daisy waved to me and kept walking, then suddenly turned around and dashed across the street to me. "What in the world do you have there?" She pointed at the kitten in my arms.

"This is Hops."

"I didn't know you had a cat."

"I didn't until two days ago." I told her about finding Hops in the alley. When I mentioned her broken leg, Daisy's face turned pale.

"You found her in the alley?" she said.

"Yep. Why? Have you seen her before?"

She shook her head. "No. You should be careful with it, though. You wouldn't want it to bite you or anything."

"Hops would never do that. She's the sweetest little thing."

"Don't be so sure," Daisy said. "I know someone who was just bitten by a stray."

I told her not to worry, that Hops and I would get along just fine.

There was a short pause, then she said, "Well, I'll let you go. You probably have a million things to do." She turned abruptly and trotted up the street.

I stood and watched her until she entered her shop, then unlocked my own door and went inside, the whole time thinking what an odd conversation that had been. Although she denied it, I got the impression she'd seen the kitten before. Not that it mattered. It also seemed strange that she didn't want to stick around and chat—at least for a few minutes. Daisy was usually much more talkative.

I settled Hops into her makeshift bed in my office and put some food and water out for her, then headed to the brewery to check the fermentation tanks. The pressure and temperature gauges both had the correct readings. My brews were fermenting nicely. After that, I went to the pub kitchen to see what we had to eat, since I hadn't eaten breakfast and it was now almost lunchtime. I found a nice, ripe banana and made a slice of toast to go with it. The only thing better would have been peanut butter, which isn't one of the usual staples in a brewpub. Peanut butter and jelly might make a good addition to the children's menu, which as of now consisted of chicken nuggets and a grilled cheese sandwich.

Properly fortified, I checked on Hops again. She was sound asleep on her blanket. I had two interviews scheduled that afternoon for waitstaff, but the first one wasn't for an hour and a half. As busy as I'd been for the last couple of days, I hadn't had much time to do any investigating. Even my stakeout attempt had mostly been a bust. It had been five days since Kurt died, and I hadn't accomplished anything. I needed to do better. I owed at least that much to Kurt.

Part of my problem was that I didn't have any real suspects. Dominic Costello was the only one who had made any kind of a threat. Who else was there? I could definitely rule out Candy and Kristie. What about Daisy? I couldn't see that, either. I thought about my book group members.

Elmer was cranky, but that was it. He'd even offered to be my bodyguard. Amanda wouldn't hurt a fly. And Pearl—well, she was Kristie's mom. No way. Candy had mentioned Ken Butterfield, but I couldn't see him as a killer, either. What reason would any of them have for not wanting the pub to open?

I felt like a lightbulb went on over my head. That was the key. I needed to find out who had a reason to keep us from opening. I knew exactly where to start. I grabbed my purse, locked the pub, and headed up the street.

The Galaxy Bar was located a good block and a half from the Allegheny Brew House on a side street that crossed Butler. The exterior was a throwback to another era. The front was dingy yellow brick with tiny windows set high above the sidewalk. One window sported a neon Miller beer sign, the other advertised Pabst Blue Ribbon. The stained wood entry door had a round window and a doorknob that probably hadn't been changed since the bar had opened in 1962. It was apparent that it hadn't been cleaned since then, either. Above the door was another neon sign with the bar's name.

I paused before going in. I didn't expect Dominic Costello to welcome me with open arms. I only hoped he wouldn't pick me up and toss me to the curb. I took a deep breath and opened the door. It took a moment for my eyes to adjust to the dim interior, which was even less attractive than the exterior, if that was even possible. I was pretty sure any loss of patrons wouldn't be my fault. Dominic's customers—all two of them—sat at the bar on ancient chrome and vinyl bar stools. Both of the men looked like they'd been there since the bar opened. They didn't even turn around to see who had come in.

Dominic wasn't behind the bar. I crossed the worn linoleum floor intending to ask the men where I could find him when he pushed through a swinging door at the far side of the bar. He was carrying a jar of pickled eggs, which he set none too gently on the counter when he saw me.

"You got a lot of nerve showing your face here," he said. "Come by to steal a few customers?"

I bit my tongue to keep from saying, *What customers?* "I just wanted to stop by to say hello, Mr. Costello. We got off to kind of a rocky start and I want to fix that."

"Yeah?" He glared at me. "You can fix it by getting the hell out of my bar. Better yet, get out of my neighborhood. We don't need another beer garden here." He turned to the two at the bar. "Right?"

The two at the bar both mumbled something unintelligible.

"Mr. Costello, I'm not opening my place to compete with you or anyone else. There's plenty of room for all of us."

"You're wrong about that. Ever since I got wind of what you were doing over there, all I hear is everyone yapping their jaws about it. Talking about how you saved the brewery. About how nice it'll be to have another pub with craft beer." He used air quotes around *craft beer.* "Well, I got news for you." He shook his index finger at me. "You didn't save anything."

"I never said I did."

"For your information, those buildings burned down after those damn foreigners took over and moved to some hoity-toity city. There was nothing left to save. What do you got? A one-story office building? That ain't no brewery. Steel City was a real brewery that kept this city alive for a long time."

"Mr. Costello—"

"I don't know why all you people have to ruin everything for us guys trying to make a living. I've worked hard all my life, and I ain't giving up without a fight."

One of the men at the bar turned around. "Hey, Dom. Cut the girl some slack. She don't mean no harm."

Dominic ignored him. "I buy my beer from real breweries. The ones that've been around for more years than you've been alive. If you think you can force me to start serving your sissy beer, you're out of your mind."

The other man turned around. "How do you know her beer ain't good? My grandpap used to make a home brew that'd knock your socks off."

His cohort laughed. "I bet it's better than the swill you serve here."

Dominic slammed his fist down on the bar. "That's it. I don't need your business anymore. Get the hell out."

"Come on, Dom," the first man said. "We were only kidding."

"I wasn't," the other guy said.

"That's it. I want all three of yinz outta here."

No one moved.

"Now!"

He didn't need to tell me again. I turned and started for

the door as the other two slid off their stools. Dominic came up behind me and clamped a hand on my forearm. Startled, I froze.

"You think you can force me out? Well, you're dead wrong."

"I'm not trying to force you out," I said, knowing my words would fall on deaf ears.

"Don't you ever come in here again," he said, practically spitting the words. "I will make you sorry if you do. And if it's the last thing I do, I'm going to keep you from putting me out of business."

My heart pounded as I tore away from his grasp and almost ran outside. I stopped on the sidewalk and rubbed my arm where he'd grabbed me. Dominic Costello had already been at the top of my suspect list, and now I had a good reason to keep him there.

CHAPTER ELEVEN

"When can you start?" I asked Nicole Clark. She was my second interview of the day and I liked everything about her. The first interview had not gone well. The woman had reeked of cigarette smoke, and by the yellow stains on her fingers I could tell she was a chain-smoker. That would have meant frequent smoke breaks and neglected patrons. She hadn't even bothered to shower. Her hair was dirty and her jeans and T-shirt had seen better days. When she told me she would only work ten hours a week and insisted on full benefits, I thanked her and told her I'd be in touch.

Nicole was the complete opposite. Her shoulder-length light brown hair was clean and she was appropriately dressed in neat khakis and a pressed blouse. She was a junior at the University of Pittsburgh and happened to be a chemistry major. She not only had waitress experience, she was interested in brewing. The restaurant where she currently worked had started limiting her hours and she'd decided it was time to move on. I told her she could work as much as she needed to as long as it didn't interfere with her studies. She was ecstatic.

"I can start now if you'd like," Nicole said in answer to my question. "I was so hoping I'd get this job that I already gave my notice. My boss told me to not bother coming back."

"Are you serious? That's no way to run a restaurant."

"I couldn't believe it either at first. But now I'm glad he did it."

We decided she'd come in on Monday. The others I'd hired weren't starting for another week, but the fact that she was without a paycheck changed my mind. She wouldn't need much in the way of training other than to learn the menu and the beers we'd be serving, but there was plenty she could help me with. With the extra help, it was possible I could start growler sales before the pub opened. Kurt and I had planned on doing just that, but with his death, I'd put the idea on hold. We had a good supply of the half-gallon glass jugs known as growlers and enough beer brewed. The licensing wasn't an issue, either—I'd received that a month ago. Growler sales would also get the buzz going for the pub.

After Nicole left, I went to my office and played with Hops, who was wide-awake and sitting on top of the paperwork on my desk. Having her leg in a cast didn't seem to faze her one bit. When she tired of trying to bite my hand and settled down again, I made some more phone calls and set up a few more interviews. I then talked to several suppliers and verified deliveries for the following week. It seemed like everything was coming together for the opening. It was hard to believe it was only three weeks away. I called it a day after that, gathered up Hops and her belongings, and headed home.

𝕴 should have been exhausted, since I hadn't slept well the previous night. Instead, I found myself pacing the living room in my apartment, the encounter with Dominic Costello on my mind. I'd been able to avoid thinking too much about it because I was busy all afternoon. And this evening I'd been on the phone, first with Mom, who wanted to make sure I was coming to dinner tomorrow, then with Candy, who was miffed I hadn't called and filled her in on what she referred to as the Big Date. I assured Mom I'd be there and offered to make dessert. Although I tried to convince Candy otherwise, she still insisted Jake was interested in me. I couldn't help but wonder if she'd have been so sure if Jake hadn't been a former sports figure.

But now there was nothing pressing to keep me occupied, so my thoughts were filled with what had happened at the Galaxy. Wearing a path on my floor wasn't going to accomplish anything. I found a notepad and a pen and plopped down on the sofa. I wrote down everything I remembered about both conversations with Dominic—if I could even call them that. The first instance in Candy's bakery hadn't scared me, but the one today certainly had. He'd not only threatened me verbally, he had grabbed my arm.

But what to do about it?

I could report the incident to the police, but there wasn't much they could do about it. They would advise me to stay away from Dominic and warn him not to make threats. There was also the chance it would get back to my dad. Dad was pretty levelheaded except where his kids were concerned. I didn't want him confronting Dominic. I wanted to find proof that the bar owner was responsible for Kurt's death and the vandalism first.

The problem was, talking to Dominic myself again wasn't a good idea. I supposed I could take someone with me, but I wasn't willing to put anyone else in that situation. I thought about it awhile. The best approach might be to find out as much as I could about him, and why he was so sure I would be the cause of his business failing. I jotted down the names of neighboring business owners I could speak to.

I yawned as I stood and stretched. It was good to have a plan. Finally sleepy, I headed to bed.

My parents lived in an eighty-year-old, four bedroom, yellow-brick house on a double lot in the Highland Park section of Pittsburgh, not too far from the zoo and the reservoir. As I parked on the street, I could already hear the sounds of the pickup touch football game that broke out in the backyard just about every Sunday. It didn't matter what time of the year it was—rain, snow, cold, or hot didn't deter anyone. The number of participants varied depending on who was around. There was always a neighbor or two in addition to Dad and my brothers, and sometimes their friends. Mom preferred the sidelines, but I'd sure gotten my share of scraped knees and elbows growing up. During my years in Germany, I managed to enlist some friends to play. My apartment had been near a local park, and we'd meet up there on Sunday afternoons. The Europeans in the group never quite got the hang of playing American football. It had been fun, but it wasn't the same.

I'd just gotten out of the car when the football came sailing over the top of the two-story house. I ran across the sidewalk and into the front yard and made the catch. A few seconds later, Mike trotted around the side of the house.

"It's about time you got here," he said. "We need another running back."

I tossed the ball back to him. "That was quite a throw. Any longer and it'd be down in the reservoir." I walked back over to the car and retrieved the brownies I'd made after Mass that morning and handed a large box containing four growlers of stout to Mike. I wasn't sure how many people would be here, so I hoped four half-gallon jugs would be enough.

"I'd say I threw it, but I'd be lying. Jake hurled that one."

"Jake's here?" I glanced down at my attire. Denim cutoffs and my old Lynn Swann jersey. Great way to make an impression. Then again, it didn't really matter. Jake had seen me dressed like this every Sunday growing up. Although, if I'd known he was going to be here, I probably would have worn something else.

"Of course he is," Mike said as we headed to the house. "Thanks for hiring him, by the way. He probably didn't tell you, but no one else would even give him a shot. He must have applied at twenty places. He has the credentials, but no one took him seriously because he played hockey."

"He didn't tell me any of that. Now I'm doubly glad I

hired him." I held the front door for Mike, since he was carrying the beer, and we went inside. "He's a really good cook. It's a shame no one would give him a chance."

"Well, you did." We stopped in the center hallway. "So, are you holding up all right?" he asked. "Sean said there's a service tomorrow night?"

"I'm doing okay." And I was. Every day got a little better. It helped that I was so busy. "Kurt wasn't Catholic, but I wanted to do something for him, since there wouldn't be a funeral here."

"I'll try to make it," Mike said. "By the way, how's that water line holding up?"

I told him it was fine, and we parted ways. Mike cut through the dining room on the right and out the French doors to the patio, where I was sure a cooler would be ready for the beer. Opposite the dining room that Mike passed through was the living room, and just beyond that was a stairway to the second floor. The hallway continued past the staircase to the kitchen, at the back of the house, which was where I headed.

My parents had recently remodeled their kitchen. They'd talked about it for ten years before Mom had finally decided to part with the birch cabinets that had survived six children. The kitchen now boasted dark cherry cabinets and a laminate countertop that looked like granite. Part of the money she'd saved by not installing granite had been put toward the farmhouse sink she'd always wanted. It was my favorite item in the kitchen as well.

Mom was at the sink rinsing some dishes and watching the football game through the picture window. She jumped when I came up behind her and kissed her on the cheek.

"You really shouldn't sneak up on me like that," she said with a smile. She dried her hands and gave me a hug.

"How else am I going to keep you on your toes?" I put the pan of brownies on the counter. "What can I help with?"

"Not a thing. Dad's going to put some hamburgers on the grill. I already have a tossed salad and potato salad made." She folded the towel she'd been holding and placed it on the counter. "I am so glad you came today. How are you?"

I thought I was done with tears, but there was something about Mom asking me how I was that made me swallow hard before answering. "I'm fine."

"Are you sure about that?"

I nodded. "I won't say it's been easy, but it's getting better."

"How is it working out with Jake?"

The kitchen door opened and Jake burst in. He wore an ancient Pirates T-shirt and even rattier shorts. It was nice to see him dressed worse than I was. Somehow he managed to make them look good.

"Uh-oh. I think I just heard my name. That can't be good."

Mom and I laughed. "I was just about to tell Mom what a horrible employee you are," I said.

"And you're a slave driver," Jake said.

"Only because you're a slacker."

Mom shook her head. "I see some things never change. Can I get you something, Jake?"

"No thanks," he said. "I was really coming in to drag Max outside. Mike's team could use some help."

"So your team's winning?" I said.

Jake grinned. "We're losing. I thought a handicap—"

"Are you calling me a handicap?"

"If the shoe fits . . ." He shrugged.

I poked him on the chest. "Prepare to lose, Lambert. Big-time."

After the game—which Mike's team won—we all sat on the patio with glasses of the stout I'd brought. A few of the neighbors who'd played ball with us hung around for a while, but at the moment it was just me, Mom, Dad, Jake, Sean, and Mike and his wife, Kate. Kate wasn't a tomboy like me and hadn't participated in the game, but she'd done her part cheering from the sidelines while keeping her two girls from trying to get in on the action. Right now, my nieces—Maire, who was four, and Fiona, who was two— were rolling the football around on the lawn. They looked like miniature Kates with their white-blond hair and blue eyes. We chatted about lots of things, but we only touched on Kurt's death briefly when Sean passed on the details of the memorial service the following evening. Maire and Fiona insisted I bring Hops to visit them, and I promised to do that as soon as her leg was healed. It was a peaceful afternoon and just what I needed. Surrounded by the cocoon of my family, I could almost forget the events of the past week.

At one point, I looked over at Jake, and for a second I thought I caught him watching me, but he turned his head so fast I wasn't sure. Wishful thinking on my part. I sighed inwardly and told myself to knock it off. Even when he got over whatever had happened with his fiancée, I was still Mike's kid sister. Eventually, I got up to use the powder room. When I returned, Dad was putting the burgers on the grill and Mom and Kate were in the kitchen. Sean, Mike, and Jake were engrossed in some sports talk, so I ambled over to the grill. "Need some help, Dad?"

"Not really, but you can keep me company." He put the last patty on the grate, closed the lid, and turned the heat down. "Any more vandalism at the brewery?"

There hadn't been, so I wasn't lying when I told him no. "Has the medical examiner said any more about Kurt?"

Dad shook his head. "He won't, sweetie."

I knew that would be his answer. It didn't mean I had to like it. "I know you're sure Kurt's death was an accident, but I'm still convinced it wasn't. I'm not going to let it go. I can't."

Dad put his arm around me and pulled me close. "I wouldn't expect any less of my little girl."

Jake and I were the last ones to leave that evening. Mike, Kate, and the girls left shortly after dinner and Sean took off right after that. I helped Mom in the kitchen while Jake and Dad redd up the patio and yard. When everything was spic-and-span, Jake helped me carry the empty growlers and the leftovers Mom insisted we take out to my car.

"Thanks," I said.

He nodded. There was an awkward silence, then he said, "About the other night . . ."

I waited, mainly because I had no idea what to say.

"I want to apologize. It was supposed to be a special night celebrating my new job, and I ruined it."

"You don't have to apologize. It was a nice dinner."

"But I do." He leaned against my car. "I shouldn't let Victoria get to me like that."

"It's perfectly understandable. You were planning to marry her." I was dying to know what had happened between them, but I was afraid to ask. I didn't want to hear he was still in love with her. I asked anyway and braced myself for the answer.

"It's a long story," he said.

"So? I'd like to hear it."

"Only if you're sure."

We went back and forth like this a couple more times until I convinced him I really did want to know what happened. I needed to check on the kitten, so we decided he would follow me home. Jake made coffee while I fed Hops and made sure she hadn't destroyed anything in my absence. Fortunately, all she'd done was shred some toilet paper and scatter some litter across the floor. When the coffee was brewed, we settled down on the sofa and Hops made herself comfortable on Jake's lap.

"I think she likes you," I said.

Jake grinned. "All the women do."

I rolled my eyes. "You are so full of it."

"Murp." It appeared Hops agreed.

"So, let's hear that long story," I said.

"Maybe it's shorter than I thought," Jake said. "Basically, Victoria dumped me because I wasn't playing hockey anymore."

CHAPTER TWELVE

"Are you serious? I can't believe someone would do that."

"I couldn't believe it at first, either," Jake said. "I thought everything was great. She and her mother were looking at places for the reception, and she'd hired some famous designer to make her dress. Now that I look back on it, I should have known."

"How could you know? It doesn't sound like anything was wrong." *Other than that she was totally wrong for you.* Of course I didn't say that. I put my cup down on the end table.

"There were signs. I just didn't see them. Or maybe I didn't want to see them."

"Like what?"

"Any place that I suggested for the wedding wasn't good enough. It had to be somewhere fancy. And expensive. The more upscale, the better. She wanted me to get a custom-made tuxedo instead of renting one like everyone does around here. When I told her I wasn't going to shell out that much money for something I'd wear once, she looked at me like I had two heads. She probably had plans for me to wear it every weekend to whatever event she was going to drag me to. She and her mother are on the board of just about every charity, so there would be a lot of them."

"Good thing you were out of town so much."

"Yeah. Then she started criticizing what I wore. I bought a pair of jeans at a Walmart and she just about had a heart attack." He pointed to his shirt. "This would have given her nightmares for a week."

"Jake, I hate to say it, but you should be glad she broke it off."

"I am now, but I sure wasn't at the time. Coming home, I realized she's definitely not the one for me." He finished his coffee and put the cup on the coffee table. "I think what set me off the other night is that she's still trying to run my life. She thinks—well, it doesn't matter what she thinks. I'm done with her." He lifted Hops from his lap and placed her on the sofa. "I'd better get going. I have to be at work bright and early tomorrow or my boss might regret hiring me."

The conversation was far from over. There was a lot more I wanted to know, but he was right—it was late, and I didn't want to push him. I walked him to the door. "Your boss would understand. I hear she's a fantastic person."

Jake smiled. "That she is." He leaned down and kissed me on the forehead, which he'd done before, but this time his lips lingered just a little bit longer. "See you tomorrow," he said.

I closed the door behind him, then leaned on it, grinning stupidly to myself.

It was going to be a busy Monday, so I left Hops at home. I called Mom and asked if she could check on her sometime during the day, and she said she would. I had planned on walking to work, but with our schizophrenic May weather, the temperature had dropped from seventy degrees yesterday to fifty today—and it was raining. So I grabbed an umbrella and a jacket and headed for my car.

After parking in the lot beside the brewery, my first stop was Cupcakes N'at. The bakery was busy. Customers stood three-deep at the counter but it didn't faze Candy at all. She smiled and chatted them up, and no one seemed to be grumpy while waiting. It would have been different if Dominic had been one of them. I breathed easier knowing he wasn't. I must have been the last customer of the morning rush. When it was finally my turn, I was the only one left. "I think I scared everyone away," I said.

"You wish," Candy said with a laugh. "You couldn't scare a fly."

That wasn't exactly true. Someone was frightened enough of me to try to keep the brewpub from opening. "I'm just happy not to run into Dominic this morning."

"Don't let him bother you. I've known Dom for years. He's all talk."

"Then explain to me why he grabbed my arm and threatened me when I went to see him on Saturday." I told her what happened.

Candy frowned. "That doesn't sound like Dom. At all. I

wonder what got into him. He's always been a little grouchy, but he's never laid a hand on anyone except for drunks who got out of hand in the bar."

"I sure don't fit that category. And grouchy doesn't begin to describe the way he acted. He was livid. He accused me of forcing him out of business. I tried to explain I had no intention of doing anything like that but he wouldn't listen. He said he'd keep me from opening if it's the last thing he does."

"Do you want me to talk to him?" Candy asked.

I shook my head. "That's not a good idea. If he's the one who killed Kurt—"

"Do you really think he did?"

"Yes, I do. He's the only one who's threatened me. I haven't talked to everyone yet, but no one else seems to be dead set against a brewpub in the neighborhood."

"I wouldn't say there's no one else."

"Who, then?"

"Wait here." Candy disappeared into the back of the store and returned with a bright blue sheet of paper. "Here's at least one other person who doesn't like what you're doing."

She passed the paper across the top of the glass bakery case and I read it. It was a flyer for Save Our Lawrenceville, an organization I'd never heard of. The first sentence read:

Stop the destruction of our historic landmark.

I looked at Candy and raised an eyebrow.

"Keep reading," she said.

The last of the historic Steel City Brewery buildings is being turned into a modern restaurant and bar and scheduled to open soon. We at Save Our Lawrenceville must stop this travesty! Our former brewery proudly served the Pittsburgh area for over a century through two world wars and even survived Prohibition! It must be granted landmark status by any means necessary. Come to the meeting on Thursday evening to help us make this possible. It's not too late!

Although I wasn't familiar with the organization, I recognized the name at the bottom of the page. Frances Donovan. "Looks like she's at it again," I said.

"You know this Frances Donovan?"

"Sort of. I've never actually met her, but when I first put in an offer for my building, she'd been working to get it declared a historic landmark. She wanted to turn it into some kind of museum."

"A museum? That's ridiculous. Let me get this straight. The place used to be a brewery. It's a brewery again, but she wants to put a stop to it and stuff it full of old things?"

I couldn't help smiling at Candy's observation. "That about sums it up."

"She must have more money than brains. No wonder the city turned her down." She pointed to the paper in my hands. "What do you think she's up to now?"

"I'm not sure, but I'm going to find out."

"Does this mean Dom is off your list?"

"Not at all," I said. "He's still at the top, but Frances Donovan is a close second. Especially if her *by any means necessary* includes murder."

"So, you're going to the meeting?"

"I sure am. Care to join me?"

Candy grinned. "Honey, I wouldn't miss it for the world. This is going to be fun!"

I had a feeling it would be far from fun, but I had to see what Frances had planned. Even if she wasn't the violent type, that didn't mean she hadn't been the one breaking into the pub. Or she could have had someone do it for her. In any case, I needed to find out what this group was up to.

We chatted for a few more minutes while I paid for my blueberry muffin. She interrogated me about my dinner with Jake. She still didn't believe me that nothing had happened between us. I skipped telling her about the call from his ex-fiancée. That was Jake's business, and I was sure he wouldn't want all of Lawrenceville to hear about his love life. I definitely didn't mention the little kiss on the forehead he'd given me last night.

When I got outside, I stopped to open my umbrella and noticed that all of the businesses up and down the street—with the exception of mine, of course—had bright blue papers stuck in their door handles. The rain had slowed, but most of the flyers were wet and possibly unreadable. It didn't bode well for a large turnout Thursday night—not that I expected many of my neighbors to go. It would be interesting to see who did.

I'd already had coffee before I left my loft that morning, so I skipped my usual jaunt to Jump, Jive & Java. I'd stop later to get my favorite barista's take on Frances Donovan's quest to stop me from opening. I imagined Kristie would have a few choice things to say. After dropping my purse, jacket, and umbrella off in my office, I took my muffin to the kitchen and warmed it up in the microwave, then went back to my desk. Nicole was due in at eleven for her first day, and I worked on getting all the necessary paperwork ready for her to sign. When I had everything in order, I headed to the brewery.

This was the part of my job I liked the best. It was so peaceful here in the morning, and there was always a lingering scent of grain and yeast in the air. I checked the pressure and temperature gauges on the fermentation tanks. Everything was as it should be. I didn't have time to brew a new batch today, but I lugged the malt I'd need for tomorrow over to the mash tun. I wondered if I'd ever be able to look at the tank without picturing Kurt. I doubted it.

The morning passed quickly. Jake came in at ten. He had two part-time kitchen workers coming in for training that afternoon, which meant more paperwork. He offered to help, so I showed him what needed to be filled out for each employee. When Nicole came in at eleven, I introduced her to Jake. He took a step backward after I made the introduction, probably bracing himself in case she had the same reaction as Candy. Nicole didn't seem to recognize his face or his name. She signed all her forms, then I showed her around. She had some good ideas for making a few things more efficient.

After the tour, Nicole and I returned to my office. "One of your first duties will be to learn about the beers we'll be brewing and serving here. You'll need to know as much about them as you do the food we'll serve. Many of the people who come in here will know a lot about craft beer and they'll expect you to know more than they do. Some of them will even try to trip you up."

"And don't forget the know-it-alls who don't know a thing but think they do," she said.

I laughed. "I've met a few of those."

"I just let them think whatever they want. You can't change their minds."

"Exactly." I liked Nicole more every minute. She was going to be a great asset. I slid a sample menu across the desk. "You can start with this. There's a short description in here, and I'll have more for you later."

"Can I take this home with me?"

"Sure," I said. I had a feeling she'd have it memorized by tomorrow.

With Jake occupied in the kitchen and Nicole reorganizing the area where we'd be storing menus, napkins, and the like, I had two hours to myself before my scheduled interview.

Time to talk to more neighbors.

The Lawrenceville Good-Value Hardware Store was located next door to the Galaxy. I hoped Dominic Costello was busy in his bar and didn't have an urgent need to buy a hammer while I was in the store. I'd only met the owner, Ralph Meehan, a handful of times, but he was always pleasant enough. The small store was packed full of everything imaginable. If you needed it, he most likely had it and knew exactly where to find it in the hodgepodge. Try to get that kind of service in one of the big-box stores.

Mr. Meehan stood behind a faded Formica-topped counter at the back of the store. I picked my way down a narrow aisle. A clerk on the other side of the store was helping a customer with what appeared to be a rather large order. Mr. Meehan was on the phone. He held the receiver between his shoulder and his ear while he flipped through a four-inch-thick catalog of some sort. The way his head tilted to the side made a strand of his gray comb-over fall in the wrong direction. It was hard not to stare as it bobbed up and down with every word he spoke. Thankfully he hung up the phone before I became too mesmerized.

"Well, if it isn't the little beer maker," he said.

There was an odd note to his voice, but I couldn't put my finger on what it was.

"What do you want?" he asked.

That was definitely a tone I hadn't heard him use before. "Actually, I'm here to see you if you have a minute."

He pushed the catalog he'd been using aside. "I don't if you're here to harass me."

Harass him? "Why would I do something like that?"

"I don't know. You tell me." He crossed his arms over his navy blue polo shirt.

"Mr. Meehan, I have no idea what you mean."

"I know all about your visit next door."

The lightbulb flashed on. He'd been talking to Dominic Costello.

"You should be ashamed of yourself. I thought you were a nice young lady, but what you're doing to Dom—"

"Me? I haven't done anything."

He shook his finger at me. "He's been a good neighbor to me for more years than I can count. That bar is his livelihood—at least it was until you came along. I thought he was wrong about you, but threatening to run him out of business . . . I never thought you were that kind of person."

"Whoa. Hold on a minute." I placed my palms on the counter, mainly to keep my hands from shaking. "I don't know where you got that information, but it's not true."

"Dom told me himself. And I saw you go in there yesterday and run out not five minutes later."

I kept my voice calm and measured. "Mr. Meehan, I have never done anything to Mr. Costello. For some reason, he's gotten it into his head that I'm out to get him. Nothing could be further from the truth. I went to see him yesterday to try and smooth things over. He threatened me—not the other way around."

"Likely story."

"It's true," I said. "You can ask the two guys who were in the Galaxy when I was. He threw them out, too." I wished I'd have gotten their names, but it was too late to worry about that now. "Dominic Costello threatened to do everything in his power to keep me from ruining his business. I can't help but wonder if that everything included murdering my assistant."

Mr. Meehan's eyes narrowed. "I thought your assistant died in an accident."

"It wasn't an accident," I said. "Someone killed him."

"Now you're being fanciful. If it was a murder, it'd be all over the news."

"Not necessarily." I was kicking myself for opening my big mouth. I shouldn't have said anything at all to someone I barely knew. And a friend of Dominic Costello to boot.

"Right." Mr. Meehan's voice dripped with sarcasm. "Even if, for some reason, the news vultures didn't get wind of a murder, Dom had nothing to do with it. He's a peaceful person. He'd never kill anyone."

"If he's so peaceful like you claim, why did he threaten me?"

"Simple answer: He didn't. End of story."

I realized this was pointless. I wasn't going to change his mind. Not without proof. "I'm sorry you don't believe me, but every word I said is true."

He snorted. "You'd better leave Dom alone or else. If I hear about you harassing him anymore, you'll be sorry."

"That went well," I mumbled to myself when I was back outside. I'd gone there to find out more about Dominic Costello. Instead, I now had a second person threatening me. I turned the corner onto Butler Street and headed to my next destination. Hopefully I wasn't going to make it three.

Crazy Cards was situated next door to Beautiful Blooms. As I reached the flower shop, Daisy was arranging a new display in the window, and I waved to her. She motioned for me to come in. She darted to the back of the shop and returned with the bright blue flyer Frances Donovan had passed out.

"Did you see this?" she asked.

"Candy showed it to me this morning."

"There's no way anyone's going to let her put a museum in that building."

"Are you going to the meeting?" I said.

Daisy nodded. "Definitely. And I'm sure Adam will, too." Her voice softened and there was a hint of a blush in her cheeks when she said his name.

I put two and two together. "I didn't know you and Adam were seeing each other."

The blush became more pronounced. "Is it that obvious?" She didn't wait for an answer. "We're keeping it hush-hush for now." She smiled. "Actually, I'd like to shout it from the rooftops, but Adam thinks we should be discreet—you know how people gossip. He's afraid it would affect our businesses."

I wasn't sure how any gossip could possibly affect them, but that sounded like Adam. Image meant a lot to him. In her overalls and T-shirts, Daisy didn't exactly fit with Adam's polished look. Then there was the twenty-year age difference between them. They were certainly an interesting combination. For her sake, I hoped it worked out. "Your secret's safe with me," I said.

I asked if she'd be coming to Kurt's memorial service that evening. She said she was planning on it and she'd see me there. We talked another minute before I was able to make my exit and go next door.

Crazy Cards was a misnomer. It was more of an all-purpose paper goods store. They had a few racks of cards like you'd see in any card store, but they were known for the large quantity of handmade ones designed by local artisans. They also carried items to make your own cards, along with scrapbook and stamping supplies. Annie Simpson, the proprietor, was one of those women who made it hard to guess her age. She was slender and a head taller than me. Probably in better shape, too. She belonged to a rowing club across the Allegheny River in Millvale and rowed several times a week.

Annie sat on the scuffed hardwood floor, pulling cellophane packets of plain card stock from the cardboard box in front of her. "Hi, Max," she said, jumping to her feet.

"You didn't have to get up," I said.

"Yes, I did. My butt was getting numb." A strand of light brown hair came loose from her ponytail and she tucked it behind her ear. "What can I do for you?"

Now that I was here, I wasn't sure how to ask what I wanted to ask. Then I spotted the infamous blue flyer in the trash can beside the cardboard box. It was covered with discarded cellophane wrappers, but the bright color stood out. I pointed at the can. "I see you got one of those, too."

"I put it exactly where it belongs." Annie shook her head. "Such nonsense."

"Does that mean you're not going to the meeting?"

"I might have if I wasn't working. I have scrapbooking class that night."

"Will you be able to make it to the memorial service tonight?"

"I'd like to, but tonight is stamping class." She made a face. "I don't know why I scheduled two classes in the same week. On second thought, I do. Money. Pure and simple. I make more holding the classes than I do the rest of the week in the store. And everyone in the class needs to buy supplies for the next one, so they get them before they leave."

"It sounds like you're here a lot of evenings," I said. This was my opportunity. "Have you noticed any unusual activity around the brewery at night?"

"What do you mean by unusual?"

I told her about some of the vandalism that had occurred. I didn't mention murder, though. I wasn't going to make the same mistake I had with Ralph Meehan.

Annie tilted her head as she thought about it. "I can't say that I have. I haven't seen anyone in the neighborhood who doesn't belong here. And I haven't seen anyone paying particular attention to your place."

I was disappointed, although I'd figured that's what her answer would be. No one had seen anything. I bought a couple of packs of thank-you cards to send out to anyone who came to the service tonight. Kurt wouldn't have cared, but I felt it was the right thing to do.

When Annie finished ringing up my purchase, she said, "I just thought of something. I doubt it means anything, though."

I'd take what I could get at this point.

"It was a day last week when I was closing up. I can't remember if it was Wednesday or Thursday night. I guess it could have been, either. I was here late both nights." She paused for a second. "Wait. It was Wednesday. I remember because I went to the grocery store when I left and I was mad because it was the last day of the sale and they were out of the buy-one-get-one-free crackers."

I wanted to tell her to get to the point, but I restrained myself.

"A guy was in front of the pub. He tried the door, and when he found it was locked, he rattled it a few times. Then he looked in the window—I guess to be sure you were really closed, then he left."

She was right. It was nothing.

"I didn't think anything of it. He kept going past your parking lot and down the street."

I perked up a bit. In the direction of the Galaxy, maybe. "Do you remember what he looked like?"

Annie shrugged. "He looked vaguely familiar, like I'd

seen him in the neighborhood before. I wouldn't be able to pick him out of a lineup, though. He was an older bald guy."

"Do you remember what he was wearing?"

"Jeans and a white T-shirt. I think."

A wave of excitement went through me. An older bald guy wearing jeans and a white T-shirt. Unless Annie was describing Mr. Clean, it had to have been Dominic Costello.

CHAPTER THIRTEEN

Like it or not, I was going to have to pay the Galaxy another visit. I was itching to go now, but the rest of my day was booked. Plus, after Saturday's incident, I wasn't about to go alone. One thing I'd learned from having a police officer for a father was the importance of having backup. I didn't always take his advice, but this time I would, especially since I wanted to confront Dominic and find out why he had been trying to enter the brew house. Wednesday was the night the alarm had gone off and someone had tampered with the sink trap in the kitchen. It couldn't be a coincidence that Dominic had tried to get in that very night.

When I got back to the pub, Nicole was polishing the oak bar to a shine and the aroma of whatever Jake was cooking made my mouth water.

"I hope you don't mind," Nicole said. "I finished my other project and needed something else to do."

"Let me see. Do I mind that someone is cleaning besides me?" I tapped a finger on my lips and pretended to think about it.

Nicole laughed. "I guess not."

"Seriously," I said. "It looks great. You don't have to work so hard on your first day, though. There will be plenty for you to do once we open."

"I don't mind. I'm used to being busy."

My stomach growled just then. "Have you eaten lunch yet?" When she shook her head, I suggested we go and see what Jake was making.

I pushed through the swinging door to the kitchen, and Nicole followed. Jake stood at a stainless steel table rolling out dough. I immediately recognized what he was making when I saw half-circle pasta pillows on a tray. "Pierogies?"

Jake grinned. "You guessed it. You ladies are just in time to taste some." He wiped his hands on a towel, then lifted the cover from a pan that sat on the warmer. The aroma of onions and butter filled the air.

Nicole closed her eyes and breathed deeply. "I think I may never leave this kitchen."

Jake and I both laughed, and he said, "Maybe the boss will approve a transfer."

"Not a chance."

"Sorry, Nicole," Jake said. "I tried."

He placed pierogies on two plates, added forks, and passed a plate to each of us. "These are traditional potato-and-cheese pierogies."

The half-circles were lightly browned from being sautéed

in butter, as were the thin strips of onion. I cut off a corner with the side of my fork. The dough seemed tender and the filling was substantial. And the taste? Let's just say I cleared my plate in record time. So did Nicole.

Jake handed each of us another plate. "Now try these and let me know what you think."

These were definitely not traditional pierogies. They were still lightly browned, but sans butter or any kind of sauce. Something you could pick up with your fingers. Beside them on the plate was a dollop of ranch dressing. "I take it this would be an appetizer?"

"Yep."

"What's in it?" I asked.

Jake grinned. "Eat it and find out."

I dipped the pierogi in the dressing and took a bite. The flavor was familiar, yet not. I'd had buffalo chicken and the dip by the same name many times, but never stuffed in Polish pasta.

"Oh, wow. This is good," Nicole said with a full mouth.

I agreed. The dough was crisp, but still tender. The filling was similar to buffalo chicken dip. I could taste cheddar cheese, and Neufchâtel gave it a nice creaminess. "Jake, this is fantastic. It'll make a great addition to the appetizer menu."

"I hoped you'd say that," he said. "I've been racking my brain trying to come up with something different. I'll confess I didn't exactly invent these, but I did put my own twist on the recipe."

We talked about how to add the new items to the menu without having to reprint everything and decided we'd put the new foods on a marker board at the entrance. Instead of adding everything at once, we'd run specials and have different ones each day.

By the end of the day, I had hired a waiter, and Jake hired another cook for the kitchen. I added another interview to the two I already had scheduled for tomorrow. Things were progressing nicely.

The memorial service for Kurt was to be held at my brother's church, Most Holy Name. Afterward, I'd ask everyone to stop at the brewpub for a toast to Kurt. Jake had made enough appetizers that afternoon to feed a small army. It wasn't exactly an Irish wake, but Kurt hadn't been Irish. I figured he'd have approved anyway. After I left work at five, I'd gone home and fed Hops. I played with her for a while, and by the time I was ready to leave for the service, she was sound asleep on the bed next to my pillow.

There were about ten cars in the parking lot of the church when I arrived—more than I expected. Although I'd invited everyone in the vicinity of the pub, I hadn't really expected them all to come. It warmed my heart to know that many people had cared about Kurt. On the way down the aisle, I thanked those I didn't know all that well for coming. Candy, Kristie, and Daisy—sans Adam—sat together. Amanda Morgan and Elmer Fairbanks were in the pew in front of them. I was surprised to see Elmer and wondered if the book club members had twisted his arm to come. Elmer hated to miss anything, though, so that may have been reason enough for him to attend. Of course, Dominic Costello and Ralph Meehan were absent. I would have truly been shocked to see them here.

Mom and Dad were already seated in the first pew, and I slid in beside them. Mike and his family came in shortly afterward and took the pew behind us. Mike squeezed my shoulder and I reached up and patted his hand. I turned my head to give him a smile and saw it wasn't Mike who'd squeezed my shoulder, it was Jake, who had slipped in beside my brother. He winked at me, and the feeling that shot through me was anything but churchlike. My cheeks started to burn and I faced front again before he noticed. Why was it I could be businesslike all day working with Jake, but as soon as we were out of the pub, a mere wink could turn me into mush? Thank goodness Candy was a few rows back, or I'd never have heard the end of it.

Sean appeared on the altar just then, which saved me from pondering Jake any further. The service was short—a few prayers and some hymns. I managed to make it through without crying. After it was over, I stood at the back of the church thanking everyone as they made their way out and inviting them back to the pub. Dad was at the rear of the line, but I didn't see my mother.

"Where's Mom?" I asked.

"She went with Jake. She's going to give him a hand setting things up."

Dad and I walked to the parking lot together. "Good," I said. "It gives me a chance to tell you what I found out." We stopped beside my car. "I've been asking my neighbors some questions."

"What kind of questions?" Dad leaned against the hood and crossed his arms.

"About the vandalism. If anyone saw anything. Things like that."

"And?" His tone of voice told me he wasn't happy about it.

I filled him in on what Annie had told me that afternoon. "I'm sure it was Dominic Costello."

Dad sighed. "Honey, that description could fit any number of men. Just because Costello kind of fits doesn't mean it was him."

"Maybe not, but combine that with the threats he made—"

"Threats?" Dad straightened up. "You didn't tell me about any threats."

"I'm telling you now." Sort of. I was going to leave out some things. Most things. "Dominic doesn't like me very much. He thinks I'm going to steal all his customers. I went to his bar to talk to him and he said he'd put me out of business. Then he threw me out."

"He threw you out."

"Not physically, of course."

"Oh, of course." Dad could do a sarcastic voice with the best of them. "Was this before or after you talked to your friend?"

"Before." When he didn't say anything right away, I said, "So, what do you think? It has to be him, right?"

Dad let out a long breath. "Not necessarily." I opened my mouth to disagree and he put up his hand. "Hear me out. It could very well be that Costello is involved, but there's also a chance he's not. Just because he tried your door, doesn't mean he broke in later. Maybe he wanted to stop and talk to you."

"I'm the last person on earth he wants to talk to. He made that clear. I'm sure he's the one breaking into the pub."

"I know you are, sweetie." He put his arm around me. "But like I said, there are dozens of bald men who wear jeans and white T-shirts. Unless I can prove it's Costello, and prove that he broke in, there's not much I can do about it."

No matter what my dad thought, I was convinced Dominic had been the one Annie had seen. Dad wanted proof—well, he was going to get it. Tomorrow I'd make another visit to the Galaxy.

By the time I got to the pub, Jake and my mother had appetizers and plates arranged on the bar. Candy must have made a trip next door, because there was also a platter of cookies. Mike had retrieved pint glasses from the kitchen and was placing them near the taps. I crossed the room and went behind the bar. He'd ditched the tie he'd worn to church and the sleeves of his blue shirt were rolled up to his elbows.

"It's about time you got here," Mike said. "Mom put me to work. That means I get the first brew, right?"

"Of course you do—after me." I grabbed a glass and poured myself a lager. That afternoon I'd tapped a lager and a spring Maibock-style beer in addition to the stout that had already been tapped. By the time the brew house opened, I'd add the hefeweizen and the IPA. I handed Mike a glass. "You can even pour it yourself."

"Gee, thanks. Next you'll tell me I'm bartender for the night."

I patted him on the shoulder. "What an excellent idea. I don't know why I didn't think of it. You've got yourself a job." I ducked out of the way before he swatted me like he used to when we were kids. He didn't grumble too much so

I knew he'd have fun with it, especially since he'd volunteered to man the taps a couple evenings a week. I made the rounds then, moving from table to table and made sure everyone had something to eat.

Mom and Dad were seated with Kate and my nieces. Fiona was on Mom's lap paging through a picture book, and Maire stood behind her mother trying to braid her hair. It didn't look all that bad considering it was being styled by a four-year-old. Kate grinned at me. "You're next, Max."

Maire stopped and put her hands on her little hips. "I can't fix yours, Aunt Max. You have boy hair."

"Maire! Aunt Max does not have boy hair," Kate said.

I laughed and reached up and ran my fingers through my hair. "It's not that short, Maire."

"It's not princess hair, like Mommy's and mine." She sniffed and put her nose up in the air in a pretty good imitation of real royalty. "I like princess hair. You should get some."

"Maybe someday," I said, even though I couldn't imagine it. The last time my hair had been past my shoulders was in grade school. Between Sister Anne telling me to get it out of my eyes and my brothers pulling on it, I'd decided short hair was the way to go.

Maire went back to playing with Kate's hair, and I turned to my mother. "Thanks for helping Jake with the food."

"It's the least I can do," Mom said. "He's quite a cook. I was impressed."

"He's very impress—" I stopped myself and felt my face get hot.

Mom had a twinkle in her eye. "You two seem to be getting along nicely."

Trying to save face, I said, "He's an asset to the brew house."

She smiled. "That's not what I meant, but yes, he seems to be." She squeezed my hand. "You should let him know."

"I've already told him I'm glad I hired him."

"Not that. Let him know how you feel. He likes you, Max."

"Like a sister, maybe." I spotted Jake coming our way. He'd not only ditched his tie like Mike had, he'd changed into a black T-shirt and tan khakis. "Let's drop this, okay?" I said to Mom.

Dad finally spoke up. "You could do a lot worse, you know."

Great. Did everyone know how I felt? I went to intercept Jake before Maire decided to start singing, *Jake and Max sitting in a tree, k-i-s-s-i-n-g.*

"Thanks for everything," I said when I reached Jake. "Your food is a big hit."

"You're welcome. It was nice to have a little tryout."

"Just like in training camp, huh?"

"Not quite. There's no getting checked into the boards here."

"That could be arranged, you know."

He wiggled his eyebrows. "You can body check me any time."

The temperature in the room went up about twenty degrees. That certainly wasn't a brotherly remark. Could Mom be right? I didn't want to get my hopes up. But I could still flirt with him. "You couldn't handle it, Lambert."

"Oh, really?"

I tried to hold back a grin. "Especially if you play hockey

like you play football. As I recall, I pretty much kicked your butt."

"Ouch. You really know how to hurt a guy," Jake said with a laugh. "I think I'd better go see Mike before you damage my ego any further."

I stood for a moment and watched him walk to the bar, then finally headed to the table where Candy was holding court. I took a seat in the empty chair next to Ken Butterfield and thanked him for coming.

"I wouldn't have missed it," he said. "Kurt was a good guy."

"Yes, he was."

"Amen," Kristie said.

Ken waved an arm. "Your place is fabulous. Looking at it now, it's hard to believe it was just an empty run-down shell. I'm so glad you decided to stay."

I wasn't sure what he meant. "Of course I'm staying. Why would you think otherwise?"

"Right around the time Kurt died, I heard you were putting the place up for sale."

Candy chimed in. "That's the most ridiculous thing I ever heard. Max isn't going anywhere."

"Where in the world did you hear that?" I asked. Daisy had mentioned something similar when I'd gone to see her last week. I glanced across the table at her and she was texting furiously on her cell phone.

Ken thought for a moment. "To tell you the truth, I'm not really sure where I heard it. It was probably someone talking about it in the deli." He smiled. "I hear a lot of things that way."

The first person I thought of was Dominic Costello, but

I didn't think he'd say I was putting the brew house up for sale. His method was more hands-on than that. Then the lightbulb came on—Fran Donovan. She'd never wanted me to buy the building in the first place. If she started a rumor I was leaving, she'd be able to drum up support for her museum idea. "If you happen to remember," I said to Ken, "would you let me know? I'd kind of like to set them straight."

"Will do." He stood. "I really have to get going." I thanked him again and he promised me he'd be back for the opening.

Things wound down after that. Mom and Kate helped Jake clean up in the kitchen while Dad watched the kids. Mike and I put the pub and bar area back in order. Between the growlers I'd taken to my parents' house and the popularity of the stout tonight, I needed to switch out the barrel. It could wait until tomorrow, but I figured I may as well get it over with. Especially since Mike offered to help me.

I pushed through the door into the brewery with Mike right behind me and switched on the light. I stopped so quickly he ran into me.

"Hey, next time warn me when you put the brakes on like that."

I couldn't answer. My heart was in my throat. Someone was lying on the concrete floor beside one of the fermentation tanks. That someone was a very dead Dominic Costello.

CHAPTER FOURTEEN

Mike spotted him a second later. He stepped in front of me, and said, "Go get Dad."

I was frozen in place. A hundred thoughts ping-ponged through my head, but none of them made any sense. Dominic was dead. In my brewery.

"Max!"

Mike's tone was sharp enough to snap me out of my daze. "I'm going." I went back through the door we just entered. Dad sat with a grandchild on each knee and looked up when he heard me come in.

"Can you get Kate to take the girls?" I sounded calmer than I felt. "We need you in the brewery.",

Dad studied my face. "Is something wrong?"

"You could say that."

He seemed to know I didn't want to say anything in front

of Maire and Fiona. "Something to do with your latest issues?"

"Yep."

Dad slipped the girls off his lap, took them by the hand, and led them to the kitchen. He returned seconds later. "Want to tell me what's going on?" He fell into step beside me.

"Dominic Costello . . ." My voice caught.

"Honey, we had this conversation already."

"Not this one, we haven't." I pushed open the door and pointed to where Mike stood near the body. "It's Dominic Costello."

Dad went into what can only be called *cop mode*. He ordered both Mike and me out of the brewing area, and told Mike to ask Mom to take Kate and the kids home. While my brother did as ordered, I considered it a mere suggestion. I hovered just inside the brewery door. Dad pulled out his cell phone and called it in.

"White male, approximately sixty to sixty-five years of age. Blunt force trauma to the head."

To hear it described that way made my stomach lurch. No one deserved to have that happen to them. He requested the medical examiner and also asked dispatch not to send it out over the radio. I knew the reason for that was to keep the media away for as long as possible. It also kept all the neb-noses with scanners from listening in. Then he disconnected and made another call.

"Hey, Rich." Richard Bailey was one of the other homicide detectives. He and Dad went back a long way. "Dispatch will be calling you." As he explained what we'd found, he looked my way and spotted me. "I'll fill you in on the rest when you get here." He slipped the phone into his pocket and came toward me. "I thought I told you to wait in the pub."

"You did. But this is my brewery and I need to know what's going on." My voice was steady. "I can't do that from the other room."

Dad put a hand on my shoulder. "I'm not trying to banish you. Like it or not, this is a crime scene."

"I won't touch anything."

"That's not the point. I can't do my job if I'm looking over here every two minutes to see if you're all right. I don't want to be distracted." He pushed the swinging door and held it open. "Go. I promise I'll keep you posted."

I was tempted to stomp out like I had when I was sent to my room as a kid. Deep down, I knew being mad was dumb, but it was better than focusing on Dominic Costello lying on the floor. Mike sat at the bar and I crossed the room and took the stool beside him.

"Jake's making coffee," he said.

"Good."

"You okay, sis?"

"Okay? There's a dead person—the second one in a week, I might add—in my brewery and you ask me if I'm okay? I am definitely not okay."

Mike stared at me. "Why are you so mad?"

"I have to be."

"That makes no sense at all."

"I'll tell you what doesn't make sense. Someone breaking in here and killing people. This is my brewery. My life. I don't understand why this is happening. . . ." My voice cracked. "If I'm not angry, I'm going to fall apart." I burst into tears.

Mike slid off his stool and folded me into his arms. It seemed like I cried for a long time, but it was probably only a few minutes. I was pulling myself back together when the front door opened and Rich Bailey entered, followed by a crew from the medical examiner's office. I wiped my eyes with a paper napkin, and Mike and I went to greet them. Mike showed them to the brewing area while I went back to my seat at the bar.

Jake came in carrying a stack of take-out cups and a stainless steel pump pot that I assumed was filled with coffee and set them on the bar.

"I should have helped you with that," I said.

"No way." He poured coffee into two paper cups and passed one to me.

My hand shook when I took the cup from him. "Thanks."

He put his hand on my shoulder. "What else can I do?"

I liked that he didn't ask me if I was okay. I couldn't have handled it. "Nothing," I said. "You've done enough. More than enough. You can go if you want."

He slid onto the stool beside me. "I'll stick around if you don't mind."

I nodded. We sat in silence sipping our coffee until Mike came back. He told us he'd given Rich his statement and he was officially dismissed. I assured him I'd be fine, so he went to check on Mom and Kate. They were probably worried, and Mike could let them know what was going on.

I only wish I knew what was going on. How had Dominic Costello ended up murdered—and I was sure he was—in my brewery? "It doesn't make any sense."

"No, it doesn't," Jake said.

I didn't realize I'd spoken the words aloud.

"Want to talk about it?"

I wasn't sure I did. I hadn't told Jake my theory that Dominic had been the one behind the vandalism and the one who'd killed Kurt. The only one I'd mentioned it to was my father. Not that my theory mattered anymore.

"Then let me start," Jake said. "There's a dead guy in the brewery. I have no idea who he is or why he was back there, or even how he got there."

I let out a sigh. "And you work here and have a right to know. I'm sorry. I didn't mean to shut you out like that. It's Dominic Costello. He owns a bar up the street."

"What was he doing in the brewery?"

"I don't know." I told him how Dominic thought I was trying to run him out of business, and that he'd threatened to stop me. I didn't tell Jake that Dominic had gotten physical with me. There was no point to it now. "I was so sure he was the one breaking in here, but obviously I was wrong."

Jake shifted to face me. "Maybe not."

"How do you figure that?" I said. "If he was the one breaking in, and the one who killed Kurt, he wouldn't be lying back there dead."

"What if he wasn't alone? He could have had an accomplice."

I immediately thought of Ralph Meehan, but he didn't strike me as the violent type. As disagreeable as he'd been when I'd spoken to him, he'd seemed almost protective of Dominic. Meehan thought I had been the one making threats to Dominic, not the other way around. I mentioned this to Jake.

"Do you think someone was really threatening Costello, or that he only told Meehan that?"

"I don't know," I said. "But what if someone really was? That person could be our killer."

"Our killer?"

"You know what I mean." I didn't get a chance to tell Jake what I was thinking. My dad and Rich Bailey came through the door from the brewery. Dad talked to Jake and asked him a few questions while I went to my office with Rich and gave him my statement. I told him about everything—the vandalism, Kurt, the threats from Dominic, and even Ralph Meehan saying Dom had been threatened. By the time we finished, mostly everyone had cleared out except for a few forensic techs who were still doing their thing in the brewery.

Dad and Rich headed to the station while I waited for the others to finish up. Jake insisted on staying with me even though I told him I was fine by myself. It wasn't that I didn't want his company—on the contrary—but I didn't want him to think I was some helpless female.

After the forensic crew left, I helped Jake gather up the empty coffeepot, sugar, cream, and unused cups and took them back to the kitchen. He was rinsing out the pump pot when his phone, which he'd set on the counter, rang. "Can you see who that is?" he said. "My hands are wet."

I peeked at the display. "It says it's unregistered."

"Ignore it, then. There's no one I want to talk to this late, anyway."

By the time he'd finished cleaning the pot and dried his hands, the phone rang again and once again he didn't answer. When it happened a third time, he snatched the phone off the counter and snapped, "Who the hell is this?"

His fingers tightened on the phone and he jammed his

other hand into the pocket of his pants. He wasn't happy about whoever was calling him. I didn't think it was merely a telemarketer, especially this late at night.

"Victoria. This isn't a good time."

Definitely not a telemarketer. I motioned to Jake that I'd be in the pub and left him to talk to his ex in peace. Not that I wanted to. I'd rather have listened in to the conversation, but it really wasn't any of my business. Jake had made it clear it was over. If he wanted me to know why she was calling, he'd tell me.

And I didn't believe a word of that. She'd broken it off with him. Not the other way around. What if he still had feelings for her? She could have been calling to say she was sorry and she wanted him back.

Jake pushed through the kitchen door. "Sorry about that."

"That's all right."

He sat on the chair beside me. "That was Victoria."

"So I heard."

"She called from a friend's phone since I wasn't taking her calls. If I'd have known it was her, I wouldn't have answered."

"You can't avoid her forever."

"I can try," Jake said. "Don't you want to know what she wanted?"

I was dying to know. "It's none of my business."

"Someone she knows owns an upscale restaurant in Manhattan and is looking for a chef. She told him I'd be perfect for the job."

I didn't think it was possible for this night to get any worse, but it just had. Jake was leaving. Going back to New York, and probably back to Ms. Supermodel. At that moment, I wished he'd never come back to Pittsburgh, because it was going to hurt too much when he left. I'd gotten by for years keeping my feelings for him at bay. I should have kept it up. I never should have hired him knowing how I felt. I should have known this would happen. "That's great news," I managed to say. "You deserve a place like that."

"I turned her down."

I'd been staring at a spot on the wall across the room so he wouldn't see what was written all over my face. I turned to look at him. "You what?"

"I told her I have no interest in going back to New York."

I couldn't believe it. "But it's a great opportunity. A fancy Manhattan restaurant? You could really make a name for yourself there."

"I don't need any of that."

"Maybe you should think about it."

"Why?"

"Would you consider it if Victoria hadn't been involved?" I asked. "Would you be interested if the restaurant manager didn't know her and had called you directly?"

"No. Maybe. I don't know." He got up and went over to the front window. "I can't see me being anywhere but here, but you're right. I should think about it." He walked back over to me. "How about we call it a night?"

I felt sick. I didn't actually want him to consider the job. I wanted him to say he was staying in Pittsburgh and had no intention of leaving. Ever. That he didn't need to think about it at all. That he'd told Victoria to take a flying leap. Why had I opened my big mouth? I mentally kicked myself while I locked up.

It was only after Jake walked me to my car that it dawned

on me that neither the alarm nor the motion detectors had gone off while we were at the memorial service. Could I have forgotten to arm the system when I went home at five? It had become second nature to set it, but for the life of me I couldn't remember one way or the other. Jake and Mom had been the first to arrive after the service. I'd have to ask Jake if it had been on. Even if it had been activated, it wouldn't have been the first time someone had broken in and not set it off. But the motion sensors should have worked. I made a mental note to call the alarm company to check the system.

Dad hadn't said it, but Dominic had to have been killed sometime between when I'd closed up at five and the end of the service at eight. I was still bewildered as to why he had been in the brew house. I had been so sure he was behind everything that had happened. Maybe Jake was right that he had an accomplice. And if he had, it had to be Ralph Meehan. But why would Ralph kill Dominic? It didn't make any sense.

Until we'd been interrupted first by my dad and Rich, and then by Victoria, I'd meant to tell Jake that if someone really had been threatening Dominic, that person had to be the killer. If Dominic thought I had been the one making the threats like Ralph Meehan said, he may have gone to the brew house to see me. But I didn't get why he'd do that after he'd warned me to stay away from him. I thought about that for a while. Maybe the killer had lured him there somehow. But surely Dominic would have seen that no one was there and left. It was possible he'd never gotten a chance to leave. He went to look for me in the brewery and then . . . I shuddered, picturing him lying on the floor. That must have been it. He'd never gotten the chance to leave. The killer struck first.

I remembered what Annie told me about the man trying to get into the pub the same night the kitchen drain had been tampered with. I was more sure than ever it was Dominic who'd attempted to enter. I wondered if someone had lured him there that night as well. That night the door had been locked, though. He'd never made entry. Dominic had tried the door, found it locked, and left.

I was too exhausted to think about it anymore. I didn't even bother washing my face or brushing my teeth. I gave Hops a few treats, then collapsed into bed with the kitten curled up beside me.

CHAPTER FIFTEEN

I hoped the previous evening had been a bad dream, but it was hard to ignore the yellow crime-scene tape strapped across the door to the brewing area. Until my dad and Rich Bailey released the scene, I was basically banned from my own brewery. I wasn't looking forward to it, but I needed to get in there today, tape or no tape.

The neighborhood was quiet when I arrived at six a.m. It was barely light out and the businesses were closed, except for Kristie's—she opened at five-thirty for the early risers. The bakery opened at seven, so Candy was likely putting the final touches on her wares.

I had tossed and turned all night, with weird dreams of Kurt's face morphing into Dominic's alternating with dreams of Jake getting back together with Victoria. I finally gave up on sleep. After a brutally strong cup of coffee and a hot shower, I headed to work. It was going to be a long day, and I didn't want to leave Hops alone again, so I brought her with me. I locked the door behind me, and after I deposited the kitten in my office, I went to the kitchen to make coffee. I could have gone across the street, but I wasn't ready to talk to anyone yet. Although the murder had been kept quiet so far, surely someone had noticed all the police activity. It was just a matter of time before everyone—not to mention the media—found out. The longer I could put it off, the better.

When the coffee was done, I took a mug back to my office and sat at the desk. I slid a notepad in front of me and thought about what I needed to do today. My pen tapping on the desktop was like a beacon to Hops, who jumped up to investigate. It still amazed me she could do that with one leg out of commission. I gave her the pen to play with and picked up another one.

First on the list was to call Nicole, then the other staff we'd just hired. I also had an interview to reschedule. I didn't want prospective employees coming in when there was crime-scene tape still hanging. By the time seven o'clock rolled around, I had twenty things to do on my list. That required the kind of fortification that only Cupcakes N'at could provide.

The bakery was busy for a Tuesday, but one of Candy's part-timers was helping behind the counter. As soon as she spotted me, Candy told her she was taking a short break and practically dragged me into the back room. I braced myself for the inevitable bear hug.

"It's so terrible, Max," Candy said as she released me. "I can't believe it happened again!"

"I can't, either." I didn't ask how she found out. Her grapevine could give the NSA a run for its money.

"Poor Dom," she said. "What in the world was he doing there?"

"That's the question of the day."

"To think he was lying there while we were sitting in the pub." She shuddered. "It's creepy."

I couldn't disagree with that. "I don't understand how he got in without setting off the alarm."

"Are you sure you set it?"

"I don't remember. I thought I did. I'm absolutely positive I locked the door, though. In any case, I need to have the alarm company come out again. If I did activate it, either I'm doing something wrong or it's not working right."

"Or someone is bypassing the alarm."

Candy never ceased to amaze me. "Wouldn't there be some evidence of that?"

"Not if it's done right."

"And you know this how?"

She shrugged. "I read a lot."

One of these days I was going to have to find out what kind of work she'd done before she became a baker. Espionage wouldn't surprise me in the least. I hadn't considered the possibility of someone bypassing the system. It was a question I'd have to ask the alarm company. "Who would know how to do something like that?" I said.

"Certainly not Dom," Candy said. "We'll figure it out, though. I suggest we get together later and brainstorm."

The last brainstorming session at our book club meeting hadn't accomplished anything. I wasn't sure a repeat would be any better. "I don't know when I can fit it in. I have a lot to do today."

"I'm not taking no for an answer." She raised a hand

when I objected. "I've already discussed it with Kristie and Elmer. We'll do whatever it takes to figure this thing out."

Elmer, too? I tried to blink away the tears in my eyes but Candy saw them. She crushed me to her black-and-gold chest.

"Don't you worry, Max," she said, patting my back. "It's going to be all right."

With friends like this, how could I go wrong?

"What do you mean I can't go into my own brewery yet?" I said to Rich Bailey later that morning. "I need to check the fermentation tanks and start another batch."

"It's only for another hour. Surely you can wait that long."

"I don't understand why."

Rich scratched his salt-and-pepper mustache, a gesture I'd seen him do a thousand times. Mostly when faced with an obstinate reporter on TV. I had called my dad earlier and left a voice mail asking if I could take the tape down. Instead of calling me back, he'd sent Rich. "We want to take one more look to make sure we didn't miss anything. As soon as your dad gets here, we'll be out of your hair as quickly as possible," he said.

Another hour wouldn't make or break me, but I was tired and cranky. I wanted to take control of at least one thing— even something as minor as checking my tanks. "I really need to get in there."

"One hour." Rich could be as stubborn as my dad, so arguing further wouldn't do any good.

"Fine," I said, and stalked back to my office. I was glad I'd told Nicole not to come in—there wouldn't have been anything for her to do. I'd spoken to Jake earlier and assured him that I was all right. I'd tried to talk him into taking the day off as well, but he wouldn't hear of it. He was coming in at one.

Hops was sound asleep on a pile of invoices on the top of my desk. As good a reason as any not to pay bills today. I had worked my way through most of my list after returning from the bakery that morning. Someone from the alarm company was coming at four to check the system and go over a few things with me. As I sat there, I thought more about what Candy had said—that maybe the alarm had been tampered with. It was the only explanation that made sense. It didn't explain, however, why Dominic had been in the brewery to begin with.

I glanced at the clock on the wall. Since I had an hour to spare, maybe I could try to find out. I locked my office door behind me so the kitten didn't escape if anyone came looking for me. As I crossed the pub, I spotted the Channel 11 news van through the window. A blond-haired reporter was setting up with a cameraman right in front of the door. Great. That was the last thing I needed. It was just a matter of time before the other stations sent reporters, and I didn't want to talk to any of them. I turned around, cut through the kitchen, and slipped out the back door.

I stayed in the alley that ran parallel to this section of Butler Street. The alley happened to end at the cross street where the Galaxy and the Good-Value Hardware Store were located. I took a deep breath before I entered the hardware store. There were no customers at the moment and Ralph Meehan looked up expectantly when the bells on the door jingled—until he saw me, that is.

"You have a lot of nerve showing yourself here after what happened to Dom. If it wasn't for you, he wouldn't be dead." He reached for the phone on the counter. "I'm calling the police."

"Go ahead. I'll be happy to wait." I pulled my cell phone out of the front pocket of my pants. "I'll even call them for you."

That must not have been the response he expected because he put the receiver back down. "Don't bother. Just tell me what you want, then get the hell out."

I took a seat on one of the stools in front of the counter. "I want to know why Dominic broke into my brew house last night."

"I don't know what you're trying to pull. Dom never broke in anywhere."

"He most certainly did."

"Bull. Dom showed me the note you left for him."

"Note? I never sent him a note."

"I saw it with my own eyes. You told him you wanted to settle things once and for all and to meet you at the brewery at seven o'clock."

A chill went through me. "That wasn't from me."

"It had your name at the bottom."

My voice shook. "Mr. Meehan, I never sent Dominic any kind of note."

"I told you I saw it—"

"Whatever you saw wasn't from me. Last night was the memorial service for Kurt. Everyone knew I'd be there—and most of my neighbors as well. Whoever sent him that note knew the brew house would be empty at seven. It was probably the same person who was threatening him, and the same person who's been vandalizing my place and making it look like Dominic did it."

"Anyone ever tell you you're pretty good at making up stories?"

I wasn't getting through to him. "I'm not making this up. I've made police reports about the vandalism."

Ralph snorted. "That doesn't mean anything."

"Think about this then. Dominic was worried that my pub would do well and run him out of business. If that were the case, all I'd have to do is wait it out. I had absolutely no reason to threaten him."

"But that's not what you did," Ralph said. "You wanted him out of the picture so bad you resorted to smearing his good reputation. When that didn't work, you sent him threats. And because of that, he's dead."

"Whether you believe me or not, someone is doing everything they can to keep me from opening the brew house. I'm convinced that same person killed Kurt, and now Dominic."

Ralph stared at me. "You're delusional. The police said he died from a head injury. No one said anything about murder."

"I'm so sorry. I just assumed you knew."

"I bet you're sorry. I've had enough of this conversation. If—and that's a big if as far as I'm concerned—Dom was murdered, we both know who did it." He pointed at me. "You did. And you can bet I'm going to let the police know all about you, and the threats you made to Dom. You're not going to get away with anything."

"Mr. Meehan . . ."

"Get out of my store."

I didn't want a repeat of what had happened when Dominic had thrown me out of his bar, so I turned and left. I should have realized Ralph Meehan would react badly to Dominic's death. They were friends, after all. While I didn't expect him to welcome me with open arms, I never thought he'd accuse me of murder. He couldn't possibly think that I'd killed Dominic. The idea was totally ridiculous. The more I thought about it, the angrier I became and the faster I walked.

"Miss! Wait a minute."

I stopped and turned around. It was the clerk who'd been helping a customer the last time I was in the hardware store. He jogged down the alley until he reached me.

"Thanks for waiting." He paused to catch his breath. "Sorry. I'm not used to running like that."

"That's okay," I said, at the same time wondering why he'd run after me. Maybe Mr. Meehan sent him.

"I was in the storeroom and I overheard your conversation with Ralph," he said. "Don't take what he said literally. He's just upset."

"I know he is, but that's no reason to call me a murderer."

"That's why I wanted to talk to you."

I had no idea where this was going.

"I mostly keep to myself when I'm working, and I hear a lot. People forget I'm even there because I don't say much."

Unlike now. I wished he'd get to the point.

"When Costello came to see Ralph, he was really bent out of shape. He kept ranting about that note Ralph told you about, saying "that little girl has a lot of nerve" and "she's gonna be sorry she messed with me.""

"That's nothing new," I said. "Dominic said as much to my face."

"Ralph didn't tell you that he and Costello had an argument about it. Costello was going to take that note to the police but Ralph told him that wouldn't do any good. Told him the only way he was going to settle things once and for all was to meet up with you. He even told Costello he'd go with him."

"Did Mr. Meehan go with him?"

"I don't know," he said. "I was done work at five and went home. I just thought you'd want to know the whole story."

"I appreciate it."

He nodded. "Don't pay Ralph no mind. He's usually real nice. I'm sure he didn't mean what he said to you."

I thanked him for the information and we went our separate ways. So Ralph Meehan had talked Dominic out of reporting the note he'd received to the police. And Dominic hadn't been going to show up at the pub until Ralph talked him into it. Was it possible Ralph had written the note? But why? Dominic was supposedly his friend. If Ralph wrote the note and accompanied Dominic to the brewery, that meant only one thing: Ralph Meehan had killed him.

Back at the brew house, I went to find my dad and Rich. I was happy to see that the news van was gone and none of the other local stations had shown up to take its place. At least not yet. Not that I wished for anything bad to happen, but I hoped they'd find a more sensational crime elsewhere.

My dad exited the brewery just as I reached the door.

"There you are," he said. "I was wondering where you got to." He put an arm around me. "Rich told me you were a little annoyed with him."

"He wouldn't let me into the brewery." It seemed petty now. "But that's okay," I added quickly. "Is he still here? I should probably apologize."

"He left a few minutes ago. We're all done in there. I wanted to make sure we didn't miss anything, especially since . . ." He didn't finish the sentence.

"I know that look." It was the same expression he used to get when he didn't want us kids to hear what he was talking to Mom about. "Since what? What aren't you telling me?"

"Let's have a seat." He took me by the elbow and we sat at the nearest table.

"It must be bad if you're making me sit down."

"First, I owe you an apology," he said.

"For what?"

"For not taking you seriously when you were convinced Kurt's death wasn't an accident."

"You don't need to apologize. If I know you, you were looking into it anyway."

"Only because you're my daughter."

I gave him a little smile. "That's one benefit of having a father who's a homicide detective, I guess. So, what did you not want to tell me? That can't be it."

Dad leaned back in his chair. "Are you sure you want to hear this?"

"Of course I do—especially if it has to do with Kurt."

"I spent most of the morning with the medical examiner. To make a long story short, he now thinks it's possible the weapon that killed Costello was also used on Kurt."

CHAPTER SIXTEEN

I was tempted to tell him—again—that I'd known all along Kurt hadn't hit his head on the tank, but since he'd already apologized, I bit my tongue. Instead, I asked him what the weapon was.

"We're not sure at this point. Possibly something metal, like a crowbar, a bat, a pipe, or even a tool of some kind."

"What kind of tool? A hammer?"

He shook his head. "No. That would . . . well . . . it wasn't a hammer."

A hardware store was full of them. Ralph Meehan's access to so many tools definitely put him at the top of my previously nonexistent suspect list. I told Dad about my visit to the store and what the clerk told me in the alley.

"That would explain why Costello was here," Dad said. "But we didn't find any kind of note. And there wasn't one with any of his personal effects. Meehan said he saw this note? And the clerk heard them talking about it?"

"Yes."

Dad stood. "I'd better have Rich go talk with him."

"Why not you?"

"He's top dog on this one, since the murder occurred here."

"Oh." I should have known that. Since I was his daughter, the powers that be wouldn't want him leading the investigation. They could have pulled him off entirely, so I had to give them credit for not doing that.

I walked him to the door and went to my office. While I played with the kitten, I thought about what I knew so far. Someone didn't want me to open the brew house. When the vandalism didn't drive me out, he killed Kurt. When I didn't close up after that, the killer made Dominic think I was out to get him and then lured him here. But why? If the killer wanted me to blame Dominic for all that happened, why did he murder him? It made no sense to me at all. He had nothing to gain by doing that, especially if the killer was Ralph Meehan. Why would Ralph want the pub shut down?

The phone ringing interrupted my thoughts. It was Candy asking—actually more like demanding—that I meet up with her, Kristie, and Elmer at Jump, Jive & Java at two o'clock. That didn't give me much time to get a few things done. I put the kitten on her bed. "Sorry, Hops, but I have work to do."

"Murp." She circled a few times, then plopped down and closed her eyes. I was tempted to join her. I headed to the brewing room instead.

I pushed through the swinging door and switched on the

overhead lights. "Oh, no." I froze, my hand still on the light switch. I anticipated there would be some mess, but this was beyond that. The room was a disaster. There was fingerprint powder on everything. And I mean everything. Crime-scene tape was crumpled up in a ball and left on the floor. There were footprints in the dust left by the fingerprint powder all over the concrete floor that I took great care to keep so clean you could eat off it. I used every swear word I knew in both English and German, and even one or two in Gaelic, as I gathered up what supplies I needed to clean things up.

I stood there with bucket and hose in hand. I didn't even know where to start. I mumbled more choice words to myself as I sprayed water from the hose into a bucket. Then I spotted the blood on the floor. Dominic's blood. Heat shot to my face. How could I be so callous to worry about the mess when two people had been murdered?

I put the hose down and sank onto one of the steps to the mash tun. For the first time, I wanted to quit. I'd known opening my own place would be hard, but I hadn't counted on all that had happened. My eyes burned as I fought back tears. "I can't do this."

"Yes, you can," Jake said.

I hadn't heard him come in. I remembered the phone call from Victoria last night. Jake possibly leaving was one more thing I couldn't deal with. "No, I can't."

He took a seat beside me on the step. "Why don't you go back to your office and let me do this, then?"

He thought I meant cleaning up, but it was much more than that. I swiped at a tear that escaped and ran down my cheek. "Why did I think I could open a brewpub anyway?

It's caused nothing but trouble. Two people are dead. And for what? So I can brew beer? Maybe it's time to throw in the towel. Give it all up."

"I never took you for a quitter, O'Hara."

"I'm not. But this is too much."

He took my hand in both of his. "If you give up, the killer wins, you know."

I wasn't sure it mattered. "It seems to me like he's going to win anyway."

"There's a chance of that, but there's no sense in handing it to him without a fight. Think about everyone who wants you to succeed. You'd disappoint a lot of people if you quit now."

Mom, Dad, my brothers, Candy, Kristie—even Elmer.

"There are too many people who care about you, Max," Jake said. "Me included."

I slipped my hand from his and stood before he noticed his comment had turned me to mush. He was right. I couldn't throw it all away now. I put my hands on my hips and turned back to Jake. "If I'm going to open this place on time, I'd better get to work. I have a huge mess to clean up."

Jake stood and grinned. "That's my Max." Then he ruffled my hair.

And I didn't mind a bit.

He offered to clean the brewery alone. As much as I would have liked to hand it all over to someone else, it was my responsibility, so we worked side by side until it was time for Candy's meeting. I asked Jake to come with me, but he declined. Smart move on his part. I wished I could do the same.

* * *

Glenn Miller's "Elmer's Tune" drifted from Kristie's sound system as I took a seat next to Elmer Fairbanks. "They're playing your song," I said to him. Today he'd traded his Stetson for a 101st Airborne ball cap.

"I hate that song," he said. "One night back in forty-four a bunch of us were sittin' in a café in Gay Paree. I was making time with a cute little mademoiselle. At least I was until this song started playing and my buddies decided to sing along. Between their singing and my red face, she made tracks outta there."

I gave him a quick kiss on the cheek. "I would have stuck around."

"Not if you'd heard them singing," he said. "Good thing they were better at jumping out of airplanes."

"I'd like to hear more about that," I told him.

"The history lesson is going to have to wait until another day," Candy said. "We have some brainstorming to do."

"Or brain drizzling in her case," Elmer muttered.

I suppressed a laugh.

"Did you say something, old man?" Candy gave him a look that would have melted steel.

Elmer grinned and winked at me.

Fortunately, Kristie came to the table carrying a tray before fisticuffs broke out. She passed a decaf to Elmer, a mocha to me, and a plain black coffee to Candy. She took the seat next to Candy. "Did I miss anything?"

"Elmer was telling us about a girl he met in Paris during the war," I said.

"Ooh, sounds romantic." Kristie leaned forward. "I want to hear all about it."

Candy loudly cleared her throat. "Can we keep on track here, please? We're here to help Max, not hear about Elmer's escapades."

Hearing about Paris in 1944 was a lot more interesting.

"It really pains me to say it but she's right," Elmer said. Agreeing with anything Candy said had to be a first for him.

"I call this meeting of Max's Marauders to order." Candy rapped her spoon on the table.

I almost choked on my mocha. "Max's Marauders?"

"I told her it was a bit much," Kristie said.

"We need a name. Every group has a name." Candy held her nose in the air. "I happen to like it."

"It's stupid," Elmer said.

I waved my hand in the air before another argument broke out. "It's fine. Let's get on with this." The sooner we did, the quicker I could get back to the brew house. Candy whipped a yellow legal tablet and a black pen from her bag. "So, what do we know so far?" She didn't wait for answers. "One—someone doesn't want Max to open her pub." She scrawled this down on the pad. "Two—two people have been killed. Three—"

"This is a waste of time." Elmer snatched the pad and pen from Candy. "We know all this crap. What we need is a strategy. Just like in the big war. Ike didn't sit around yapping about what he already knew."

"And what exactly do you propose, General?" Candy asked. "If you're planning an invasion, I've got news for you—"

"Let him have his say," Kristie said. "He does have a point."

"And I have to get back to the brew house," I chimed in.

Candy leaned back in her seat and crossed her arms over her chest. "Well. Looks like I'm outnumbered."

"Okay," Elmer said. "I ain't gonna rehash what we know. I ain't no cop, but it's pretty obvious that the same person killed Kurt and Dominic. Why?"

"I don't know," I said. I held off mentioning the new information about Ralph or what the medical examiner had told my dad. I wanted to hear their thoughts first.

He sketched a quick diagram of the street and all the businesses. When he finished, he pointed to my place with the pen. "I've been thinking a lot about this. What's so important about the old brewery and who wants to keep it from opening?"

"That lady who plastered the blue flyers all over the place," Kristie said.

Elmer nodded. "Yeah, I saw those flyers. I propose we all go to that meeting."

"We're one step ahead of you," Candy said. "We were already planning to go."

I caught Kristie's gaze and we both rolled our eyes. If those two didn't knock it off, I was going to have to bang their heads together. Either that or give them boxing gloves and have them duke it out.

"So what other reasons?" Elmer said. "This is supposed to be a brainstorming session, you know."

Kristie chimed in. "Maybe the killer wants the building for some other reason."

"Maybe he wants to open his own brewery," Candy said.

The three of them went back and forth with ideas. I tried to interrupt several times to tell them what I knew. I finally gave up and sat quietly. This was going nowhere. They could make a list a mile long, but it was all pure speculation.

Candy finally noticed I wasn't contributing. "Something wrong, Max?"

I didn't want to hurt their feelings, but if I didn't tell the truth, Candy would see right through me. "I appreciate everyone's help," I said. "But I don't think this is working."

"Why not?" Kristie said.

I continued. "They're all good reasons, but there's no way to tell which one is right—or even if one is right. And none of the ideas take Dominic into account. I thought he might have been the killer, but it turns out he had nothing to do with the brewery, other than that he thought I was bad for his business."

"The girl's right." Elmer patted my hand. "Don't take this the wrong way, but Kurt's death at least makes sense. It was a way to get to you."

I smiled at Elmer. "No offense taken. And you were right that the two murders are related." I relayed what the medical examiner had told Dad, then filled them in on my conversation with Ralph Meehan and what the store clerk had said. "I think Dominic was lured to the brewery. If that's true, though, I can't figure out why he was killed—especially since it seems like the killer wanted me to think Dominic was behind everything."

"If Kurt and Dominic were killed with some kind of tool," Candy said, "and Ralph went with Dominic last night, that gave him both means and opportunity." Once again I wondered about her previous career. I'd never heard anyone outside of law enforcement use those terms.

"That's true," I said. "But I can't figure out what his motive would be. I can't think of any reason why Ralph would want to stop the brewery. Or why he'd kill someone who was supposedly his friend."

"Maybe Costello's murder wasn't planned," Elmer said. "What if Ralph got him there to set him up, but Costello figured out what he was doing? He had to be eliminated or he'd blow the whistle."

He was onto something. "That makes sense," I said.

Kristie spoke up. "It still doesn't tell us why he'd want to keep the brewpub from opening. I'm not buying it."

She was right. Until I could figure out a motive for Ralph, I needed to consider other suspects as well. But who?

"So we're back to the question—who doesn't want the brewery to open?" Elmer pointed the pen at me.

The blue flyers came to mind again. "Frances Donovan."

"Who's that?" Elmer said.

"The blue-flyer lady," Candy said.

I explained who she was and what she wanted to do with the building.

"Sounds like a nutcase," Elmer said. "Now that we got a couple of suspects, what's our plan?"

Candy lifted the pen from Elmer's hand. "I know exactly what we're going to do. Pass me that tablet, old man."

Ten minutes later—even with Elmer's grumbling about Candy taking her own notepad back—we had a plan. Or rather, Candy did. I didn't especially like it—except for going to the Save Our Lawrenceville meeting on Thursday

night. At this point, I was too tired to argue. The three of
them planned to take shifts when they could to keep an eye
on the brewery. Kristie was going to watch in the early
evening from her viewpoint inside the café. Candy was going to take the late evening and planned on sitting in her car
in the parking lot, where she could see the back door. My
job was to canvass the neighborhood like I'd been doing.
And Elmer? Well, starting the day after tomorrow, Elmer
planned on sitting in the brew house. All day long. It seemed
I now had a ninety-two-year-old security guard.

*I*nstead of going straight back to the brew house, I headed
to the deli up the street to pick up some sandwiches. It
was almost three and I hadn't eaten lunch. I didn't think Jake
had, either, since he'd been stuck finishing the cleanup. This
time of day, the deli wasn't crowded. Adam Greeley sat at
one of the tables with a man I didn't recognize. They were
engaged in what appeared to be an intense conversation,
with Adam waving his bandaged hand around. I figured I'd
wait to say hello.

Ken Butterfield was at the counter. "I heard the news,
Max. I couldn't believe it happened again. Is there anything
I can do?"

"I don't think so, but thanks for asking." I ordered two
turkey sandwiches with the works. After I had my order and
paid for it, I turned around to leave. The man talking to
Adam suddenly slammed his fist down on the table.

"I told you no." He stood so quickly he almost knocked
his chair over. The man straightened his chair, then tugged
his black polo shirt into place. There was some kind of logo

on the left side, but I couldn't see exactly what it was. "Don't ever ask me something like that again." He stormed out.

I looked at Ken, who shrugged. He didn't know what it was all about, either. Adam sat rigid in his chair, then reached up and pressed his palms against his eyes. I went over to his table. I said his name twice before he noticed I was speaking to him. "Is something wrong?" I asked.

He smiled, but the smile didn't quite reach his eyes. "Nothing I can't handle," he said. "Just a little business issue that didn't go my way."

"Oh." I didn't know what else to say. I settled for the same thing Ken had asked me. "Anything I can do?"

Adam stood. "Only if you can turn back time, which I think is out of your league."

I watched him leave, thinking that had been a strange thing to say, even for him. Whatever had gone on between him and that other man really wasn't my problem. I put it out of my mind and headed back to work.

Jake and I sat in my office eating the sandwiches I'd bought at the deli while I filled him in on Candy's plan.

"It doesn't sound like much of a plan to me," Jake said. "Isn't it basically what you've been doing already?"

I chewed what I had in my mouth before answering. "Pretty much. For me, anyway." Hops sat on top of my desk, and I watched as she sniffed a piece of turkey that had fallen out of my sandwich and onto the paper wrapper. She decided it might be edible, licked it, and started nibbling.

Jake picked off a tiny piece of cheese from the last bite of his sandwich and dropped it beside the turkey. I was glad he didn't have a problem with a cat sharing our lunch. "It's nice they want to help, and at least it gives them something to do." He grinned. "Especially Elmer. I think he has a thing for you."

"I hope you're not serious."

He crumpled up his wrapper and dropped it into the trash can beside my desk. "Of course I am." He stood and walked to the door. "How could anyone possibly not have a thing for you?"

I stared openmouthed at the door after he left. Did Jake's words mean what I thought they did? Or was I reading something into them? "What do you think, Hops? Did I hear that right?"

Hops looked up from her treat, decided my question wasn't worth answering, and went back to eating.

"You're a lot of help." I let out a sigh. It had to be wishful thinking on my part. I needed to get the idea out of my head that Jake's feelings would change. Especially now. He hadn't said any more about the job offer in New York. If he'd made a decision either way, he'd tell me. And it had to be his decision. As much as I wanted him to stay, I couldn't interfere.

The kitten finished eating, jumped down from the desk, and plopped onto her blanket. It was almost four, so I gathered up the rest of the sandwich debris and tossed it in the can, then I closed my office door behind me and headed back out to the pub.

Gary, the alarm guy, was right on time. I watched as he opened the panel and checked everything there was to check. "I don't see any problems here," he said. "Let's take a look at your keypad." He had me set and deactivate the alarm several times. It worked just fine.

"I don't get it," I said. "Could someone have tampered with it?"

Gary shook his head. "If anyone messed with it, it would set off a tamper alarm. You have motion detectors, don't you?"

I told him I did and explained that they had actually been set off the night the kitchen drain had been disconnected.

He crossed the pub to the motion detector that faced the brewery door and pointed to it. "There's your problem. It's turned toward the ceiling. Not gonna get any motion there." He checked the others. All three had been pivoted on their mounting brackets to face upward.

CHAPTER SEVENTEEN

My anger hadn't dissipated much by the time Gary left. He'd repositioned the motion detectors and advised me that I might want to add a surveillance system. When he told me the cost, I advised him that I couldn't afford one.

Jake listened to my ranting without complaint. We sat at the bar after he drew two glasses of stout. Which he did perfectly, I might add. "So moving the motion detectors explains why the alarm hasn't gone off," I said, "but it doesn't explain why there's no sign of a break-in."

"No, it doesn't," he said. "Any ideas?"

"None. I'm totally stumped."

"The motion sensors were activated once, right?"

I nodded. "The night I found the kitchen drain disconnected."

"Maybe that's the night they were moved."

"That makes sense, depending on how long it took for the police to respond," I said. "The alarm company called me first to make sure it wasn't a false alarm. I think it took me about fifteen minutes to get here and the police only beat me by a minute or two."

"Then it was probably another couple of minutes before you entered. Definitely enough time to move them."

I glanced up at the nearest motion sensor. "You wouldn't even need a ladder. I saw how easily they swiveled. You could use the end of a broom."

Jake finished his beer. "I think you should consider the surveillance cameras. There's a good chance this person will just do the same thing again."

"I know what to look for now. Besides, money is tight as it is. Those cameras are way out of my budget."

"Not if you let me help you out."

"Absolutely not."

"And why not?" Jake went behind the bar, rinsed his glass, and placed it in the other side of the sink.

"Because it's not fair to you." Especially if he was thinking about not being here. "It's my responsibility."

He leaned across the bar. "It's not like you're forcing me. It's fair if it's something I want to do."

"That's not the point."

"Then what is?"

I pushed my drink away. "This place—this brewery—is my dream. Not yours."

"You don't know that."

But I did. "Hockey has always been your dream. For as

long as I've known you, you never wanted to be anything but a hockey player."

"Well, things changed. That dream is over."

By the set of his jaw, I knew he didn't want to talk about it. I wasn't going to let him change the subject this time. "So, what changed, Jake?"

He stared across the room, and for a minute I thought he wasn't going to tell me. Finally he came around the bar and took the seat beside me. "I guess you have the right to know." He took a breath and blew it out. "You're right. I never wanted to do anything but play hockey—ever since my dad took me to my first game. Even before that I loved flying across the ice on my skates. I never feel so alive as when I'm on the ice. I guess I should be happy I had the chance to play on a professional team."

He still hadn't said why he wasn't playing anymore. I didn't want to push him, so I waited.

"Two years ago, I was tripped and my head slammed into the boards."

Jake must have seen me wince, because he said, "Yeah. I blacked out and had to be carried off the ice. I had a concussion and didn't play for half the season. When I finally returned to the ice, I still wasn't a hundred percent. Every once in a while, my vision would blur, or I'd see double."

"And they let you play like that?"

"They wouldn't have if I'd have told them."

"Jake! You should have—"

He put his hands up. "I know I should have, but you know what they say about hindsight. I didn't even tell Victoria. Not that it would have mattered. Even if she realized how serious it was, she wouldn't have stopped me from playing. It would have ruined all her plans."

The more I heard about the ex-fiancée, the more I disliked her.

"Anyway, I made it through the rest of the season thinking all I needed was some rest. I was right for the most part. My vision improved and I thought everything was okay, and then halfway through last season I got hit again."

"Oh no." My heart went out to him. I took his hand without even thinking about it and he squeezed mine.

"It was worse this time. In addition to another concussion, I had to be treated for a blood clot in my brain. The doctor told me I was lucky I didn't die. And then he gave me the really bad news. If I kept playing and got hit again, there was a good chance it would kill me." He gave me a little smile. "I kind of like being alive, so I opted for a career change."

"I am so sorry." I never in a million years imagined it was anything so serious. No wonder he didn't want to talk about it. I thought about us playing football in my parents' yard. It was touch football, but I was worried anyway. "Are you out of danger now?"

"Yeah, I am. I just can't play hockey." He stood. "Don't look so sad. It's not the end of the world. I had at most three or four more years before I'd have to retire anyway. And I do love what I'm doing now." He put his hand on my shoulder. "Especially working here. I couldn't ask for a better place to be."

I had to ask. "Does that mean you've decided to stay?"

"Definitely. Victoria called me again. It seems she had

an ulterior motive—no surprise there. That chef position also entailed being in a reality show. And guess who'd get her big shot at being on national TV—as my fiancée, no less?"

"I guess she wasn't too happy with you."

Jake laughed. "I never knew she could swear like that."

Good thing he hadn't gotten to the brewery any earlier this morning, or he would have heard cussing in three languages.

We talked a while longer. Jake offered to buy me dinner, but I asked for a rain check. Not only was I exhausted, I had to get the kitten home. She'd been stuck in my office all day, which really wasn't fair to her. My workdays weren't going to get any shorter, so I needed to come up with a way to accommodate both of us.

After Jake left, I gathered up Hops, set the alarm, and locked the door behind me. Adam Greeley had just exited Handbag Heaven, and I waved to him. He didn't acknowledge me and kept walking toward the parking lot next door.

Seeing Adam reminded me of Daisy, so instead of going to my car, I turned in the other direction. Daisy looked up when Hops and I entered Beautiful Blooms.

"You still have that cat?" She sounded surprised.

"Yep." I scratched the kitten on her head. "Hops and I are pretty good friends now."

"I never took you for a cat person. Didn't you tell me it's a stray? It could be vicious."

I laughed. "You've got to be kidding. She's very sweet." I held Hops out to her. "Would you like to hold her?"

Daisy backed away and waved her hands. "No, thanks.

I'm not taking any chances. How is everything over there today? I saw the TV news van. You didn't have to talk to them, did you?"

"No, thank goodness," I said. I gave her a rundown of my day. "So, we're managing, and if someone tries to break in again, the motion detectors should work."

"That's good." She glanced at her watch.

"Am I keeping you from something?" I asked.

She blushed. "Not really. I mean . . . it's just . . . I'm supposed to meet Adam."

"I saw him leaving his store right before I came in. I think he was headed for the parking lot."

"I'd better get a move on then," Daisy said, reaching for her keys. "I don't want to keep him waiting."

We walked to the door together, and while she locked up I asked her where Adam was taking her.

"Oh, we don't go out." She blushed again. "We're not ready to make our relationship public yet."

More like Adam wasn't. I was sure it wasn't Daisy's idea. It's one thing keeping your feelings to yourself when you know the other person doesn't feel the same way, but I didn't understand why Adam wouldn't want anyone to know he was seeing Daisy. Maybe he was one of those guys who had a wife in another city. Or maybe my imagination was running away with me.

I didn't want to see Daisy get hurt. Hopefully Adam would come to his senses, declare his love, and they'd live happily ever after.

Right.

There was about as much a chance of that as Jake doing the same.

* * *

Hops and I were both glad to get home. I played with her for a while, then fed her dinner. I didn't feel like eating, which was good, because I didn't feel like cooking. Ice cream and cereal were the only things I had that didn't require cooking. Not that there was anything wrong with eating cereal for dinner. I'd done it many times. Ice cream would be a bonus.

I stretched out on the sofa. I owed my mother a call—I'd only talked to her briefly that morning, but I didn't feel like talking to anyone. The kitten climbed up and made herself comfortable on my stomach. She purred as I stroked her head. I closed my eyes thinking I'd just rest them for a minute.

I woke up two hours later. Hops was still asleep, so I gently lifted her and placed her back on the couch after I got up. I fixed a bowl of cereal and took it to my desk in the bedroom, where I switched on my laptop. If computers had feelings, this one would surely feel neglect because I rarely used it. I either used my phone or the computer at the pub, since I was there most of the time. Also the one at the pub was much newer. And faster.

I wasn't sure what it would accomplish, but I'd decided to Google every business on my block of Butler Street, as well as the hardware store and Dominic's bar. I probably should have done it days ago, but this was really the first large chunk of time I'd had to devote to it. I started with the Galaxy. Nothing much came up, other than an old article in the paper about the police responding to a bar fight. The only thing on Dominic was one of those sites that read, *We found one Dominic Costello in Pittsburgh*, then try to get you to pay to get his phone number.

There wasn't much on Ralph Meehan, either, other than that he was on Facebook. The hardware store didn't have a website. Neither did Ken Butterfield's deli. Crazy Cards, Jump, Jive & Java, Beautiful Blooms, and Cupcakes N'at all had websites. I spent way too much time checking out Annie Simpson's craft classes. When the pub was established and I was able to take a night off here and there, I'd have to sign up for one. I liked the idea of making a scrapbook about my time in Germany. Nothing in my search of the store owners stood out.

I found two articles about Adam Greeley's boutiques. The longer of the two featured in the *Pittsburgh Times* was mostly about his This and That store, which carried a little of everything. The writer raved about the imported silk scarves and blouses and mostly neglected the other items. The article only briefly mentioned Fleet of Foot and Handbag Heaven and how one could get designer shoes and handbags for a fraction of what they cost elsewhere.

I also found a couple of complaints about Adam on a review site. He'd fired one of his workers after accusing her of stealing. She not only wrote the bad review, she filed a complaint with the employment commission. I didn't know how to search whether or not the commission had found in her favor, but two other employees—anonymous, of course—backed up her story on the review site. I already knew Adam was a little paranoid regarding his staff, so none of this came as a surprise. It was interesting, though.

Two hours after I started, I came to the conclusion that this was all a massive waste of time and logged off. I washed my face and brushed my teeth, then stretched out on the bed and finally called Mom back. We talked for quite a while about nothing in particular, but it was comforting nonetheless. By the time we hung up, I could hardly keep my eyes open. Despite my earlier nap, I fell asleep in record time.

Hops seemed to know she wasn't going to the pub with me. As I got dressed after my shower, she burrowed under the covers on the bed as if to say, "Just try and get me out of here." It also gave me an excuse to not make the bed—always a good thing.

I'd awakened early thanks to the nap and getting a decent night's sleep, so I decided to treat myself to breakfast. The problem with having cereal for dinner is that it doesn't keep hunger at bay for very long. It was a gorgeous morning, so I left my car at home. There was a diner that was open twenty-four hours on my way to work, so I stopped there and had the best vegetable omelet I'd ever eaten. I would probably regret eating the large mound of home fries the next time I got on the scale, but at the moment it was worth it. I planned to brew today, so I'd burn off a few of those calories lugging beer ingredients from the storage area to the brewery.

When I turned the corner onto Butler Street, I spotted some new blue flyers stapled to telephone poles advertising the meeting tomorrow night. It wasn't enough to completely ruin my good mood of the morning, but it did tamp it down a bit. I realized Frances Donovan was the one person I hadn't researched last night. I needed to do that. Maybe it would give me a hint as to why she was so dead set on turning the old brewery into a museum. To my way of thinking, a working brewery was not only better use of the space, it paid homage to all those who had made brewing what it is today.

I waved to Candy, who was at the counter in the bakery as I passed. Across the street, Kristie's coffee shop looked busy. Even Adam was an early bird this morning. I could see him unloading merchandise from boxes inside Handbag Heaven.

After I deactivated the alarm, the first thing I did was check the motion detectors to make sure they were in the same position. I was relieved to see that they were. Maybe Dominic's death—whether intentional or not—had been enough to make the killer think twice about coming back. Probably not, but I could hope.

I dumped my purse and keys on my desk and headed for the storage area. With summer on the way, I thought I'd brew my own version of a summer ale. I chose hops that would give the beer citrus notes and lugged the hops and malt to the brewery. After I got the grains into the mash tun, I checked the gauges on the hefeweizen and the IPA in the fermentation tanks. It wouldn't be long until they'd be ready for kegging. I then returned to the storage area to check the inventory. I wanted to get a little ahead on the brewing before the pub opened. It would be terrible to run out of beer.

At one time, the storage area had been a garage. It was located at the far end of the brewery and, just like the kitchen, opened to the alley. During the renovation, the contractor wanted to get rid of the double garage door, but I talked him into replacing it instead. The large opening made it much easier when supplies were delivered. The trucks could back in or back up to the door and unload.

As I made notes of the items I'd need, I thought I smelled smoke. Figuring someone had just walked down the alley with a cigarette, I ignored it. Instead of dissipating, the odor got stronger. I put my pen and paper down on an empty spot on the steel shelving and walked over to the garage door. Wisps of gray smoke seeped under the bottom of the door. I raced through the brewery and the pub, and into the kitchen. I flung open the door to the alley. The Dumpster that always took up the spot on the other side of the alley had been pushed against the garage door. And it was fully engulfed in flames.

CHAPTER EIGHTEEN

I ran back inside and called 911 from the kitchen phone, then yanked the fire extinguisher down from the wall and sprinted back to the fire. My fingers slipped off the pin. My hands shook so much, it took three tries to get the pin out. I got as close to the fire as I could, but when I sprayed the extinguisher, it didn't reach the top of the Dumpster. I tried again with the same results. I frantically searched the alley for something to stand on. Nothing.

I remembered the two-tiered step stool in the storage room and dragged it out into the alley. I was tall enough now, but the extinguisher barely made a difference. Sweat trickled down my neck from the heat. My eyes burned from the smoke and I coughed as I got a lungful. The thick smoke finally drew people from the neighborhood. Candy was the first to arrive, followed by Ken Butterfield, plus a few people who must have been just passing by. One of them took the extinguisher from me, and Kristie showed up with one from the coffee shop and passed it off to Ken. Candy took my arm and pulled me back away from the fire. "Stay here," she demanded, then went to help the others.

I bent over and sucked in fresh air. My throat was raw and parched. When I could breathe again I straightened and saw the flames licking the wood frame surrounding the garage door. I was going to lose everything! I couldn't let that happen. I went toward the Dumpster as the fire department arrived.

While the firefighters worked on putting out the fire, I spotted Jake running this way down the alley. He reached me and pulled me into his arms. "Are you all right? Please tell me you're okay."

I heard Jake's heart pounding as he held me. "I'm fine." My voice was raspy.

"Thank God," he said. "When I saw the smoke and the fire truck . . ."

I pulled back so I could see his face. His expression certainly wasn't the usual kid-sister-of-my-best-friend one I'd seen numerous times. This was different. "I'm fine," I said again.

"What the hell happened?"

"I was doing inventory in the storage room and smelled smoke. When I checked, someone had moved the Dumpster up against the door and set it on fire."

"That son of a—"

"I tried to put it out, but it was too far gone."

It wasn't long before the firemen had it under control, and the fire captain came over to where Jake and I stood.

"Excuse me." He looked at Jake. "Max?"

I stepped forward. "I'm Max." I wondered for the ump-teenth time why my parents hadn't named me Mary. It would have made things so much easier.

"Oh. I wanted to let you know we got the fire out. We'll be moving the Dumpster away from your door, just in case it starts up again."

"Thank you," I said.

"That's a stupid place for a Dumpster, by the way. It shouldn't be up against your door like that."

No kidding. "That Dumpster belongs on the other side of the alley. Someone moved it in front of my door. That fire was set deliberately."

"Now, we don't know that, young lady," he said. "Don't you go starting rumors like that."

"Rumors, my ass," Jake broke in. "That fire was arson, and I want to know what you're going to do about it."

Apparently, Jake had more sway than me because the fire captain said, "I'll have the arson investigator have a look-see."

"What a pompous, condescending"—I fished for a word that wasn't vulgar—"idiot," I said to Jake after the fire captain walked away. "And he actually called me *young lady*!"

Jake laughed. "That is what you are."

I jammed my hands into the front pockets of my jeans. "That's not the point and you know it."

"Of course I do." He put his arm around me and kissed the top of my head. I felt like something changed between us, but I wasn't sure what. I didn't have time to analyze it now.

With the Dumpster out of the way, I got my first glimpse

of the damage to the building. It was bad, but it could have been much worse if I hadn't discovered the fire when I did. The paint on the steel garage door had blistered badly from the heat. It would need to be replaced as well as the frame around it. The best news was that the brick structure was undamaged except for some soot on the bricks.

Kristie and Candy stood with Ken Butterfield, Daisy, and Annie from the card shop. The Good Samaritan bystanders were already gone. Somehow, I missed the arrival of Daisy and Annie. I thanked them all for their help.

"We didn't really do anything," Candy said.

"Yes, you did," I said, "and I appreciate it." I invited them all inside. "It's a little early for beer, but I can make coffee." I would have some cleaning up to do in the storage area, but it could wait until later.

"I've tasted your coffee, Max," Kristie said. "I'll go get some."

"Hey, I can make coffee," Jake said.

"Not like mine you can't. I'll be back in two shakes of a lamb's tail as my mother likes to say."

"And I'll get some donuts," Candy said.

Ken wasn't about to be left out. "I'll send over some sandwiches for lunch."

Daisy and Annie looked at each other. "I guess we'll just mooch," Annie said.

I was behind Daisy, Annie, and Jake at the kitchen door, and I glanced down the alley. Ralph Meehan was heading this way. I did a double take to be sure it was him. He had a lot of nerve. Jake had been the first through the door, so I told Annie to let him know I'd be a minute.

My anger reached the boiling point by the time Ralph

reached me. "If you came to gloat, you'll be disappointed to know it didn't work."

"What are you talking about?"

"The fire. The one you set in that Dumpster. That fire destroyed my garage door and could have burned down this whole building." It wasn't the smartest thing to say if Ralph was the killer, but I'd had enough. "You're not going to get away with it. There's going to be an arson investigation—"

"Hold on there, young lady." Ralph held up his hands. "I didn't set any fire."

"I don't believe you."

"Why would you even think something like that?" He seemed puzzled, but it could have been an act.

"To drive me away. Because for some reason you don't want the pub to open."

"That's ridiculous. Next you'll be accusing me of killing Dom and your friend."

I was about to do just that. Instead I said, "Then why are you here?"

"I came to apologize." He ran a hand through his comb-over. "I have to get back. I'm by myself today and I don't want to stay closed for long. When I saw that smoke and saw where the fire engines were going, all I could think about was what you told me, and about Dom."

I wasn't buying the apology. "That fire was set deliberately."

"It had to be." He paused like he wasn't sure what to say next. "I'm sorry for giving you such a hard time before. I meant to talk to you sooner. Detective Bailey came to see me after you left the store. He asked about the note."

"And?"

"For some reason, the detective thought I might have come here with Dom that night. Believe me, I wanted to, but once I persuaded Dom he needed to talk to you, he insisted on going alone."

Not convinced, I waited for more.

"If Dom had gone to the police instead of listening to me, he'd still be alive. That's something I'll have to live with for the rest of my life. You don't know how much I regret not going with him. I should have closed the store early."

"You were at the store when Dominic came here?"

Ralph nodded. "I was. I had to show Detective Bailey my surveillance tapes to prove it."

The anger I'd felt minutes ago settled like a ball of lead in my stomach. "You didn't kill Kurt and Dominic."

"Sorry to disappoint you." The corners of his mouth turned up.

Now I was the one who was puzzled. "Why the turnaround? You threw me out of your store. I just about accused you of murder, and now you want to apologize. I don't understand."

"Believe me, I was mad as a hornet when Detective Bailey questioned me. You have him to thank for making me see things clearly. He vouched for your character and told me everything that's been happening here. I didn't believe him at first, but the more I thought about it, the more I realized I was wrong."

"Apparently, so was I." Boy, was I ever.

Ralph stuck out his right hand. "How about we call a truce and start over."

I shook his outstretched hand. "Agreed."

"Anyway, as my way of setting things right, I want you

to let me know what you need to fix this up. It'll be on the house."

I had as much reason to apologize as he did. There was no way I'd let him do that. "I'll let you know what I need, but I'm paying for it."

Ralph smiled. "We'll see about that, young lady."

What was with the *young lady* stuff today? I promised to keep him posted and went inside to join the others.

The moment I entered the kitchen, I remembered the grain in the mash tun. I glanced at the clock on the wall, surprised to see only a little over an hour had passed. I wasn't too late. Jake sat at a table in the pub with Daisy, Annie, and Ken. Candy and Kristie hadn't returned with coffee and donuts yet. I explained that I needed to tend to the batch of beer. They all offered to help, but the saying about too many cooks spoiling the broth also applies to brewing.

I left Jake to hold the fort and went into the brewery. I drained the liquid from the bottom of the mash tun and recirculated it through the grain, then added heated water to make sure all the sugars were removed. The next step was the brew kettle. When it was boiling, I started adding hops.

Daisy came through the door just then and held up what she was carrying. "I felt bad you were in here while we were all scarfing down donuts, so I brought you one."

"Thanks."

Her gaze roamed the room. "This is the first time I've been in here. It's pretty impressive. I've never seen beer brewed before."

I explained what I was doing.

"I never realized how much there was to it," she said.

"It doesn't seem like a lot when it's something you love to do."

"I guess not."

I told her more about the process while I put the rest of the boiling hops in. When I finished, I asked her how her evening with Adam had gone last night.

She sighed. "All right, I guess."

"You don't sound like it was."

"I just wish he'd make up his mind about what he wants. One minute he's like the nicest guy in the world, and the next he ignores me. Frankly, I'm getting tired of it."

"Have you tried asking him what he wants?"

"Of course I have. He always says"—she deepened her voice—"'I want you, baby.'"

Yuck. I recalled what he'd said when I ran into him at the deli. "Is he having business problems? That could be worrying him."

"He's been having trouble getting some of his inventory, but he told me he had that all under control and it wouldn't be a problem much longer."

"That's good. He must have gotten a delivery, then. I saw him through the window of Handbag Heaven unloading some boxes when I came in this morning."

"You saw him this morning?" Daisy said.

I nodded.

"Are you sure?"

"I'm positive. Why?"

She frowned. "He sent me home early last night because

he had a six a.m. flight to New York this morning. He said he had a meeting with some new suppliers."

"Maybe he changed his mind, or the meeting was cancelled," I said, although I didn't believe it myself. There was no doubt in my mind Adam was giving her the runaround.

"That must be it, but I wonder why he didn't call me."

I hoped she didn't expect me to supply an answer.

"He probably didn't have time," she said. "If he called the shop, he'd get my machine because I've been here," she said. "I guess I'd better go check."

He should have called her well before she showed up to help me. My guess was that he had no intention of taking an early morning flight to New York or anywhere else. Poor Daisy. I watched her leave thinking she was in for a whole lot of heartache.

𝕵 finished the batch of ale and it was now in the fermenting tank where it would stay for about two weeks. By late evening, Jake and Mike had replaced the framing and the garage door. Ralph Meehan didn't carry that size door, but he contacted a company that did and Mike picked it up in his truck. Ralph supplied everything else we needed, and since I insisted on paying, he gave me a big discount.

While they worked, I made a quick trip home to feed Hops and play with her a bit, then got my car and returned to the brew house to clean and sanitize the brewing equipment. The brewing part was fun. The cleaning afterward, not so much. At ten o'clock, the three of us finally sat down

and ate leftover sandwiches from the platter Ken Butterfield had sent over for lunch. Mike took off right after he
wolfed down two sandwiches, and Jake and I weren't far
behind him.

Jake stood beside me while I set the alarm and locked
up. "Thanks for everything today," I said. "Especially for
working on the garage door. That was definitely above and
beyond your job description."

"Maybe you should add that one to it." He grinned.
"Manual labor as needed."

"Maybe I will. But only for brawny, ex-hockey players."

"Ooh, she thinks I'm brawny. That's good, isn't it?"

I laughed for the first time that day. "Definitely."

We were both parked in the lot around the corner, and
when we reached my car, Jake put his hand on my shoulder.
The butterflies that suddenly took flight in my stomach
weren't sure what to make of it.

"Max . . ." There was a long pause. Instead of saying
whatever it was he was going to say, he squeezed my shoulder. "I'll see you tomorrow, boss."

That wasn't what I expected. On second thought, maybe
it was. It certainly wasn't what I hoped he'd say. It was on
my mind all the way home. After this morning, I was under
the impression his feelings had changed. That he saw me
as more than Mike's baby sister. Now I was confused. When
he put his hand on my shoulder and said my name tonight,
I hadn't expected a declaration of undying love, but I sure
thought it would be something different than "I'll see you
tomorrow." Apparently I'd read too much into his concern
for me. It was just as well. Who had time for romance,
anyway?

* * *

𝔍 slept like a log until Hops batted my face with her cast. I groaned and looked at the clock. It was after eight, and she wanted her breakfast. Immediately. I hadn't intended to sleep this late. I dragged my rear out of bed, fed the kitten, and headed to the shower. Thirty minutes later, I felt almost human. I wasn't brewing today and I had interviews scheduled, so I dressed in black slacks and a short-sleeved turquoise jersey instead of the jeans and T-shirt I wore on most days.

It was another beautiful morning, so I left my car at home. I'm not usually an anxious person, but as I got closer to the pub my stomach started doing flip-flops. The fire yesterday seemed to have been more of a warning than an attempt to burn down the building. But what kind of warning? What was this person trying to accomplish? And why? I was at a complete loss. Especially now that Ralph was no longer a suspect. Kurt's and Dom's murders, the vandalism, the fire—none of it made any sense. If this person was trying to drive me out, it wasn't going to work.

With a new resolve, I unlocked the door and went inside. I went from room to room and checked everything twice, then opened the new garage door and checked the alley. Much to my relief, everything was fine. I headed across the street to celebrate with an iced mocha. With extra whipped cream.

Kristie was behind the counter working her magic as usual. She'd changed her hair color since yesterday. Some of her hair color, anyway. The burgundy dreadlocks were now streaked with blue. The early-morning crowd had come and gone, but the next wave that usually included writers and students hadn't arrived yet. There was only one person in line ahead of me. When it was my turn, I told Kristie I'd like extra whipped cream.

"What's the occasion?"

"Only that no one tried to burn down the pub this morning."

She grinned. "Are you sure it's not because of your hockey man?"

I felt heat creeping into my face. "Absolutely not. There's nothing going on there."

"Uh-huh. Sure there isn't."

"Seriously. We're just friends."

Kristie squirted a large dollop of whipped cream on top of the cup. "I don't believe that for a minute. I saw how worried he was yesterday. That hug he gave you wasn't a just friends hug."

She drizzled squiggles of chocolate syrup on the whipped cream, then sprinkled jimmies on the top. She didn't believe in adding a maraschino cherry like other places did, because they were bad for you. Like the chocolate and whipped cream weren't.

"And your feelings are written all over your face," she said. "You've got it bad." Just then the door chimed. "Well, speak of the devil."

I glanced over my shoulder. It was Jake.

"We were just talking about you," Kristie said.

I was sure my face had turned bright red.

"Uh-oh," Jake said. "That can't be good."

Kristie grinned. "That kind of depends. I was just telling Max you—"

"—were a great cook," I said. I shot Kristie a look that told her to button her lips. Or else.

"Oh, he can cook all right." I could tell she wasn't referring to food at all.

Jake looked from Kristie to me and back to Kristie again, like he was missing something. Thank goodness he was.

She passed my mocha over the counter, then took Jake's order for a plain coffee with an extra shot of espresso. I didn't dare leave, afraid Kristie would tell him exactly what we'd been talking about, so I waited for him. As we left, Kristie sang out, "You two behave, now."

I was going to wring her neck.

"What was that all about?" Jake asked.

"Nothing," I said as we jaywalked across the street. "Kristie's imagination runs wild sometimes."

"In other words, I don't want to know."

"Yep." I unlocked the door to the brew house and we went inside. "You're here early. I didn't think you were coming in until this afternoon."

"I thought it was a good idea to be here."

I stopped in my tracks. "I don't need a babysitter."

"I know you don't. That's not what I mean."

"That's what it sounds like."

Jake set his cup on the bar. "I just thought you might want some extra help today. Nothing more."

Before I had a chance to respond, the door opened and Elmer Fairbanks came in. I fought the urge to groan. I'd completely forgotten he was coming in today. Great. Now I had two babysitters. This was ridiculous.

"I heard about that fire yesterday," Elmer said. "If I'd have been here, it never would have happened." He snapped the 101st Airborne ball cap from his head. "So, where do you want me?"

Anywhere but here, I wanted to say. How in the world was I supposed to get anything done? I wouldn't be able to leave the pub without one of them shadowing me. I didn't want to hurt his feelings, but I had to say something. "I appreciate your wanting to help, Elmer, but I really don't need looking after."

"Maybe you don't, but this place sure does," he said. "Break-ins, murder, arson. Maybe you want to take bets on what's gonna happen today."

I heard Jake snicker. Traitor.

"Nothing is going to happen," I said. "I have interviews scheduled, so there will be people going in and out all day. I have new employees coming in to learn the ropes. And Jake will be here, too. It's perfectly safe."

"Yeah? That's what we thought in the Ardennes before everything started exploding. No such thing as a safe place."

Now what? I looked at Jake, who was doing all he could to keep a straight face. Then I came up with an idea that would get them both out from under my feet. "Good point," I said to Elmer. "Jake, why don't you show Elmer where the fire was yesterday and get him acquainted with the layout of the pub. Then you can talk to him about any security concerns."

"Me?"

It was my turn to suppress a smile. "You did say you came in early to help, didn't you?"

CHAPTER NINETEEN

Ididn't feel a bit bad about leaving Elmer with Jake. He deserved it. Contrary to what he'd told me, I was positive Jake hadn't come in early to see if he could help with anything. I had five older brothers and a sometimes-overprotective dad. I could spot Protection Mode a mile away. With any luck, Jake and Elmer would hit it off and both of them would stay out of my way. Since there was no guarantee that would actually happen, I downed the rest of my mocha, slung my purse over my shoulder, and snuck out the front door.

There were three places I hadn't visited yet, all belonging to Adam Greeley. So far, I'd mostly struck out trying to find anyone who had seen suspicious activity near the pub. Annie had been the only one who'd seen anything even remotely out of the ordinary. Since Adam's stores were directly across the street, I was hopeful that at least one of his staff had seen something. And frankly, I was curious about the situation between Daisy and Adam. Daisy was a lovely person, and I was annoyed with Adam for treating her the way he was. Not that I could do anything about it, except maybe put in a good word for Daisy.

I remembered the article I'd read in the *Pittsburgh Times* about This and That, so I decided to start there. Many of the boutique shops in the area were funky, fun places. Although this one had a mix of merchandise, This and That, as well as Adam's other two stores, was a little more high-end. It featured plush carpets, glass and marble tables and fixtures, and soft lighting. The lone sales clerk was arranging silk scarves on a glass-topped table, and she looked up as I entered. She greeted me with a smile and I returned her good morning.

"You're from across the street, aren't you?" she asked.

I said I was and introduced myself.

"I saw the reporters over there the other day," she said, shaking her head. "They actually came over here and started asking all kinds of questions about what happened. I made them leave."

"I appreciate that."

"So, what can I do for you? I have the feeling you're not here to buy a scarf."

By this time, I had gotten pretty good at summarizing the events of the last few weeks. When I finished, I asked if she had noticed anything strange.

"I can't say that I have," she said. "But you might want to talk to Mr. Greeley. He keeps an eagle eye on everything." She lowered her voice to a whisper. "And I mean everything."

I wasn't about to say that I knew that already, but I told her I'd talk to Adam.

The clerk in Fleet of Foot said almost the same thing. She hadn't seen anyone, either, but said I should talk to the boss. While I was there, I spied a cute pair of sandals and on impulse decided to buy them. They were a well-known brand and marked half off, even though it was the beginning of the season. I couldn't pass them up. While the clerk rang up my purchase, she asked me what I planned to do after the brewery closed.

"I'm usually exhausted by that time of night, so I go home and crash."

She giggled. "No, I mean after it's closed for good. You know, after you sell it."

I almost dropped the credit card as I passed it across the counter. "Hopefully, that won't happen for a long time. Possibly never. I'd like to hand it down to the kids I don't have yet." An image of a little boy who looked just like Jake flashed in my mind. *Get a grip, O'Hara.*

The clerk frowned. "Huh. I heard you were putting it up for sale. I figured it was because of everything that happened. And with those blue flyers everywhere . . ."

She didn't need to finish the sentence. "Those flyers belong in the trash." I slid my card back into my wallet. "Who told you I was selling the brew house? I'd like to set them straight."

"I'm sorry. I probably shouldn't have said anything."

"I'm glad you did. Was it Fran Donovan who told you?"

The clerk shook her head. "That's the lady with those flyers, right?" She handed me the tangerine shopping bag holding my new sandals. "Actually, it was Mr. Greeley."

I vaguely remembered something Daisy said last week. Someone had mentioned I wouldn't be opening the brew house. It made sense now—it had come from Adam. But why did he think that? He had no business sticking his nose into mine, let alone trying to start a rumor like that.

I thanked the clerk and left. I paused out on the sidewalk trying to get my anger in check. I didn't want to go barging into Handbag Heaven like I was the SWAT team. But I did want to find out why Adam was telling everyone I was selling the brew house. I took a couple of deep breaths, and when I figured my blood pressure had returned to a normal level, I went into the handbag store.

Adam stood at a marble counter on one side of the store. The counter was piled with quilted handbags of all shapes and sizes, and he was attaching price tags to their handles. "Well, to what do I owe the pleasure?" he said. "It's been a long time since you've been in here."

I wasn't sure if it was good or bad that he seemed to be in a friendly mood. "I've been a little busy," I said.

"You certainly have." He slid a pile of handbags aside and leaned on the counter. "I just got in this new shipment of Veras if you're interested." He held up one of the bags. "They're all thirty percent less than you'll find them anywhere else."

Any other time I might have been tempted. "Not today."

"I understand perfectly," he said. "I'm sure your money is tight right now, especially in light of everything that's happened over there. And that fire yesterday." He shook his head. "So horrible. You could have lost everything."

Like I didn't know that already. "My finances are fine.

Everything is coming together and we'll be opening right on schedule."

His smile disappeared and reappeared so quickly, I would have missed it if I hadn't been watching him so closely. "Well, that's certainly good news," he said.

I could have beat around the bush and hinted about what I'd heard, but I was fed up. I went for the direct approach. "If that's the case, why are you telling everyone I'm selling the brewery?"

"Where in the world did you hear such a thing?" Adam was no longer smiling.

I wasn't about to give away my sources and cause problems for them. "It came from more than one person."

He busied himself with the handbags in front of him. "I never . . . They must have misunderstood what I said."

"I don't think so. When I mentioned to them that I had no intention of leaving, they seemed genuinely surprised."

"Is it any wonder?" he said. "Death and destruction follow you around ever since you bought that old building."

"Through no fault of my own. Someone's out to get me."

He smiled again. "Why, Maxine. That sounds a bit paranoid."

Maybe it did, but it was true.

He pushed the handbags to the side. "Remember when I mentioned a week or so ago there was something I wanted to talk to you about?"

I didn't . . . Wait. I vaguely remembered him saying something like that when I'd run into him on the sidewalk outside the bakery. It had been the day his hand was all bandaged up. I glanced at his hand. There were only a couple of red marks now. Tooth marks. So he was the one Daisy had said was bitten by a cat.

Adam came around the counter. "I know you've had a bad time of it. A terrible time, in all honesty. I may have pointed out to a few people my surprise that you hadn't quit."

It wasn't quite an admission, but I'd take it.

"I have a proposal for you," he said. "I want to buy your building."

I couldn't have heard him right. "Excuse me?"

"I'd like to buy your place."

"What? Why?" It was all I could come up with.

"I've had my eye on that building for quite a while. Imagine my surprise when I came back from being out of the country on a buying trip to find it had been sold."

"The building was up for sale for over a year. Why didn't you make an offer if you wanted it?"

He shrugged. "I was waiting for the price to come down. It seems like I waited a little too long."

"Is that why you've been telling people I'm closing down?"

"Wishful thinking on my part, I suppose, although I never actually said you were leaving. I only hinted at it." He gave me his biggest salesman smile. "So how about my proposal?"

I shook my head. "I'm sorry, Adam, but the brewery isn't for sale. Not now and not ever. I've put too much time, money, and sweat into that place to give it all up."

The bell on the door chimed as a customer came in.

"You know where to find me when you change your mind."

As I went out the door, I heard Adam pitching for another kind of sale. "Mrs. Patterson! How lovely to see you. Wait until you see the new Veras I got in my shipment yesterday . . ."

At least I now knew why Adam was spreading rumors about the pub shutting down. That was one mystery solved. If only I could figure out the rest as easily.

"Find out anything interesting?" Jake asked when I returned to the brew house. He sat by himself on a stool at the bar. Nicole wasn't due in yet, and I didn't see Elmer.

"How did you know what I was doing?" I held up the bag holding my shoes. "I could have just been shopping."

"Right. If that were the case, you could have taken Elmer with you instead of passing him off to me. Nice move, by the way. I'll have to remember that." He grinned. "Of course, if that's lingerie in the bag, I'm glad you didn't take him with you. You wouldn't want to give the old guy a heart attack."

Jake mentioning lingerie made my hand shake. I put the bag down on the bar. "Where is Elmer?"

"He went to the bakery. He said he had—and I quote—'a hankering for something sweet.'"

Drat. I'd hoped he'd gotten bored and gone home. "So he'll be back?"

"Afraid so."

I let out a sigh. "Great. I know he means well, but I can't have him underfoot and following me around all day. It's going to drive me nuts."

"Just find something for him to do. Some busywork. Nicole will be in soon. Maybe he can help her."

"Maybe."

"I saw you leaving the store across the street. Did you learn anything?"

I filled him in on the Adam situation, then I picked up my bag. "I'll be in the office if you need me. I have to get some paperwork done before the interviews this afternoon."

Jake touched the shopping bag. "Are you going to tell me what you bought?" He had a wicked gleam in his eyes. "Some lacy getup, maybe?"

I yanked the bag out of his reach. "Wouldn't you like to know?" I spun around before he could see my flaming cheeks. I went down the hallway thinking maybe I should have bought something besides shoes.

The rest of the day passed quietly. Nicole and Elmer hit it off. It turned out her grandfather had been in Elmer's unit during World War II, so they had a lot to talk about. My interviews went well, and I hired two more people. I now had enough to cover both lunch and dinner shifts, as well as into the evening. Since we wouldn't have a full-service bar, I didn't need to hire bartenders. I'd likely cover the taps myself with occasional help from Mike and my mom and dad. And Nicole, too. Between the kitchen staff Kurt had hired and more that Jake had, everything seemed to be under control.

Then why did I feel like it wasn't?

The phone on my desk rang and I absentmindedly answered it.

"Hi, sweetie." It was Mom. "I just wanted to check on

you. Mike said he and Jake replaced your garage door yesterday."

I hoped he hadn't told her why I needed a new door.

"He also told me about the fire."

Darn that brother of mine. What a tattletale.

"Max, you should have told me."

"I didn't want you to worry, especially after everything else."

"I worry more when you keep things to yourself. Besides, I'm your mother. I'm going to worry no matter what."

She had a point. To make up for trying to keep her in the dark, I told her about the conversation I'd had that morning with Adam. I asked if Dad had learned anything new, and she told me no, that he'd been working on two new homicides. After that, she brought up the meeting of Fran Donovan's Save Our Lawrenceville group that evening and asked if I was planning to attend.

"Candy, Kristie, and I are going. Would you like to come with us?"

"I'd love to." She said she'd meet us there. Right before I hung up, she said, "Did you ever notice the abbreviation for Save Our Lawrenceville is SOL?" I could hear the smile in her voice.

I laughed. One could only hope.

When Candy, Kristie, and I reached the meeting room at the library, we weren't sure we were in the right place. There were only five people in a room that could have held thirty, and they were all crammed into the front row.

We stepped through the doorway and I spotted my mother sitting on the left side in the back of the room. We took the seats beside her.

A man in the front row turned around, his eyes widening when he saw us. He quickly whispered to the woman beside him, who did the same to the woman next to her. It made me think of the kids' game where the last person recites what they heard and it's different than what the first person said. In this case, the last person didn't recite anything—he turned around and stared.

"How rude," Candy said, loud enough for the front-rowers to hear. The staring man faced front again.

Kristie shushed her. I wanted to melt into the floor. Mom squeezed my hand. "It'll be all right," she said. "We have a right to be here. It's your neighborhood, too, and your brewery."

I heard a distinct harrumph from someone up front. One of the women said, "Well, I never!"

"I'll bet you haven't," Candy said.

I poked her with my elbow. "Stop that! We're here to find out what's going on, not to antagonize these people."

"You're no fun at all."

I turned around as the door closed behind us. A tiny woman with dove-gray hair and wire-rimmed glasses marched to the front of the room. Her height was well below my five foot two, and a strong wind would likely blow her away. Her light blue gauzy skirt was almost ankle length and she wore white anklets and purple sneakers. Her pale yellow oxford shirt didn't match either the skirt or the sneakers. Candy looked downright fashionable next to her.

She stepped onto a small stool at the podium. She took

a piece of paper from her skirt pocket, unfolded it, and spread it out in front of her. "Welcome to this very important meeting of Save Our Lawrenceville. I expected a much bigger turnout, but thank you all for coming."

Considering her appearance, I expected her voice to be squeaky and strident, but it was smooth and strong.

"There is a blight on this community and we must put a stop to it."

"Blight my patootie," Candy whispered.

I jabbed her with my elbow again.

"Every day we are losing more of our heritage. As the saying goes, those who ignore history are doomed to repeat it. We can't let this happen."

The front-rowers nodded in unison like bobbleheads.

"I need the support of each and every one of you. Call the mayor. Write letters to the editor. If we have to, we'll march up and down Butler Street with signs."

Kristie leaned across Candy so I could hear, and whispered, "I'd kind of like to see that."

Fran Donovan folded the paper and put it back in her pocket. "Does anyone have any questions?"

Candy's hand shot up.

Oh no.

Fran pointed at Candy. "You in the back row."

Either Fran hadn't spotted me, like her cohorts had, or she had no idea who we were.

Candy stood. "How does restoring an old, abandoned building and returning it to its intended use destroy history? If you make it into a museum, you'd be doing the very thing you're spouting off about."

Two people in the front row whispered to each other.

"Something doesn't need to be a museum to show history," Candy continued. "There's no better way for people to get a glimpse of the brewing history of our city than seeing an actual working brewery."

I sat up straighter. I couldn't have said it better myself.

Fran pursed her lips. "That's not the point."

One of the whisperers in the front row said, "I think the cupcake lady made a good point. I hadn't thought of it that way. Maybe she's right."

"Cupcake lady?" Fran said. Her gaze went back and forth across our row and finally rested on me. "You!" She hopped down from her step stool. "You're the one who stole my brewery!"

Candy looked ready for a fight. I stood and touched her arm. "I appreciate your support," I said to her, "but I need to handle this."

She took her seat again.

"I didn't steal your brewery. The Steel City Brewery has been gone a long time. I bought the only remaining building and restored it. Would you rather have it remain empty and abandoned?"

The front-rowers whispered among themselves.

"If your group really wants to save Lawrenceville and its history, you should be in favor of what I'm doing."

"Get out." Fran pointed to the door. "You're not welcome here."

"I'd really like to stay and talk to you," I said as calmly as I could. "I'd like to know more about you and your group."

"If you're not leaving, then I am." She marched to the door. "Meeting adjourned."

"Ms. Donovan," I said. "You don't have to leave."

She did anyway, followed by her friends in the front row. The four of us looked at one another. Finally, Kristie said, "That went well, didn't it?"

We stopped for ice cream, then went our separate ways. On the way home, I remembered I'd left my sandals in my office. I could have waited until tomorrow to get them, but since I was passing the brew house anyway, I figured I might as well pick them up. I couldn't stop thinking about how Fran Donovan had acted when she discovered that I was present at her meeting. My grandma would have said she was one card shy of a full deck. I'd have to agree. There was no reason she couldn't have stayed and talked things over in a reasonable manner. At least the meeting had been sparsely attended. If the people in that front row were her only supporters, I didn't have anything to worry about.

I parked on the street in front of the pub and unlocked the door. Once inside, I disarmed the security system, then flicked on one of the wall sconces. As much as I loved the quiet of the place, the din of the crowds I hoped for would be even better. I couldn't believe anyone in her right mind would want this to be a museum. It was exactly what it was supposed to be. Candy was right. There was no better way to honor the brewers of the past.

I went back to my office to retrieve my purchase. While I was there, I checked my to-do list for tomorrow. Not quite as busy as today, so I'd probably have time to get another batch ready to brew. I left the office, and as I crossed the pub I spotted something on top of the bar. Funny. I didn't remember seeing anything there when I came in, but the lights had been dim. I just hadn't noticed it, I guessed. I went closer. It was a paper lunch-sized bag with the top rolled down. I lifted it, unrolled the top, and peeked inside.

I dropped the bag, jumped back, and screamed.

There was a dead rat inside.

CHAPTER TWENTY

At least I hoped it was dead. I ran outside, fishing my cell phone from my purse as I went, and called 911. The dispatcher asked me to calm down three times before she understood what I said. I'm not sure she believed a dead rat was an emergency, but she promised to send a car right away. While I was talking, I scanned the street in search of whoever might have done this. The sidewalks were busy for a Thursday night. The bakery and coffee shop were closed, but Adam's stores were open, as well as the deli and the card shop. I didn't see anyone who looked like they'd just dropped a dead rat on my bar.

I opened my car door and sank down onto the passenger seat. I was sure that bag hadn't been on the bar when I'd first gone inside. Whoever had done this had come in while I was back in my office. The realization that I could have ended up like Kurt and Dominic wasn't lost on me. That someone could get so close and I didn't even know they were there scared the crap out of me. I started shaking, and I was still shaking when the police arrived.

It was the same officer who'd responded the night the alarm had gone off, so he knew a little about what had been going on. When he told me to wait outside, I was perfectly happy to let him check the building alone.

It wasn't long before he came out carrying the paper bag. "It's all clear." He reached into the bag and pulled the rat out.

I jumped back.

"It's all right," he said. "It's not real. It's only rubber."

I swallowed the screech I'd almost let loose.

He laughed. "Someone's idea of a practical joke, I guess."

Some joke. It would take days for my heartbeat to return to normal. Rubber or not, it was disgusting. The fake rat was the kind you'd see in a Halloween display, complete with a knife sticking out of it and painted-on blood all in one piece.

"Wait. There's something else in here." He lifted out a slip of paper. His smile disappeared as he read what was written on the paper. "This may not be just a joke."

"What do you mean? Can I see it?"

I expected him to pass it to me, but instead he held it up so I could read it. A chill went down my spine. It definitely wasn't a joke. The note read, *This could have been you.*

It took a while before I stopped shaking enough to drive home after the officer took my information for the report. The rat had been bad enough, but the fact that the person who'd killed Kurt and Dom had been that close to me really creeped me out. The note was right. It could have been me. I didn't understand why the killer had let me off with a warning. As frightened as I was, I knew I couldn't let my fear get the best of me. I pulled into my parking spot in the lot and turned off the ignition.

Maybe that was the point. Someone wanted me to be afraid. Scared enough to give up the brew house. It couldn't be a coincidence that this happened right after the meeting tonight. Fran Donovan had accused me of stealing the brewery from her. Storming out of her own meeting wasn't exactly normal behavior. A reasonable person would have stuck around to hear what I had to say. That's how these meetings are supposed to work. And judging by the sparse turnout, she didn't have a whole lot of support for her contention that what I was doing was a bad thing. Heck, Candy had almost convinced one of the guys in the front row that Fran was off base. Even so, Fran still had seemed convinced she was going to stop me—possibly by leaving that rat and the note for me to find. A Halloween prop didn't equate to murder, however. I thought about that. She was small, but that didn't mean she couldn't have killed two men, especially if she took them by surprise. I didn't quite buy that theory, but it was all I had at the moment.

I pulled my phone out of my purse and Googled her name to get her address. Her home was only a half mile away, on a side street off Penn Avenue. I started up the car again. Fran Donovan was going to have a surprise visitor of her own.

* * *

The narrow one-way street was difficult to navigate even by Pittsburgh standards. Some cars were parked with two wheels on the sidewalk, probably to avoid having their side mirrors sheared off. The vehicles with owners brave enough to park correctly were mostly overly large trucks and SUVs. It was almost like they were saying, *Go ahead and hit me. I'm bigger than you. See who comes out of this one unscathed.* I was able to maneuver around them, and I made it to the end of the block without doing damage to my car or anyone else's. I found a parking spot on nice, wide Penn Avenue instead, even though I had to walk a block.

The houses here weren't row houses, but they may as well have been, since they were built so close together. Only a few had front yards, but almost all were well kept. It wouldn't be a bad place to live unless you were claustrophobic. Fran Donovan's house was one of those with a yard, but instead of grass, she'd filled it with perennials. Nothing was in full bloom yet, but in another month it would be lovely. I hadn't envisioned her as a gardener. My first impression was of someone more at home in a dusty archive somewhere.

I went up the two steps to her small porch and rang the doorbell. For a split second I wondered if I was doing the right thing, but it was too late to turn back now. I waited and rang a second time.

"Hold your horses. I'm coming." Seconds later she swung the door open. "You!"

"I know it's late, but I need to talk to you," I said.

Fran was already dressed for bed, and she pulled the neck of her pink chenille robe closer together, then yanked on the belt to make it tighter. "I have nothing to say to you. You have a lot of nerve invading my space like this."

"Invading? Like how you invaded mine?"

"I have no idea what you're talking about. I want you to leave now or I'm calling the police."

I crossed my arms over my chest. "Why don't you do that. Maybe you can explain to them why you put that bag with a rubber rat in it on my bar."

Fran had the door half closed but she stopped. "What?"

"You put a fake rat in a paper bag with a threatening note and left it on top of the bar in my brew house." I enunciated each word slowly.

The little bit of color in her face drained away. "I did no such thing!"

"I don't believe you. It's too much of a coincidence that it happened right after that meeting—the one you left early because you were so upset to see me there. You waited until I unlocked the door and turned the alarm off, then snuck inside when you saw me go back to my office."

"I would never do anything like that," she said. "That's so . . . so . . ." Her voice faltered. "Mean."

"Then talk to me. Please."

She took a step back and I thought she was going to close the door, but instead she opened it all the way. "You're right. We need to talk. Come in."

I hesitated a moment. Her shock at what I'd told her seemed genuine, but what if it wasn't? I couldn't very well back down now, though. Just in case, I lifted my phone from my purse and clutched it in my hand as I went inside.

The door opened directly into her living room, which

was bigger than I thought it would be considering how small the house looked from the outside. There were hardwood floors under a well-worn oriental rug. The furniture was similar to what I'd inherited from my grandmother, but unlike mine, hers actually looked like it belonged in the room. What really surprised me, though, were the items that filled display and bookcases plus the numerous photos on the walls. I felt like I'd just entered a museum, but not just any museum. This room showed the history of the former brewery that my building had once been part of.

One display case held beer bottles ranging from the 1800s all the way to the last ones produced by Steel City Brewing. Another case held cans, many of them decorated with Pirates and Steelers designs. There was assorted memorabilia in other cases. I turned to Fran. "This is fabulous."

"Yes."

She stepped aside when I moved to get a closer look at the photos on the walls. Every aspect of the brewing process was documented. There were photos of local celebrities of the past standing by stainless steel tanks. A few of the photos were autographed. Candy would be in seventh heaven if she saw the ones with her beloved Steel Curtain of the seventies Steelers, especially the one on which some-one had written "DEFENSE!"

Much older photos were displayed on the next wall. These were all black-and-white. The first one dated to the beginning of Prohibition—kegs of beer were being busted open by feds with axes. The next ones showed ice cream, and I remembered reading that the brewery had survived through that era because of their versatility. They'd produced ice cream and soda pop instead of beer.

I turned around. "Where did you get all this?"

"My father." She motioned to the sofa and I followed her lead and took a seat.

"This all belonged to your father?" I finally understood her attachment to the brewery and why she thought it should belong to her.

She nodded. "My father worked in the old brewery from the time he turned thirteen. He started just before Prohibition. It was the only place he ever worked, and it almost killed him when they made him retire. Anyway, he collected all these things over the years. Every time a new bottle design came in, he always saved one of the bottles. Some of the oldest ones he found at flea markets or estate sales."

"What about the rest of it?"

"The same thing. Anytime there was an article in the paper, he'd cut it out and save it. And the photos—he was a bit of an amateur photographer. Whenever there was any kind of event, he made sure to capture it. He became the company's photographer. Unofficially, of course."

"What did your father do at the brewery?" I asked.

"Anything and everything. He was just a boy when he started, so at first he mostly ran errands. He did whatever was needed. Eventually he became a brewer."

"Like me."

"Don't flatter yourself," Fran said. "My father would never have brewed those fancy beers. You people are just glorified home brewers."

I bit back a smart remark, and said, "My beers are pretty simple. I mostly brew in the German tradition. I don't use artificial flavorings or unusual ingredients."

She seemed surprised at that. "So, what do you use?"

"Water, yeast, hops, and barley. Sometimes wheat."

"Oh."

Not exactly an enthusiastic response. "It's really the same as what your dad did but on a much smaller scale." I could tell from her expression that she didn't want to believe that.

"Enough about that," Fran said. "That's not why you're here. I want to know why you accused me of such a horrible thing."

I gave her the full rundown beginning with the vandalism before Kurt was murdered. "After the meeting tonight, I went back to the brew house to pick something up I'd forgotten earlier. I checked a few things in my office, and when I went to leave, I saw a paper bag on top of the bar that hadn't been there when I came in. When I opened it, there was a dead rat inside. At least I thought it was a dead rat. It turned out to be made out of rubber."

"Oh my," Fran said. "You must have been frightened."

I nodded. "But that wasn't the worst. There was a note in the bag that said, *This could have been you*."

"That's terrible! You've really had a bad time of it," she said. "I had no idea all this was going on. Your friend's death didn't even make the paper, and when I heard about the bar owner's murder, I assumed it was because of his unsavory business."

I wasn't quite sure how she'd come to the conclusion that making the beer was okay but serving it was bad.

"You really thought I was behind all this?" she asked.

"I did—at least between leaving the brew house and arriving here."

"I didn't realize I came off the way I did, but you need

to understand that brewery was my father's entire life. Before I'm gone, I need to make sure the legacy he entrusted to me goes on. A museum—a real museum would do that."

I suddenly had an inkling of an idea how I could help her, but I'd have to think about how to make it work. I kept it to myself for the time being.

"Although I guess it's possible my father would have liked to see his old brewery operating again." Fran gave me a slight smile.

Was it possible I had actually won her over?

"Back to the trouble you've had," Fran said. "You said someone is getting in, even though there's no sign of a break-in?"

I nodded. "It's so frustrating. I can't figure it out. And neither can the police or the alarm company."

Fran smiled. "I believe I can."

That was even more far-fetched than me thinking I'd won her over. "I don't want to burst your bubble, but if the police don't know how someone's getting in . . ." I didn't finish the sentence.

There was a twinkle in her eyes as her smile got wider. "The police don't know everything."

I was starting to think I was wrong about her. Maybe she really was the nutcase I thought she was earlier. The only thing she could possibly know that the police didn't was if she was the killer. My phone was still in my hand, and I wondered how fast I could dial 911.

Fran stood and walked over to the wall, where she removed one of the photos. "They don't know about this." She handed the picture to me and returned to her seat.

It was a grainy black-and-white shot of a cavernous brick

room filled with wooden kegs. I didn't understand. "What does this have to do with the brew house?"

She clapped her hands together, very pleased with herself. "If you look at the date on the photo you'll see it was taken in 1928, well before the end of Prohibition."

"So?" I had no idea where this was going.

"Those kegs are filled with beer, and not *near beer*, either."

Near beer was an almost nonalcoholic beer that some breweries had produced back then. "I still don't see what you're getting at."

"So how did the brewers get that bootleg beer out of the brewery?"

I blew out air in a big sigh. "I have no idea."

"They did it the same way your murderer is going in and out." She leaned forward. "By using the tunnels."

CHAPTER TWENTY-ONE

"What tunnels?" I said. Fran wasn't making any sense.

"There are tunnels that run under the brewery."

What a ridiculous notion. It wasn't possible. "I would certainly know about it if there were tunnels under the brew house," I said. "It would have been disclosed when I bought the building. That's not something a real estate agent is going to keep from you."

Fran leaned back in her seat. "The real estate agent wouldn't have known about them. They're not on any building plan, since they were illegal. But they're definitely there. I've been in them."

I still didn't buy it. "Then where is the entrance? My basement walls are concrete block." Then I remembered the old shelves on the walls. Could it be behind one of those?

"It's there. I'm sure of it."

I couldn't wrap my mind around it. If she was right, how could I not have known about this? It was my building, for heaven's sake. "Tunnels. Under the brewery."

"Yes. Do you want to hear about them?"

"You bet I do," I said.

Fran told me that despite—or maybe because of—the ban on alcohol, there was a huge demand for it, and the ice cream and pop business wasn't enough to keep the business afloat. They needed a way to get beer to barges on the Allegheny River, and a series of tunnels was the safest way. After Prohibition was repealed, the tunnels were used for a while until shipping by boat was no longer cost-effective. The tunnels were eventually closed off and forgotten, except by the old-timers like Fran's father, who'd taken her to see them when she was a girl.

One thing about this story bothered me. The building that housed the actual brewery was gone. My brew house was in the former office building. I mentioned this to Fran.

"There were half a dozen ways to enter the tunnels. And that's only the ones I knew about. From what I remember my father telling me, there were entrances from some of the other businesses in the area. Alcohol came in as well as went out."

"You're sure there's one under my building?"

"Positive."

All this made sense now. Someone else knew about these tunnels and was using that knowledge to get in and out of the brewery without being detected. Except for the one time the alarm had been activated, of course, when he'd solved that problem by repositioning the motion sensors. I needed to see these tunnels.

Fran agreed to meet me at the brew house at ten the next morning to show me the entrance. It was going to be a long night.

I arrived at the pub before seven a.m. raring to go. I'd spent a sleepless night thinking about those tunnels and trying to figure out where the entrance could be. Even though Fran said they'd been closed off years ago, it was amazing nothing had been discovered during the renovation. I'd had all the interior partitions removed, the exterior walls taken down to the bricks, and the hardwood under the old linoleum refinished. There wasn't anything special about the basement. There were old steel shelves along the walls, but I didn't store anything there because it was damp and I was afraid mice would get into the grain. The rest of the space was empty except for an ancient six-foot-tall safe that was too heavy to move. If I ever expanded into this space and made it a rathskeller, it would make an interesting conversation piece. The combination lock on the safe was missing, so it was no longer useful for much more than that.

When Jake arrived at seven-thirty, he found me in the cellar on my hands and knees examining a space under one of the built-in shelves. "Hold that pose a second while I get out my phone. I have to get a picture."

"I hope you want a new phone, too, 'cause you're gonna need one." I pushed myself to my feet.

He laughed. "What are you doing down here?"

"Looking for a secret door."

Jake raised an eyebrow. "Let me guess. You found a bunch of those old Nancy Drew books you used to read as a kid and you're reenacting *The Mystery of the Secret Door*."

"Did anyone ever tell you you're a smart aleck?" I said as we climbed the stairs.

"All the time."

"And for the record, there's no Nancy Drew book with that title."

He slid onto a bar stool. "What are you really doing?"

"I just told you."

"You're serious?"

I took the seat beside him. "Yep. Remember that meeting I went to last night?"

He nodded.

"It didn't go very well." I told him about Fran storming out of the meeting and what happened after that. As soon as I got to the part about the rat, he interrupted.

"I thought you were going to call me when you were going to be here late."

Good thing I skipped telling him about the note. "I stopped on the spur of the moment and I thought I'd be in and out."

"That's not the point. It could have been much worse. You could have been hurt."

"I know that, but I'm not going to let someone scare me out of my own brewery. If I'd planned on being here more than a minute or two, I would have locked the door and set the alarm."

"I'm not going to lecture you—not that it would do any good. But call me the next time," he said. "What happened after that?"

I filled him in on my visit to Fran Donovan's house and what she told me about the tunnels.

"It's kind of hard to believe," Jake said. "Are you sure this Fran isn't just making all this up?"

"That's what I thought at first. I didn't think it was possible. I've never seen any kind of door—even one that had been closed off—in the basement. She's adamant about it, and she even showed me an old photograph of this large space that she swears is part of the tunnel. Anyway, she's coming here at ten to show me where the opening is."

"So that's why you were down on the floor."

"Yep."

"Great." He stood and slipped his phone out of his shirt pocket. "Can you do that pose again? I really want to get a picture."

I jumped up and snatched the phone from his hand. "You were warned, Lambert." I skipped around to the serving side of the bar.

He leaned over the wide bar top trying to get the phone from my hand. It was just out of his reach. "Give it back, Max."

"I don't think so." I sidled up to the other end of the bar. We were both laughing as Jake kept grabbing for the phone.

"You're going to be sorry," he said.

"Ha! You have to catch me first."

Jake vaulted over the bar and landed in front of me, only inches away. My pulse accelerated, much like a car going from zero to sixty in two seconds flat.

"What was that about catching you?" he said.

Still holding his phone, I put my hands behind my back. He reached around me and grasped my hands. Any retort I had caught in my throat, because the next thing I knew, Jake was kissing me.

We parted a minute later, both of us breathless. "I told you you'd be sorry," he said.

"Who said I'm sorry?" My voice was shaky.

I was pretty sure he was about to kiss me again when I heard "Ahem."

We jumped apart.

"Little early in the morning for hanky-panky, isn't it?" Elmer said with a big grin on his face.

"It's not what you think," I stammered.

"I may be old, but there's nothing wrong with my vision, you know," Elmer said.

"Maybe not," Jake said. "But you do have rotten timing." He put his palm out and I gave him back his phone. He squeezed my hand. "I'll be in the kitchen. I have another recipe I want to work on."

Elmer grinned again. "Looks to me you were cooking something right here."

I heard Jake laughing as he went through the door to the kitchen. I went around the bar and dropped into a chair.

"I knew something was going on between you two." Elmer took a seat on the other side of the table.

"There's nothing going on," I said. "We're just friends." Meanwhile, my brain was screaming, *Jake kissed me!*

"Whatever you say. Where do you want me today?"

I told him about Fran and the tunnels.

He nodded. "I heard rumors about them, but I figured they were just stories. Who would have thought there were bootleggers in Pittsburgh?"

Indeed.

*   *   *

Once again, Candy discovered what was going on before I had a chance to tell her. This time I blamed it on Elmer, who'd gone to the bakery to get some sweet rolls. It was a little after nine when she tracked me down in my office, where I was struggling to fill out a report of brewing operations for the state. It was my first one, and it didn't help that my thoughts kept wandering back to Jake.

"Why didn't you call me?" She stood in the open doorway to my office. "I had to hear this secondhand."

I laughed. "That's a first, isn't it?"

"And it better be the last. You know I like to keep informed."

"You're just nosy."

Candy held her hands over her heart. "You wound me, Max. I am not nebby. No one around here would know what to do if I didn't keep up on things." She pulled a chair up to my desk. "So spill. Elmer told me a little bit—that Fran Donovan told you about some tunnels. How did you get her to talk to you?"

"I didn't tell Elmer everything because I didn't want him hovering any more than he already is." I told her about coming back here and what I'd found—including the note, and that was why I'd paid a visit to Fran. "When I accused her of leaving that little present, she was appalled that I thought she'd do something like that and she invited me in." I told her the rest of the story.

"I can't believe I never thought of tunnels," Candy said.

"You knew about them?"

"No, I didn't," she said. "I didn't grow up in Lawrenceville. But entering inside the building instead of the outside is the only thing that makes sense. It's so simple and it explains why I didn't see anything the couple of nights I sat in the parking lot."

"You actually staked out the place?"

"Of course I did."

I just shook my head. We talked for another minute or two, then she had to get back to the bakery. Before she left, she made me promise to keep her informed. I didn't have much choice in that matter—she'd find out somehow, like she always did.

I tried to get back to working on the report, but I couldn't concentrate. I got up and went back to the brewery. While I checked the gauges, I kept thinking about Jake. I'd wanted that kiss since forever, and now that it had happened, I wasn't sure what it meant. I wanted it to be the beginning of something, but what if Jake didn't feel the same? Maybe he only kissed me because I was convenient. A spur-of-the-moment impulse that didn't mean a thing to him.

Which was probably true. Sure, he'd shown concern for me at times, but he'd never voiced any notions of a romantic relationship. We were good friends. Good friends who shared a kiss. A kiss that didn't mean anything.

Oh, who was I kidding? It certainly meant something to me. But if Jake didn't feel the same, well, so be it. It wouldn't be anything new. I'd just carry on as I always had and keep my feelings to myself.

Fran Donovan arrived promptly at ten. Jake was still in the kitchen. I wasn't sure what he was working on, but I smelled tomato and garlic. Elmer sat at one of the tables, and he'd begun telling me another war story when Fran opened the door and peeked in.

I went over to greet her. "Thanks for coming." I then introduced her to Elmer.

She looked around the room. "This isn't what I expected."

"It ain't the den of iniquity you thought it would be?" Elmer said.

"Elmer!" If Fran weren't standing between us, I would have elbowed him.

Fran smiled. "Not exactly."

I waited while she took everything in and asked Elmer to see if Jake could join us.

She finally turned to me, and said, "This is very nice. It's hard to believe this used to be offices."

"Would you like to see the brewery?"

"I would. Very much."

I led her through the swinging door and into the brewing area.

"Oh my." She touched one of the gleaming stainless tanks. "It's beautiful. Just like I remember from the old brewery, except they were larger." She walked to each tank and peered at the gauges. She appeared years younger when she turned to me. "My father took me to work with him sometimes. He showed me quite a bit about brewing."

When she asked, I explained what was fermenting and when it would be ready for kegging.

"I take it you don't bottle any of this," she said.

"No. At least not for the near future. To tell you the truth, I'm not sure I want to grow that much."

She seemed surprised at that. "Why not?"

"I like the personal touch. I want to keep my hand in

every aspect of the business, and I don't think I'd be able to do that if we were producing hundreds or thousands of bottles. I just want this to be a place where people can come and relax. Come and have a good beer and some good food. I don't need more than that."

She reached over and touched my arm. "I need to apologize to you. I'm afraid I misjudged you terribly."

"You don't need to apologize."

"But I do. I wasn't sure what I would find when I came here. I was almost afraid to be right, that this would be a horrible place." She smiled. "A den of iniquity, as your Mr. Fairbanks said."

"Elmer does have a way with words."

"You've brought this place back to what it should be. A museum would be wrong here."

"You haven't given up on that entirely, I hope. All those things you showed me last night were amazing."

"I'll find a place for them," she said.

"That's something I want to talk to you about." Before I could tell her my idea, Elmer swung open the door and poked his head through the doorway.

"Are you going to show us these tunnels or not? Let's get this show on the road." He went back out.

"Definitely a way with words," Fran said. "Shall we?"

Jake was sitting with Elmer when we returned to the pub. I'd never felt awkward with him before, but now it was hard not to think about that kiss when I looked at him. I was glad we weren't alone, because I could keep my thoughts on the matter at hand. I introduced him to Fran, and after a little small talk, Fran turned to me.

"It's so different in here than when it was offices." She walked around the room, looking at it from different angles. "I remember a reception desk here." She pointed to an area near the door.

I led the way down the hallway, opened the door to the basement, and led the way down the steps.

"It's not the same down here, either," Fran said.

I told myself not to be annoyed, but what did she expect? Of course it looked different.

"It used to be jammed with file cabinets, old office furniture, you name it. There was hardly room to walk." She moved to the wall where the safe was. "I remember this, but I don't think it was here. And those shelves. I don't remember all these shelves." She crossed the room and confidently pointed to an area behind two shelves. "There. Right there." She turned to me. "That's where you'll find the door to the tunnel."

CHAPTER TWENTY-TWO

"I'll be right back." I jogged upstairs and grabbed the bag I kept a few basic tools in, thinking I should have brought it with me in the first place. I handed Jake a hammer and I took a crowbar. The shelves were bolted to the concrete block wall. The bolts were old and rusted, and it didn't take us long to pry the shelves from the wall. Jake moved them aside while I began to examine the wall. The old concrete blocks were mostly intact. The wall was cold and damp under my fingers. Jake, Elmer, and Fran soon joined me, and between the four of us, no spot was left untouched. There was no door, and no sign a door had ever been there.

"Hmm. Maybe it was the other wall," Fran said.

Jake and I pried the shelves from the other wall with the same result. Concrete blocks with no door or opening anywhere.

"That can't be." She shook her head. "I distinctly remember it. It may have been a long time ago, but I'm sure it was here."

"Nutjob," Elmer said, loud enough for me to hear. I gave him my sternest look.

"How long ago?" I asked.

"The last time was right before my father retired. He wanted to show me where the tunnel entrance had been. It was covered with plywood. He didn't want the history to be forgotten after he passed on."

"What year was that?" Jake asked.

Fran gave not only the year, but the month as well.

My heart sank. Over forty years ago. Forty years since she'd been in this building. Forty years to imagine something that wasn't there. Jake put his arm around my shoulder. I wanted to cry. This was all for nothing.

Fran circled the basement studying the walls closely. "I don't understand it. It should be here. I'm sure of it."

"Fran," I said, "it was a long time ago. Sometimes I can't even remember what happened last week."

"Are you telling me I'm wrong? That you don't believe me?" She sounded indignant.

"I'm only saying it's been too long to remember everything about it."

"I know what was here," she snapped. "There's nothing wrong with my memory. You saw the picture of the tunnel. And my father took me down here more than once." She stabbed her index finger in the air. "It was here."

I had seen the picture. But it was only a photo of a large space with kegs. I wanted to believe it had been taken in one of Fran's tunnels, but I wasn't sure it was. I tried to let her down gently. "There may have been tunnels here at one time. You yourself said they'd been closed up. If they're still under these buildings, we may never find them. I don't see any way into them from here."

Fran placed her hands on her hips. "The entrance is here. I did not imagine it. We just need to find it. And I know just how to do that. I'm going to look through all my father's papers and see if he documented anything about the tunnels. I also have some blueprints of the old brewery complex. I'll dig them out as well. I should have done that in the first place, but I was so excited, it didn't even cross my mind."

I wished her luck. I wasn't hopeful she'd find anything worthwhile.

Sweaty and grimy, I plopped down on a chair in the pub after she left. "Well, that was a massive waste of time."

"Maybe not," Jake said.

Elmer snorted. "You're as delusional as that woman."

I was in no mood to put up with him right now. I told him to take the rest of the day off. He didn't want to, but Jake told him he'd keep an eye on me.

"I bet you will," Elmer said, grinning.

Jake laughed, and I said, "Go home, Elmer." He grumbled all the way out. He probably complained to himself all the way home.

I leaned back in my chair and sighed. If I hadn't been preoccupied and disappointed over what I thought of as "the tunnel business," I might have felt strange being alone with Jake. The kiss was the last thing on my mind at the moment. I'd been so sure Fran would lead me to finding how the killer was getting in. I was positive that information would have somehow led me to find who killed Dominic and, more important, Kurt. I'd let him down once again. I didn't understand how Fran had been so wrong about the tunnel entrance. If there even was one.

Jake reached over the table and put his hand over mine. "Stop it."

Annoyed, I pulled my hand away. "Stop what?"

"Beating yourself up," he said. "It's written all over your face."

"I'm not beating myself up."

"Right."

"Okay, maybe I am. I just feel so stupid for thinking what I did. For believing her. There's probably no truth to anything Fran told me." Jake took my hand again, and I tried to ignore the warmth that shot up my arm. I didn't pull away.

"You're not stupid," he said. "You saw the photograph she had of one of the tunnels. And Elmer said he'd heard of them. Just because Fran was confused doesn't mean there's not another way into them."

"Where? The walls are concrete block. There was nothing there that showed where a door would have been."

"Maybe it's behind the block."

"If that's the case, that's not how the killer got in. We're back to square one."

"Then there has to be another way in," Jake said. "This building was vacant for a long time, right?"

"Yep. Several years."

"Chances are, whoever is coming in here was able to come and go as he pleased before you bought the place. He didn't have to worry about anyone seeing him. He was using the tunnels under the building for—whatever—then the building was sold and he was afraid he'd be found out."

"That makes sense, but we already assumed whoever it is was using the tunnels."

"Hear me out. If we're sticking with that theory, the guy still wanted to use the tunnels."

I didn't quite get where this was going, but I agreed.

Jake got up and paced beside the table while he talked. "He knew that whoever bought this place would see the opening, explore the tunnel, and discover what he was up to. So he covered it up."

"If he covered it up, how is he getting in?"

He grinned like a kid. "That's what we need to figure out."

"You're insane. I'm not tearing out the foundation."

"I didn't say you had to do that. My guess is it opens up somehow."

"Like a secret passageway?" I laughed. "And you accused me of playing Nancy Drew."

He stopped pacing, rested his hands on the table, and leaned over. "I never did get a picture of that."

"And you never will." He was too close, and the warmth when he touched my hand a few minutes ago was nothing compared to what I felt now. I didn't look at him because I was afraid of what I'd see in his eyes. Or, more important, what wouldn't be there. I couldn't have stood that.

I pushed my chair back and went over to the bar. The bottled water on the shelf was warm, but I opened one anyway and took a long drink. I didn't want to think about tunnels anymore. It was barely afternoon and I was exhausted already. And hungry. "What were you cooking earlier? It smelled really good."

"Garlic and tomatoes for flatbread pizza, since you have that on the menu."

"Do you have the rest of the ingredients?"

"I do. I was just about to put a couple together when Elmer came to get me."

"Great." I smiled. "Get back to work, then. I'm starving."

Jake's flatbreads were delicious. One had the typical *Margherita* toppings—tomatoes, basil, and fresh mozzarella. The second was topped with roasted red and yellow peppers, mushrooms, and goat cheese. I was glad he was trying out the menu items and taking care of the kitchen. I didn't know what I'd have done without him.

I got my second wind after I ate. I finished the report I'd been working on, organized the papers on my desk, and made a list of things I still had to do before the opening. All the staff I'd hired were scheduled to come in Monday morning to learn the ropes. I hoped a week of training would be sufficient. I wasn't worried about the waiting-tables part, but learning the beer styles and being able to suggest a beer to go with a certain food might not come easily to some. Nicole had picked it up quickly. Hopefully the others would do the same.

One of the things on my list was to check on the order I'd placed with Daisy. This was as good a time as any, so I told Jake where I was going and headed out. Daisy was putting the finishing touches on a bridal bouquet when I entered her shop. Sprays of baby's breath mingled with white tea roses, and Daisy had somehow weaved antique lace ribbon throughout the bouquet. The same lace wrapped the stem, or holder—whatever it was called—and lace streamers trailed from the bottom.

"That's gorgeous," I said. "I've never seen anything like it."

She just about beamed. "Thanks. It's my own design. The bride wanted something a little different than your run-of-the-mill nosegay."

"Looks like you achieved it."

She sighed. "Always a bridal-bouquet maker, never a bride," she said, putting her own spin on the old adage.

"I take it Adam is still being . . ." I searched for a word.

"A pain in the rear." Daisy finished it for me.

"Why didn't you tell me Adam was the one telling people I was selling the brewery?"

Daisy's face reddened. "I'm sorry, Max. I should have said something, but he didn't actually say you were selling, he said he *thought* you would."

That was the same thing in my mind. "Well, I talked to him yesterday and straightened him out. But that's not why I'm here. I wanted to check to see if everything was on schedule."

She said it was, and we discussed when she should start putting things in place. We decided on Wednesday of next week.

Before I left, she asked me how the meeting had gone. I told her about the meeting, Fran, and the tunnels.

"Ooh, secret tunnels sounds almost romantic," she said. "Can't you just picture Eliot Ness raiding the place and smashing all those beer kegs?"

I laughed. "That sounds like my worst nightmare."

"I guess it would," she said. "Keep me posted on those tunnels. If you find a way in, I'd love to see them."

"Will do."

When I got back to the pub, Jake was waiting for me with a big grin on his face. "Guess what I just got," he said.

I had no idea. "Salmonella from eating your food?"

"Ha-ha. Very funny. You can do better than that. I'll give you a hint. It has to do with ice."

"You bought a new ice bucket." I was having fun with this now.

"And sticks."

I could tell he was dying to tell me, so of course I couldn't give in to that. "I know. A snowman. With stick arms."

"Ice and sticks. What does that make you think of?"

"Popsicles? Klondikes? Oh, wait. Klondikes don't have sticks. Plus, they're ice cream."

He groaned. "Max, you're killing me."

"I give up," I said.

"I just got off the phone with a guy I know in the Penguins' front office. He's holding two tickets for me for the playoff game tomorrow afternoon."

"That's great," I said, although I didn't even know the Pens were in the playoffs. "Is Mike going with you?"

"I haven't asked him yet. I thought I'd see if you wanted to go first."

I considered it for a split second, then declined. I needed to keep my distance after what happened this morning. At least for the time being, anyway. It wasn't that I didn't want Jake to kiss me again—on the contrary. I probably wanted it too much, and that was a problem. Until I knew the kiss wasn't just a fluke, it was hands-off. I didn't make up an elaborate excuse, I just told him I needed a day to do nothing. He seemed to accept that and went to call my brother.

The phone rang as I was getting ready to leave for the day. Jake had already gone and, by four, I'd decided to call it quits, too. I was tempted to let the call go to voice mail, but I made myself answer it. I wished I hadn't. It was someone from the Bureau of Building Inspection. I'd called days ago to schedule the final inspection, and now they wanted to know if I'd be available tomorrow morning. They usually worked only Monday through Friday, but they were backed up and were trying to schedule some of the inspections on Saturdays. This was the big one that would permit me to open the pub, so I couldn't very well say no.

So much for a day off doing nothing.

CHAPTER TWENTY-THREE

"To make a long story short, we couldn't find a tunnel entrance," I said to my mom that evening. After I got home, took a shower and fed Hops, I gathered up the kitten and we headed to my parents' house. Mom had called and said she was making tuna casserole for dinner. Even though she didn't have to, she still made meatless meals on Fridays, and tuna casserole was one of my favorites. She always crumbled potato chips on top. Except for the one time she used cracker crumbs, which got a definite thumbs-down from the family.

We were in the kitchen. The casserole was in the oven, and I was tearing lettuce for a salad while Mom chopped a red pepper to go in it. There was a loaf of homemade honey wheat bread on the counter that she'd taken out of the oven before she put the casserole in, and the aroma was practically making me drool. I was ready to just pick up the loaf and take a bite. Hops must have been thinking the same thing, because she kept butting her head against my ankle and looking up at the counter. Or maybe she only wanted to be up where all the action was. I dried my hands and put a couple of her treats on the floor. That did the trick. She gobbled them up, then moved to her blanket in the corner of the room.

"That had to be disappointing," Mom said, dropping a handful of peppers into the bowl with the lettuce.

"Very." I took a bag of baby spinach out of the fridge and opened it. "I don't know what to make of it. I want to believe the tunnels are how that person is getting in, but . . ." I shrugged and tossed some spinach into the bowl. "Right now I'm not even sure the tunnels really exist or if they're a figment of Fran Donovan's imagination. She showed me an old photo, but who's to say it wasn't just an old warehouse?"

Mom opened a package of mushrooms. "If I know you, you'll keep digging until you figure it out. I've never yet seen you go after something you wanted and not get it."

"Not everything," I mumbled.

She'd tolerated all my years of teenage whining that Jake treated me like a kid, so she knew exactly what I meant. "He does like you, sweetie."

"As a friend. Except for the kiss today—"

"He kissed you?" She stopped slicing mushrooms. "That's wonderful!"

"Yes. Maybe. Not exactly." I told her what happened. "I'm sure it was one of those spur-of-the-moment things that he probably regrets now. He didn't bring it up or say anything about it when we were alone again this afternoon."

"Did you?"

"Bring it up? Of course not." I put the remaining spinach back in the fridge.

Mom went back to the mushrooms. "Jake could have been waiting for you to say something."

That hadn't even crossed my mind. "Why would he do that? He's the one who kissed me. I'm not going to throw myself at him."

"Of course you're not. But look at it from his point of view. You still treat him like Mike's friend—"

"But that's what he is."

"Let me finish. You're treating him the same way that you complain he treats you. He's obviously shown his interest; now he's waiting for you to return it."

Oh crap. Was she right? Was that why he asked me first if I wanted to go to the hockey game with him?

Mom smiled. "I'd say a kiss shows an awful lot of interest."

"Hey, who's kissing my little girl?" Dad crossed the kitchen and put his arm around Mom and pecked her on the cheek.

"Jake," Mom said.

"It's about time." Dad surprised me with his answer.

In short order I found out I was the only one who didn't think Jake was interested in me. Mike, Kate, Sean, and if I were to hazard a guess, Pat, Joey, and Jimmy, too. My whole family. Sheesh.

Mom got the casserole out of the oven, and I set the

dining room table while Dad sliced the bread. When he brought it to the table, I asked him if there was any progress with the investigation. The look on his face told me all I needed to know.

"We'll keep on it, sweetie," he said.

I knew he would, but it was discouraging anyway. Over dinner I told him about Fran Donovan's theory about the tunnel under the pub. Just like everyone else, my dad had heard rumors about tunnels, but no one he knew ever saw one. He said that surely someone would have discovered and used them by now. He didn't buy my reasoning that someone was using them to enter the pub.

Maybe I was still a little aggravated that Dad hadn't made any progress with Kurt's murder, because his insistence that the tunnels didn't exist made me want to prove him wrong. I still had more than a few doubts of my own, but it wouldn't hurt to do a little more investigating and try to find that opening.

I arrived at the brew house at seven a.m. I didn't want to take any chances that the inspector would find a problem with something and we wouldn't pass. I walked through each room, checking and double-checking everything from light switches to plumbing. I was relieved to find all was in order.

I had some time before the inspector was due to arrive, so I went over to the coffee shop to grab a mocha. One of Kristie's part-time baristas was at the counter, which was typical for a Saturday. We chatted while she made it, then

I took it back to the brew house with me. I had just finished my coffee when the door to the pub opened.

The inspector looked familiar, but I didn't recognize his name when he introduced himself as Lavon Reed. He showed me the paperwork and explained what he was going to look for. It was hard to concentrate because I kept trying to remember where I'd seen him before. When I stepped ahead to lead him to the kitchen, the logo on his black polo shirt jogged my memory. He was the man Adam had argued with in the deli. But why? I wished I had paid more attention to their argument. What had he said to Adam? It was something like *don't ever ask me that again.* So, what had Adam asked him?

"Congratulations," Lavon Reed said with a smile thirty minutes later. "You passed."

I could have hugged him. "Thank you. That's such a relief."

"These are the days I really like my job. I don't like it when I have to deliver bad news."

Like when he'd talked to Adam? "It's nice to get some good news," I said. "Come back after we open and your first beer is on the house."

"I'll be happy to come back, but I'm afraid I'll have to pay for what I eat and drink." He grimaced. "We're not allowed to take any freebies because it doesn't look right to the public. Someone might think we were taking a bribe or a payoff."

"I didn't think of that. Does that happen? Someone trying to bribe you, I mean." Maybe that's what Adam had tried to do.

"You wouldn't believe how often. Just last week a guy . . ." He stopped and shook his head. "I'd better not say." He had me sign off on the inspection and we chatted another minute or two, then he was off to his next job.

When he was gone, I did a little dance around the room. I couldn't wipe the smile off my face. We passed! The brew house was a go. After so much hard work and so many things that had gone wrong, we were actually going to open. With tears in my eyes, I looked up toward the ceiling. "We did it, Kurt." I could almost hear him say, *I told you so.* "I really wish you were here for this," I whispered.

I wiped my eyes with the back of my hand. The pub was going to open, but I still had some unfinished business. Kurt's killer was out there. I needed to find him.

The reality of how much work I had to do in the next two weeks set in quickly. I had a tentative schedule for training on Monday, but I went over it again and made a few notes. The inspection sheet Lavon Reed had left with me caught my eye, and I picked it up. It shouldn't have surprised me when he mentioned that people offered him bribes, but it had. I thought again about his argument with Adam. What was Adam doing talking to the building inspector anyway? And what could he possibly have asked to garner the response he had? I wouldn't put it past Adam to try to bribe someone. I shook my head, laughing at myself. Why did I care? It was really none of my concern. I had enough on my plate without worrying about someone else's business.

Tired of sitting, I got up and stretched. I hadn't planned on being here all day, but here I was. I thought I should probably go home. I could call Jake on the way and tell him the good news. It was five o'clock. The hockey game should be over by now. If Mom was right, he'd be happy to hear from me. I passed the basement door and stopped. The tunnels. I hadn't given them a thought all day.

Was it possible we missed something yesterday? We'd checked all the walls for an opening, even going so far as to remove the old shelving. The floor was solid concrete, so there was nowhere for a trapdoor. It wouldn't hurt to take one more look. I went back to my office and grabbed a flashlight just in case. I had just started down the stairs when my phone rang.

It was Jake. "You missed a great game," he said. He told me the Penguins won, and I gave him the good news about the inspection.

"Are you still at the brew house?" he asked.

"Yep. I was on my way out, then thought I'd do one last search for the tunnel entrance."

"If you wait a bit, I'll help. We're stuck in traffic, but as soon as I drop Mike off, I'll be there."

I crossed the basement floor to the first wall we'd checked yesterday. "You don't have to. I probably won't be that long—especially if I don't find anything."

"I can't let you have all the fun. I'll be there as soon as I can."

Before I could protest, he hung up. I stuffed my phone into the front pocket of my jeans. There was plenty of light in the basement, but I turned the flashlight on anyway and aimed the beam at the wall. I moved the light in a grid pattern, then did the same to the other walls.

Nothing.

I was about to turn off the flashlight when the beam lit up the area near the old safe. The safe was about eighteen inches from the wall, where it had been since I bought the building. Eighteen inches was just enough room for a person to squeeze behind it. I knew it was a long shot, but we'd checked everywhere else. I went over to the safe and shined the light behind it.

Fran had been right after all. There was a tunnel, and I'd just found the entrance.

At least I thought it was the entrance. It had to be.

The area behind the safe appeared to be the same as the block walls of the cellar, but on closer inspection I found what appeared to be painted plywood. It was rather ingenious. Someone had put a lot of work into making it blend into the wall. The area was in heavy shadow, so it was no wonder we hadn't spotted it yesterday. If it hadn't been for the beam from the flashlight, I still wouldn't have seen it. It would only have been a matter of time, though, before someone took a closer look or even had the safe moved and discovered it. It also explained why someone was trying to drive me away.

I squeezed behind the safe and slid the plywood disguise to the left. There was an old wooden six-panel door. My heart beat faster as I turned the knob and pushed it open. The hinges were as quiet as those on a brand-new door. Someone kept them well oiled.

I slipped my phone from my pocket to check the time. I had no idea when Jake would get here and I didn't want to wait. He'd have to catch up with me. I went in. I expected the passageway to be damp and full of cobwebs, but it wasn't. It was constructed well, with concrete walls, floors, and ceiling. There were no cobwebs or spiders anywhere, thank goodness.

When I'd gone what I guessed was about fifty feet, the passage widened and opened into the cavernous space from Fran's photograph. She was going to be thrilled when I showed her. From here there were three more tunnels, each going in a different direction. I walked a few feet into the one at my left and shined the light ahead. It looked like this one curved around behind the brew house, then straightened. My guess is this was the one Fran said went to the Allegheny River. I'd save it for last. I retraced my steps and checked the passageway on the right. This was likely the one that had gone to the old brewery. It was wide enough for three people to walk side by side, but it was not well kept. After I walked for a minute or so, I came to a dead end. Where a door might have been was a concrete wall. A real one this time.

Disappointed, I retraced my steps and started down the last passageway. It only took a couple of minutes to reach the end. There was a door that appeared to be well maintained. I gripped the doorknob and hesitated. I had no idea what I'd find behind it. I had to at least take a peek, then I'd go back and wait for Jake and call my dad. My scalp tingled as I inched open the door.

The room was dark. I scanned the room with my flashlight and saw that I was in a basement. Cardboard boxes lined the walls and some were stacked in the center of the room. Empty crates were tossed in a pile in one corner. My light hit an open box in the center of the room and rested on what appeared to be black leather. I tiptoed into the room. I had to see what was in the box. I lifted the item from the box. It was a black leather purse labeled with an expensive designer name. This must be Adam's basement.

Holy crap. Adam.

Thoughts clicked together in my brain like a Rubik's Cube.

His interest in my security system. Telling Daisy and some of his employees I was going to sell the pub. Not wanting Daisy to tell anyone they were seeing each other. He was using Daisy to get information about me. His argument with the building inspector. He'd probably tried to bribe him to make the brew house fail inspection.

The big question was why. He'd murdered two people to get to me. What could he possibly have against me? I wouldn't have cared if Adam used the tunnels if he'd have asked me. Unless there was a reason he didn't want me or anyone else to know. If he was doing something illegal.

Using my flashlight, I peered closely at the handbag I'd picked up. There were a few loose threads, but other than that, I couldn't find anything wrong with it. I put it back and examined the carton. There were no markings on it at all— not even packing tape. I found that odd. Surely a name brand, high-end company would have their name plastered all over the box. They also couldn't have shipped it without taping it up and addressing it properly.

I moved to another box filled with quilted handbags and totes. These were identical to the ones Adam had been stocking when I'd talked to him in his store. They seemed authentic, but again, the box wasn't labeled or taped. It dawned on me that the goods could be good-quality fakes.

If Adam was selling counterfeit goods and using the tunnel to transport them, he wouldn't have wanted me to know that. If he wanted to buy me out to keep all this a secret, he must be making a fortune on them.

My grip tightened on the flashlight. How dare he! He killed two people just so he could keep making money from selling this stuff?

Well, he wouldn't be doing it much longer.

I marched through the door, closing it behind me. When I reached my own basement, I called my dad's cell phone. His voice mail picked up.

"Hi, Dad, it's me. Call me back as soon as you get this message. I know who killed Kurt and Dominic and why." I hit the end button and called Jake. He picked up on the first ring.

"I found it," I said. "I found the tunnel."

"That's great!"

"It was behind that old safe." I started to tell him about the counterfeit goods when a voice behind me said, "I wouldn't say any more if I were you."

I spun around. It was Adam.

CHAPTER TWENTY-FOUR

$\mathcal{A}$ cold tendril of fear took root in my neck and curled down my spine. I'd been so focused on calling Dad and Jake, I only now noticed that the basement lights I had left on had been turned off. The only illumination was from the flashlight I still carried.

Adam stepped out of the darkness. "End the call. Now."

"I'll have to call you back," I said into the phone.

"Wait! Is that Adam?" Jake said into my ear.

"Yes."

Jake mumbled an obscenity. "I'll be there in ten."

"Now!" Adam demanded.

Instead of disconnecting, I pressed the button to turn the volume down. Jake would be able to hear us, but not the other way around. I pocketed the phone. "Done," I said.

He flicked the switch on the wall and turned on the overhead light. I blinked at the sudden brightness of the room. Adam held a gun in one hand and a metal baseball bat in the other. Daisy's bat. Adam had taken it. Oh God. And used it on Kurt and Dominic. My stomach knotted.

"You seem to like those tunnels, so we're going to take a little walk," Adam said.

"That's not going to happen. I'm not going anywhere with you." I wasn't going to show him how frightened I was. For a split second I thought about running for the stairs, but I'd never make it. Not with a gun pointed at me. He'd already killed two people. He'd have no qualms about shooting me in the back.

Adam moved behind me and jammed the gun into my back. "This should change your mind. I really don't want to shoot you, Maxine, but I will if I have to. It won't be all that difficult to make your death look like a robbery gone bad."

"I wouldn't count on that. Three murders in one place will look awfully suspicious. Besides, I called my Dad. He knows I found out who killed Kurt and Dominic."

"You really shouldn't lie like that," Adam said. "I heard you leave the message. You didn't tell him it was me. You didn't even give him a clue."

My heart sank. He was right. But Jake knew. He was coming.

Adam prodded me toward the opening in the wall behind the safe. Every warning my father had given me over the years ping-ponged in my brain. *Never get into a car with a stranger* was number one. If he'd thought of it, I'm sure *Never go into a dark secret tunnel with a killer* would top it. I didn't have a choice, however. If I balked, he'd kill me now. I would delay it as long as I could and hope for the best. If he took me back to his store, I'd have a fighting chance. The store was open, and if I screamed, someone would surely come running.

We reached the large open area. Instead of heading down the tunnel to his store, he pushed me toward the passageway I hadn't explored yet. The one I assumed led to the river. "Where are we going?" I asked.

"Shut up and keep walking." He jammed the gun against my back and I winced. Once we were a few feet inside the tunnel, he threw a switch and a string of lights along the ceiling flashed on. I'd wondered about that. It would be hard to move merchandise in the dark. He suddenly lifted the bat and I squealed as he smashed the flashlight out of my hand.

"You won't be needing that," he said.

I wouldn't be using the flashlight as a weapon. "This is the tunnel that goes to the river, right?"

He didn't answer.

"I figure it does, since the one that goes straight goes to your stores, and the one on the right is a dead end." I hoped Jake was picking all this up. The cell phone signal in my basement had been good, but I wasn't sure how long that would last in here.

"If you must know, yes. It goes to the river. Not that it's going to matter to you once we get there."

The tunnel seemed to go on forever, but it could only have been a few blocks. A quarter of a mile at most. As we walked, I searched for some kind of escape path but there was nothing. The only way out was back the way we'd come. We soon reached a set of concrete steps at the end of the tunnel and Adam ordered me to go up. There was a hatch at the top, and he reached overhead, slid the lock over, and pushed it open. "Out," he said.

I expected there to be buildings or something in this area, but it was eerily empty. I could barely make out Butler Street in the far distance. Between the street and where we now stood were gravel lots whose only occupants were weeds. If any cars had parked here, it had been ages ago. Railroad tracks ran directly beside us, and on the other side was a slight slope that led down to the river. My heart pounded so hard I could hear it. I had to think of something. And fast.

Jake would be here soon. I was sure Adam wouldn't hesitate to shoot him. I couldn't let that happen.

Adam nudged me with the gun again. "We're going down to the river."

"No, we're not." It wasn't the smartest thing to say, but I wasn't a good swimmer. As a matter of fact, I didn't even like the water much. Especially water where I couldn't see the bottom. The river was very deep—over twenty feet in spots, and the current was strong. I wasn't going in without a fight. I had to delay what seemed like the inevitable. I turned so my back was to the river and planted my feet. Not only was I not taking another step, but my turning this way prevented Adam from seeing Jake when he came. If he came. "I'm not going anywhere near that river," I said. "Not until I get some answers. You owe me that much."

"I don't owe you anything."

"Maybe you don't, but I'm asking you anyway. Why, Adam? I don't understand. I don't understand why you did any of this. Not the vandalism, and especially not the murders."

"Why? You want to know why?" he said. "That building should have been mine. Not yours, and certainly not that looney tunes history lady's. I had it all worked out. I was going to expand and have five more stores. I even had blueprints drawn up. Then I went out of the country, and when I came back I found you bought the building. All my plans to sell my exclusive merchandise . . . gone."

"Don't you mean your counterfeit merchandise? That's why you hid the tunnel entrance, isn't it?"

"Gee. You're as smart as you look. What else was I supposed to do?"

I caught a glimpse of Jake's head coming up through the hatch. I forced my gaze to stay on Adam so I didn't give Jake away. "I didn't even know about the tunnel until this week. I wouldn't have cared if you wanted to use it. I never would have known your stuff wasn't legit."

"It would have been a matter of time. But that wasn't the point, anyway. That building was supposed to be mine. But you had to have your little brewery."

Jake was close. He crouched down waiting to make his move.

"So you killed two people trying to drive me out."

"Soon to be three," he said. "Kurt figured out it was me. I dropped my watch that night and he found it. He knew it was mine because he admired it once. I hid and listened while he called you. I had this with me." He held up the bat. "I'd planned on using it on your tanks. Instead, I made a noise near one of the tanks, and when he came to check, I took care of him once and for all."

I was going to be sick. I took a deep breath and swallowed. Poor Kurt. Tears filled my eyes. I blinked them away. I was not going to let Adam see me cry. "What about Dominic Costello?" My mouth was so dry, I could barely get the words out.

Adam shrugged. "A convenient patsy. He was the perfect fall guy, since he was so vocal about opposing you. But once again, my plans were ruined. I was in the brewery trying to decide what to smash that would be blamed on him. I planned to be long gone before he showed up, but he was early. When he didn't see things my way I had to take care of him, too." He motioned with the gun. "I've had enough of this. Time for you to take a little swim."

This was the moment Jake had been waiting for. He sprang up and tackled Adam from behind. They crashed to the ground. The gun flew from Adam's hand and skittered down the slope. It made a splash as it fell into the water. I watched in terror as they rolled on the ground. Jake was much bigger, but Adam was strong. The bat lay on the ground near them but I couldn't get close enough to get it.

Jake was on top of Adam with one hand on his throat holding him down. He drew his other hand back for a punch. Adam grabbed Jake's wrist and used it for leverage to pull Jake off him. Adam jumped to his feet. He grabbed the bat and swung it down toward Jake's head. I screamed. Jake rolled away at the last second and the bat struck the ground with a clang. Jake kicked the bat out of Adam's hands. It rolled to my feet and I snatched it up.

Before Adam could go after Jake again, I drew the bat back with both hands and swung with all my might. The bat hit Adam's elbow and I heard the bone crack. He fell to the ground screaming in pain. Then he passed out.

The bat dropped from my hand and Jake caught me before I did the same. He held me and we stood like that until we heard sirens. "You called the police?" I said.

"As soon as your call dropped I called your dad. He got your message and was trying to call you back. I told him what little I knew about Adam."

"Thanks for coming to my rescue." His arm was still around my shoulders, and I leaned into him.

He kissed me on my head. "I should be thanking you. That was one hell of a swing."

I looked up at him. He was grinning. "What?" I said.

"Want to know what my first thought was when he hit the ground?"

"Sure."

"She shoots and scores!"

We were still laughing when my dad and the cavalry arrived.

CHAPTER TWENTY-FIVE

Mike stood on a chair and tapped his spoon against the top of his glass. No one heard it over the din. I was behind the bar, and so far, opening night had been everything I'd dreamed it would be. We had a packed house. Every table was full, and it was standing room only at the bar. My entire family was there, including all my brothers. Mom was in seventh heaven with all her kids in one room. Mike tried again to get everyone's attention, to no avail, so my brother Joey stood, put two fingers in his mouth, and let loose an ear-splitting whistle. The crowd fell silent in an instant.

Mike shook his head. "Man, I really need to learn how to do that." He was greeted with laughter. "Anyway, I just wanted to congratulate my baby sister over there. . . ." He pointed in my direction. "Max has worked like a demon. . . ."

"Bad choice of words," Sean hollered. He got a bigger laugh than Mike had. I guess no one expected a priest to be funny. They obviously didn't know much about my eldest brother.

"Sorry," Mike said. "Max has worked really hard for this. For those of you who don't know her, she trained for years to be a brewer, and if you've tasted the beer tonight, you know it's paid off."

Someone yelled, "Hear! Hear!"

"She's had a rough few weeks, but she didn't quit. She didn't give up her dream. Thank you all for turning out and supporting her."

My face grew hot at the round of applause that followed. Mike jumped off the chair and headed my way. When he reached the bar, I wrapped my arms around him. "You are the best brother in the world," I said. "But don't you dare tell anyone I said that."

"Your secret's safe with me. Why don't you take a break? I'll tend the taps for a while."

I protested, but he wouldn't take no for an answer. I rinsed and dried my hands, then went to mingle with the customers. I went from table to table and tried to talk to as many people as possible. Everyone, with few exceptions, not only raved about the beer but loved the food as well. Jake's buffalo chicken pierogies were the hit of the night. That made me so happy for Jake, who had been stuck in the kitchen most of the night. I was pleased at the comments about the waitstaff, too. At one point I overheard Nicole talking about our brews with a table full of guys who thought they were beer experts. She didn't falter once, and she may even have won them over. I caught her eye and gave her a thumbs-up.

We closed the kitchen at eleven, and by midnight, there were only a few stragglers—most of them my family and friends. Two young guys sat at the bar trying their best to impress Nicole, who had taken over the taps. My sisters-in-law and my nieces and nephews all left at the same time. Sean had left an hour ago because he had early Mass in the morning, but my other brothers stuck around. Elmer had even put in an appearance earlier. Ken Butterfield had stopped in for dinner and so had Ralph Meehan.

I sank onto the chair beside my mother at the table where she was sitting with Candy, Kristie, and Fran Donovan. Dad was at the next table with my brothers, and it sounded like he and Patrick were exchanging cop stories.

Mom squeezed my hand. "I am so proud of you, sweetie. Tonight was wonderful."

"It was, wasn't it?" I said. "I can't believe it finally all came together."

"Kurt would have been pleased."

He certainly would have been, even though we didn't serve his *kirschtorte* tonight.

Jake came up behind me, and a thrill went through me when he rested his hands on my shoulders. "It was a great night."

"I can't help thinking it almost didn't happen," Candy said. "That creep was right under our noses and we didn't see it. It makes my blood boil."

"And poor Daisy," Kristie said. "Has anyone heard from her?"

"I talked to her yesterday. She brought the rest of the plants over, but she's not ready to face the public. She's keeping the shop closed for another week." Daisy and I'd had a good cry together yesterday. She truly loved Adam and was devastated that he had used her the way he did. We talked for a long time. "I think she'll be okay," I said. "She's just hurting right now."

Mom got up and excused herself to corral the guys and call it a night. Jake took the seat she'd just vacated. He pulled the chair closer to mine and put his arm around me. We hadn't talked about it, but his actions since the close call with Adam made me think he really did like me. And not as his friend's kid sister.

Fran Donovan was quiet, and I asked her if something was wrong.

"I still feel terrible," she said. "If I had told you earlier about those tunnels . . ."

"Adam would have found another way in," I said. "What he really wanted was this building. Besides, you didn't build the tunnels." I hadn't told her my idea yet, and I figured now was the perfect time. "You know how you talked about a museum here?"

"I'm sorry about that," she said. "That was wrong of me."

"No, it wasn't." I smiled. "Actually, I think it's a great idea."

Everyone at the table looked confused except for Jake, who knew all about it.

Fran said, "I don't understand."

"Despite what happened, those tunnels are part of this place and part of this city's history. They need to be preserved. I propose we turn that big chamber down there into your brewing museum. Fix it up the way you see fit." I grinned at the surprise on her face. "It's all yours."

Fran worked her mouth but no words came out. A tear made a track down her face. Finally, she simply said, "Thank you."

𝕴t was three in the morning and everyone was gone except Jake and me. We both stood behind the bar putting glasses away. I turned to Jake. "Do you believe I didn't have a single glass of beer tonight?"

"I didn't, either." He picked up two glasses. "We need to remedy that." He filled the glasses with hefeweizen and handed me one.

"This calls for some kind of toast," I said, "but I think I'm too tired for words."

"You're speechless. I should write that down. It doesn't happen too often."

I laughed. "Very funny. Would you like to wear that beer?"

"I'd much rather drink it. I have a toast." He held up his glass. "To Max. The prettiest brewer I know."

"I believe I'm the only brewer you know. How about . . . to Jake. The best hockey player–chef I know."

"You forgot to say I was brawny."

I laughed. "Okay. To the best brawny hockey player–chef I know."

He shook his head. "That won't work, either. Okay. I have one." He held up his glass with one hand and placed his other hand on the small of my back and pulled me closer. "To the future and whatever it brings."

That I liked. I especially liked something I saw in his eyes. "Prost," I said in German. I clinked my glass against his.

"Cheers," Jake said. "To the future."

BLACK FOREST CAKE
(kirschtorte)

This is similar to the cake Kurt was trying to perfect, although he would have baked his from scratch.

*1 box chocolate cake mix, plus ingredients to prepare
(or bake from scratch)
2 20-oz. cans tart pitted cherries
1 cup sugar
¼ cup cornstarch
1½ tsp. vanilla
3 cups whipping cream
⅓ cup confectioner's sugar*

Preheat oven to 350 degrees. Grease and flour two 9-inch round cake pans.

Prepare cake mix according to directions on box. Pour

batter into prepared pans. Bake according to package directions. Cool in pans on wire racks for 10 minutes, then remove from pans and cool completely. Drain cherries, reserving ½ cup liquid. Combine reserved liquid, cherries, sugar, and cornstarch in saucepan. Cook over low heat, stirring constantly, until thickened. Stir in vanilla. Split each cake layer in two lengthwise (so you have four), then crumble one layer and set aside.

Make frosting: Beat 3 cups cold whipping cream and ⅓ cup confectioner's sugar in a chilled bowl at high speed until stiff peaks form. Set aside 1½ cups for decorating.

Place first layer on a plate. Spread 1 cup frosting over cake. Top with ¾ cup cherry mixture. Repeat with second layer. Top with third layer. Frost sides of cake with remaining frosting, then pat crumbs around sides. Put reserved frosting into a decorating bag with a star tip and pipe around top and bottom edges of cake. Place remaining cherry filling onto top of cake.

Refrigerate until serving time.

BUFFALO CHICKEN PIEROGIES

**This is the appetizer that wowed everyone
at the Allegheny Brew House.**

JAKE'S FILLING:

1 cup cooked shredded chicken (or 1 can chunk chicken)

⅓ cup Frank's RedHot sauce

1 8-oz. package cream cheese

½ cup ranch dressing

¾ cup shredded cheddar cheese

Heat chicken and hot sauce in saucepan. Stir in cream cheese and ranch dressing and heat until cream cheese is melted and mixture is hot. Mix in cheddar cheese and cook until cheese is melted and mixture is hot and bubbly.

BASIC PIEROGI DOUGH

(Makes 12 to 15)

2 cups flour

1 tsp. salt

1 egg

½ cup sour cream

¼ cup butter, softened

Mix flour and salt. Beat egg, then add to flour mixture. Add sour cream and butter and work until dough loses stickiness. Wrap dough in plastic wrap and refrigerate at least 30 minutes, or overnight.

Boil water in large pot. Roll dough on floured surface to ⅛-inch thick. Using a large glass or a cookie cutter (3- to 4-inch diameter), cut dough into circles. Place 1 Tbsp. filling on each circle. Wet edges of circles, fold, and seal completely using fingers or tines of a fork.

Place pierogies in boiling water. When they float to the top, remove with slotted spoon and drain. (At this point, they can be frozen until later, if desired. Place in boiling water again to defrost.)

Heat 2 Tbsp. canola oil in a nonstick pan. Add pierogies and brown on each side. Drain on paper towels.

Arrange on a plate and serve with ranch dressing for dipping.

Keep reading for a special preview of
Joyce Tremel's next Brewing Trouble Mystery . . .

TANGLED UP IN BREW

Coming soon from Berkley Prime Crime!

I looked at the printout in my hand one more time, then checked the number spray painted on the gravel in the formerly empty lot in Pittsburgh's Strip District. "Thirty-eight. This is it," I said to Jake Lambert, my assistant and chef—and more importantly, my boyfriend.

Jake dropped the poles and tent parts he'd lugged from his truck. "Thank goodness. I was starting to think they skipped us." He swiped at his forehead with the back of his hand. It was only nine in the morning and already the temperature had hit eighty. Not unusual for a mid-July day, and we'd dressed for the heat. Jake wore khaki shorts and a white tank top, while I opted for my ancient denim cutoffs and teal tank.

It had taken us twenty minutes to find the designated spot where we were to set up our tent for the inaugural Three

Rivers Brews and Burgers Festival. My brewpub, the Allegheny Brew House, was one of the fifty breweries and brew pubs invited to participate in what everyone hoped would be an annual event. There would be prizes for the best beers and for the best burger creation. I was entering three beers in the competition—a chocolate stout, an IPA, and my newly developed citrus ale.

So far, Jake was keeping his burger recipe top secret. Even my friend, Candy Sczypinski, who owned the Cupcakes N'at bakery next door to the brewpub couldn't get it out of him. And Candy had an uncanny knack for learning everyone's secrets. Her information network rivaled the NSA's. Maybe it was the fact she looked like Mrs. Santa Claus—if Mrs. Claus was a devout Steelers fan, that is. In any case, she'd never failed to get the scoop on anything going on in our Lawrenceville neighborhood—until now.

Jake stuck his hands into the front pockets of his shorts. "Do you want me to start setting up?"

Before I answered, a model-thin woman with an auburn ponytail and carrying a clipboard came up to us. She was dressed a little less casually than we were, in white capris and a navy and white cotton blouse. She reached out her hand. "Ginger Alvarado. You must be Maxine O'Hara. We spoke on the phone."

I shook her outstretched hand. "Call me Max. It's nice to finally meet you in person." I introduced her to Jake.

"The hockey player, right?" she said.

"Retired." Jake smiled although I was sure he knew the inevitable question was coming.

"Aren't you a little young for that?"

"It just leaves me more time for my second career." It

had become his standard answer even though it wasn't the reason he'd had to quit a few years early.

"I'm looking forward to tasting whatever masterpiece you've come up with." Ginger turned to me. "And tasting your beer. I've heard a lot of good things about your pub."

"Thank you," I said. "I'm happy to hear that."

Ginger slid a paper from her clipboard and passed it to me. "These are some general suggestions on getting your tent up and situated today. You can pull your vehicle up to unload, but move it to the lot next door when you're finished. If you're going to tap your kegs today, I don't recommend leaving them here overnight. We've hired some off-duty Pittsburgh Police officers, but only for the festival itself. Definitely don't leave anything valuable in your tent." She pointed to an area behind us. "Most of the temporary electric you'll need is set up and by the end of the day we should have all of it in place."

"Jake, the kitchen is over there." She pointed to a large white tent at the far end of the lot. "There are twenty-five chefs registered for the contest, so you'll all be sharing the prep space under the tent. There are plenty of both charcoal and propane grills surrounding the tent thanks to some generous donors. The burger tasting will begin at noon, and the field will be whittled down to five finalists by four o'clock. From that five, three will compete next weekend in the final. The beer judging will be ongoing since there are so many brewers, and everyone attending the festival will get a scorecard to mark their favorites so they can vote online in addition to scoring by our three judges."

Ginger glanced at her clipboard. "Feel free to roam around and meet the other vendors. I know you probably know some of them, but there are quite a few from out of town. Give them a real Pittsburgh welcome. If you need anything, my cell phone number is at the bottom of the page."

After she moved on to the next brewer who had arrived, Jake turned to me. "I'm a little nervous about the competition."

"Maybe if you tell me about your burger, I can help you decide whether or not to back out."

Jake grinned, showing the dimple I liked so much. "Oh, no you don't. I know what you're trying to do."

I gave him my most innocent look. "I'm not trying to do anything. I just want to help my most trusted employee make the proper decision."

"Right." He laughed and a curl of Irish stout–colored hair slipped onto his forehead and I reached up and pushed it back. Not an easy feat since at six foot three, he was a foot taller than me. He rested his hands on my shoulders. "I thought Nicole was your most trusted employee," he said.

Nicole was my part-time hostess-waitress-bartender, recently promoted to manager. I was leaving the pub in her capable hands while we were at the festival. "She is. But you're a close second," I teased. "So. About this burger . . ."

Jake ruffled my hair just like he did when we were kids and took a step back. "I'm not falling for it, O'Hara. You'll have to wait to be awed by my creation like everyone else."

I finger-combed my short black pixie into place. "Did anyone ever tell you how mean you are?"

"All the time." He leaned over and picked up one of the metal tent poles. "Any idea how we put this thing together?"

*   *   *

An hour later we had the ten-foot-by-ten-foot canopy tent up and Jake's truck unloaded. We had a banquet size folding table that I covered with a white paper tablecloth. We weren't bringing the kegs until tomorrow—the first day of the festival, but I brought several large coolers filled with ice and growlers. There was a good chance the brewers would want to sample each other's products. At least that was what usually happened at these things. I also opened a package of plastic cups and placed them on top of the table.

I stood back to admire my handiwork. Many of the other vendors had arrived by that time, and the previously empty lot looked like a sea of white canopies. The only color was the Pittsburgh skyline and the bright yellow David Mc-Cullough bridge (which everyone still called the Sixteenth Street Bridge) in the background. I definitely needed to find something to make my booth stand out, but I wasn't sure what. I had brought a printed list of my beers with me, but that wasn't enough. At the very least, I needed to make a colorful poster board with the list and put it in front of the tent.

Jake had already gone to check out the kitchen, so I decided to make the rounds and talk to the other brewers. I'd waved to a few while we were setting up and I really looked forward to talking shop with them. Since the brewpub opened two months ago, I'd been too busy to do much else. Not that I was complaining. I was thrilled the pub was a hit so far.

The spot beside us was still vacant, so I strolled over to the next one where Dave Shipley was having a tug-of-war with the tent canopy as he tried to slip it over the metal corner. As I reached him, the opposite side of his tent swayed and I grabbed it and pulled. The tension was just enough for Dave to attach his end.

"Thanks, Max," he said. "When the directions said pop-up, I didn't think I'd need help putting it up."

"Are you here by yourself?" I held the pole while he secured it with a stake.

"Yep. I couldn't spare anyone today. The Pirates play tonight." Dave owned Fourth Base, a popular brewpub on the North Shore between PNC Park and Heinz Field. It was a prime location—he got baseball fans in the summer and football fans in the winter. He brewed pretty good beer, too. He was one of the first brewers I met when I moved back to town and he'd been a big help when I had questions on starting up the brewery and the pub.

"What about tomorrow?" I said.

"Cindy and Tommy will be here." Cindy was his wife and Tommy his eighteen-year-old son. "Tommy's gonna enter that burger thing."

"That's great. I didn't know Tommy could cook."

Dave's grin lit up his bearded face. "The kid's never cooked a thing in his life, but he's spent the last two weeks trying out different hamburgers on us. They're not bad, either. Except for the one he stuffed with hot jalapenos and pepper jack cheese, then topped with hot sauce. My mouth didn't cool off for days."

I laughed. "I can imagine."

He snapped open the legs on a folding table. "So, what's Jake come up with for the competition?"

"I wish I knew. He's keeping it top secret."

"Must be something pretty good, then."

We talked for a few more minutes until a white cargo van pulled up to the empty space between our tents. I fought the urge to groan aloud when the driver got out of the vehicle. Dave mumbled an expletive.

Dwayne Tunstall was the last person I'd expected to see here. On second thought, maybe I wasn't all that surprised. Dwayne had a habit of turning up where no one wanted him, which was pretty much everywhere he went. The man was a leech. He was well-known in the brewing community, and not in a good way.

Dwayne walked over to where we stood. "Well, if it isn't my two favorite brewers."

"I wish I could say the same," Dave said, ignoring the hand Dwayne had extended.

Twelve years of Catholic school had taught me if I couldn't say something nice to not say anything at all, so I stayed silent.

"I must say, I'm surprised to see you here, Maxine," Dwayne said.

I gritted my teeth at his use of my given name. "It's Max. Only my grandmother called me Maxine." And the nuns, but I left that out. "Why are you surprised? Where else would I be?"

Dwayne ran a hand through his sandy-colored mullet. Between the hairstyle, and the jeans and muscle shirt he wore, he looked like a wannabe Billy Ray Cyrus. I wondered where he found a barber who was stuck in the eighties. It was someone to be avoided at all costs.

"I figured you'd be keeping an eye on your pub," Dwayne said. "Not to mention that you're new to this whole brewing gig. Not like me. And Dave here. You don't have a snowball's chance of winning anything."

"Max has a better shot than you do," Dave said.

Dwayne laughed. "I'm going to be the one taking home that Golden Stein."

"Who'd you steal the recipe from this time?" Dave snapped the legs open on his banquet table. "I know it wasn't mine. I learned my lesson the hard way."

"I never stole anything. It was a coincidence."

Dave straightened and put his hands on his hips. "You're a real piece of work. You expect me to believe you just happened to come up with the same beer right after you helped me brew a batch." He shook his head and turned away.

Dwayne looked at me. "I suppose you'll take his side."

I didn't say anything. I didn't have to.

"Fine. You just wait and see who wins the competition. Everyone will come flocking to my place. I guarantee it." He strode to the back of his van, yanked open the door, and started unloading.

I wasn't about to let Dwayne or anyone else ruin my weekend. Hopefully I'd be so busy serving up samples I wouldn't even know he was here. I told Dave I'd see him later and moved on to visit some of the other brewers.

An hour later, Jake and I were sitting on folding chairs back in our booth and wondering what to do with ourselves. Occasionally another vendor stopped and one of us poured a sample, but otherwise we had nothing to do. There was no sense in both of us being bored, so I suggested to

Jake that he return to the pub and come back later in the day. He wouldn't hear of it.

Dwayne Tunstall had tried to engage me in conversation several times, asking questions about my brews. I'd tried my best to ignore him without success. I ended up answering his questions curtly without telling him much of anything.

Jake watched the exchange in silence, then finally said, "Maybe he wants to try a sample."

"No, he doesn't," I said.

Dwayne raised his hands in the air. "I know when I'm not wanted." He spun on his heel, then turned back. "You're wrong about me, you know."

I didn't say anything and he walked away.

"What was that all about?" Jake said. "Other than the guy's a little weird. He seemed harmless."

"It's a long story."

Jake reached into a cooler and lifted out two bottles of water. "It's not like I have anything else to do. It could even keep me from dying from boredom."

I opened the bottle he passed to me and took a swig. "Hey, you had your chance to leave. You're stuck here now."

"So fill me in."

"Dwayne has a bad reputation. Some of the brewers have had problems with him in the past."

"What kinds of problems?"

"Stealing," I said. "Back when Dave was getting started, Dwayne worked part-time for him, as well as part-time for Cory Dixon over at South Side Brew Works. They didn't know it at the time, but Dwayne was filching the beer recipes. As soon as he got what he needed, he quit. The whole time he worked for Dave and Cory, he was in the process of starting up his own place. Dwayne didn't even bother to put his own spin on the brews."

"What did Dwayne mean when he said you were wrong about him?"

I recapped my bottle and put it on the ground beside me. "He insists it's coincidence that his beer just happens to taste exactly like the others. If they were merely similar, maybe I could buy it. But identical? No way. Every ingredient would have to be the same, and in exactly the same proportions—not to mention the brewing times and the fermentation."

Jake finished his water and tossed the bottle into the bag I'd brought for recycling. "Kind of makes you wonder why he's here."

"What do you mean?"

"Well, he's a pariah in the brewing scene," he said. "Why would he want to be where no one wants to have anything to do with him?"

"Good point." I thought about what Dwayne said earlier. "He's here for the competition. He told Dave and me he's going to win the Golden Stein. He sounded sure it was going to be him."

"Sounds more like he's delusional."

I shook my head. "No. I don't think so. But I wouldn't put it past him to do something underhanded to make sure he walks away with that trophy."